NORTH of HAPPY

Also by Adi Alsaid:

Let's Get Lost
Never Always Sometimes

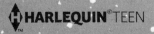

NORTH
of HAPPY

ADI ALSAID

ISBN-13: 978-0-373-21228-6

North of Happy

To Laura. There's no one I'd rather share a meal with.

PROLOGUE

THE PERFECT TACO

2 ounces pork al pastor

1 teaspoon lime juice

1 slice pineapple

1 pinch chopped onion

1 pinch chopped cilantro

1 warm corn tortilla

Salsa, to taste

METHOD:

The day before Felix died, he'd flown in from Asia craving tacos.

As usual, the two of us and Mom went to our favorite taco joint, a chain in a neighborhood near our house. It was one of those places that offered English menus and had TVs in overhead corners. We gorged on every kind of taco on the menu, made hungrier by Felix's cravings.

But when the waiter cleared our plates, Felix wasn't satisfied. The tacos, he said, were overpriced and bland, the atmosphere too sterile. "You love food so much, I'm shocked you still come to this place." Felix told me casually. I knew he didn't mean anything by it, but I also knew I'd never be able to enjoy the restaurant again.

"Meet me outside of school tomorrow. I'll find us some real tacos."

And the next day, there he was, wearing that threadbare once-white shirt that seemed on the brink of disintegration. Even now that he's dead, that same shirt stained red with his blood, I always think of it as it was then: colored not by the violence of Felix's death, but by the shape of his life. He claimed to wash it in the shower himself, which grossly explained the yellowish hue of old sweat and cheap soap. In that one color I can still see my brother in all his exuberance.

"So, where we going?" I asked. I'd been antsy all day, eager to spend time with him before he ran off again to wherever the hell he was going next.

Felix just smirked and led us toward the hospital down the street, where there's a "secure" taxi stand everyone from school uses. Instead of asking for the price to a certain destination, though, he took us past the huddled taxi drivers and around the corner, into unexplored territory. The neighborhood around the campus was not particularly safe. Rumored to be gangland, even. The bodyguards who hung out outside my international school were a constant presence, though Felix always insisted it was rich-people paranoia.

"Uh, where we going?" I instinctively reached for my phone. I'd heard teachers got mugged here on the way to the subway. One of the houses on the walk was rumored to be a drug dealer's, painted bright blue to stand out against the drab gray buildings around it.

"There's a taco place I saw on the way up here. I bet it's way better than that shit we ate last night."

I readjusted my backpack. "I thought you used to like Farolito."

"Sure, when I was in the bubble." Felix slung an arm around my shoulder, slight pang of body odor coming off him. "The world is a much bigger place than you realize," he said with a smile. "We're going to explore it."

We sat down at one of three plastic-tablecloth-covered tables, and a small, smiling man walked over with two menus. Felix waved him away, calling out our order: two tacos al pastor, everything on them (pineapple, onion, cilantro, salsa; I'm sure the words strung together could make a poem).

Then he asked me for a pen, and took a napkin from the metal holder in the middle of the table. He drew three imperfect columns, labeling them Restaurant/Stand, Location, Reaction. "One taco each per spot. We don't stop until we find the perfect one."

I could almost see the day ahead as if it were shot by the Food Network, some Anthony Bourdain–narrated exploration of the city. I tried to contain my glee.

The tacos arrived and Felix clapped his hands, smiling warmly at the waiter/owner. The man smiled back and asked what else he could bring us. I was about to stammer some apology for only getting one taco, maybe cave in and get something else, but Felix spoke up. "Nothing today, thanks. We are on a quest, un tacotón."

We paid the miniscule bill, recorded our reaction (meh), followed the curving street down to a massive set of stairs and then to a subway stop. It marked the first time I had ever been on the metro, I was embarrassed to realize. To my surprise, the metro was not the dangerous hellscape I'd envisioned. It was actually kind of soothing—to move around the city without the ubiquitous traffic, the manic chorus of horns employed at the slightest annoyance or whim, to disappear into a station and reemerge in a part of the city I barely even recognized.

Toward the southern end of the city, in a neighborhood called Coyoacán, we sat at a small place with red plastic tablecloths and a taco named the Chupacabra. "We should get that," I said. "It's their specialty."

Felix waved the little columned napkin in my face. "Important research going on here, man." He turned to the server, again asked for two al pastor, everything on them.

I rolled my eyes and asked for a beer, since I was with him and it seemed to fit the mood.

"No," Felix interrupted, changing the order to a bottle of water instead. "Beer's gonna fill you up. We have a lot of eating to do today."

Two minutes later the tacos were served, and we ate the same way: an extra dabble of salsa, a squeeze from a lime wedge, heads tilted, the first bite taking out nearly half the taco. Felix chewed slowly, not talking, taking the task of assessment seriously.

"What do you think?" I asked, wiping at some salsa on the corner of my mouth.

He held up a finger as he finished chewing. Every time he came back from his travels his hands were rougher, his skin cracked and worn by a foreign sun. "Solid, but lacking something."

"Like, maybe the ingredients in their specialty taco?"

Felix widened his eyes comically. "Who said you're allowed to be funny now? I'm the funny one."

A surge of joy flowed through me, because after all those years of being abandoned in favor of exciting adventures, I was still the little brother. Reflexively, I checked my phone to see whether I should be letting Mom and Dad know where I was. The habit was so ingrained that it even felt rebellious to not call and at least lie to them.

"Put it away," Felix grumbled. "They don't need to know your every move."

The night wore on. The metro got unbearably crowded, people pushing in, literally packing each other into the carts. The trains slowed, and getting on and off became a struggle, each "excuse me" bolstered by force as we pushed others out of the way. We escaped at the Salto de Agua station. An indoor market was half a block away.

Our list of tacos sampled had grown to nearly ten, and a couple had come close to perfection, at least in my opinion. But each time I'd thought we'd found it (crispy, juicy meat, warm doughy tortilla, perfect spice and zing to the salsa, the grilled pineapple sealing it all with its sweetness), Felix would shoot it down.

"We're not looking for *great*, man. We are striving for perfection! Nothing short of it will do."

"And what makes a taco perfect?"

"Beautiful question," Felix said. "It's a taco that tastes as good as the idea of a taco itself. A taco that'll hold steadfast through memory's attempt to erase it, a taco that'll be worthy of the nostalgia that it will cause. A taco that won't just satisfy or fill but will satiate your hunger. Not just for tonight but for tacos in general, for food, for life it-fucking-self, brother. You will feel full to your soul.

"But!" he added, a callused index finger pointed straight up at the sky. "It's also a taco that will make you hunger for more tacos like it, for more tacos at all, for food, the joy of it, the beauty of it. A taco that makes you hungry for life and that makes you feel like you have never been more alive. Nothing short of that will do."

I walked in awe beside my brother. I was starting to feel the discomforts of so much food, a tiredness in my feet. I still had school tomorrow. Mom had already called a handful of times; lately she'd been trying every twenty minutes. It was so hard to break the momentum of the night, though. Maybe one or two more stops, just until traffic died down. Then I'd tell Felix we had to turn back around. Fun could still be enveloped by responsibility. Maybe that feeling Felix had described did exist, was to be found in one of these unassuming stands, joy encapsulated in three bites. A shame not to try a little longer to find it.

Most of the stands were starting to shut down. The fruit and vegetable vendors packed their produce into wooden crates. Butchers hosed down their chopping blocks. Only the taco and birria and ceviche stands still had customers crowded around on stools or on foot, two guys in aprons working the grill, one more at the big slab of pastor. No real sinks in sight, one pump bottle of hand sanitizer for customer use.

Mom would weep if she saw us here, if she knew how many similar spots we'd visited throughout the day. She'd run to get us typhoid shots, never let us leave home again. I was proud of this, for some reason.

"Dos con todo, por favor!" Felix called out as we elbowed for room at the counter.

"This might be the spot," I said.

"Oh yeah? How can you tell?"

"The size of the pastor. They know they're going to sell a lot. Line of people is always a good sign. The limes are fresh. More than three salsas, which means they take some pride in what they provide. The girl making the tortillas back there from scratch." I pointed out the little details I'd started noticing, clues as to whether or not the place might be worthy. "That cook just spotted a bad piece of meat and threw it out right away, so they care about quality. They have some sort of special mix of seasoning they use on their arrachera, not just Worcestershire and Maggi sauces like lots of the other places."

I knew I was rambling, but Felix rambled too. I continued. "Look at how good that guy is at catching the slices of pineapple inside the taco. He's looking away while he does it. He must have served a shitload of these every day for years."

Felix smiled, surveyed the scene. "You want me to talk to one of these guys? Get you a job?"

"Shut the fuck up."

"Why? All you watch is those cooking shows."

"Sure, yeah. Except, what would I tell Mom and Dad? 'Oh hey, remember my SAT prep courses? My internship with Dad? College next year? Yeah, never mind. I got a job at a taco stand!'"

"Why not?" Felix asked. He was serious too. "You think they'd love you less?"

"Probably," I joked and then said, "Last stop?" just to get off the subject.

"Are you kidding? The best spots only start setting up now. I guarantee that the perfect taco doesn't go to bed until four a.m."

The napkin list was running out of room, heavy with ink and pock-marked by holes from the pen on uneven surfaces. "Dude, this has been great. But I really have to get back home."

"No, you don't," Felix said.

I shoved my hands into my pockets, staring resolutely at my brother, trying to come up with something to convince him otherwise. Felix led us somewhere near the historic downtown area, where homeless men lined the streets in thick blankets, surrounded by empty bottles.

Another taco stand, who-knows-where in the city. Extra dab of salsa, squeeze of lime wedge, head tilt. My worry had drifted away, especially after Mom stopped calling. I'd stopped looking at the time, stopped thinking about the homework I didn't do. I listened to Felix's stories, gave myself up to those little cheesy diatribes about living life as you wanted to, to laugh loudly and love often. Felix could sound like a Hallmark card, like boxed inspiration, but he was earnest enough to make you fall for it. One in the morning on a school night, and clearly the perfect taco was not necessary for perfection. "What a world," he kept saying.

We were both full to the brim, laughing about not being able to stomach another bite and yet forcing ourselves to keep eating when a nearby argument turned to shouting. My heart began to race. Then, pops like pinecones in a fire, a stray bullet knocking Felix to the ground. Soda from his glass bottle, intact but spilling bright orange liquid behind his head. The thought, even then, of life's sudden change of course. The terrible words: *nothing will ever be the same.*

CHAPTER 1

THAI BRUSCHETTA

1 French baguette

½ pound deveined shrimp

½ cup coconut milk

2 teaspoons minced ginger

2 Thai chilies, seeded and deveined

2 stalks lemongrass

2 tablespoons red Thai curry paste

1 mango, sliced thin

1 tablespoon Thai basil, chiffonade

METHOD:

On a rooftop in the ritziest part of Mexico City, while my graduation party rages on—music and drinks and waiters delivering canapés to the two hundred people in attendance—I am trying to act like I have my shit together.

There's a pigeon perched next to me, its head tilted, eyes meeting mine, cooing suggestively. I know before it even opens its beak that it's Felix, and that he's going to tell me to escape. It's just what he does now.

The air is fresh after this afternoon's rain. Mexico City doesn't have that nice post-rain smell that other places do, like Mom's hometown in Illinois, when the storms sweep in from Lake Michigan and leave in their wake an almost herb-like scent. I wonder if anyone's ever replicated that post-rain smell in a dish.

This party is Dad's consolation to me for not letting me travel this summer, for fearing that I'd be like Felix and stay gone. It's also Mom worrying that I've been Unusually Quiet Since It Happened; it's her desperate to see me acting like myself again.

Waiters are running around delivering rum and cokes to my classmates, glasses of wine to the parents in attendance. Trays of assorted hors d'oeuvres make their way around the rooftop (ceviche in a spoon, yakitori skewers, chilaquiles sliders—getting to choose what to serve might be the highlight of the party for me). Music thumps out into the night. Neighboring buildings with their own rooftop terraces have similar soirees happening, but none are quite as loud as this one. I keep imagining that I'm not really here, that I'm floating above the party or something, watching it all from some far-off vantage point.

Poncho, Nico and Danny hold their shot glasses out in front, waiting for me to clink. The burn passes quickly. None of us really have to scowl to get the stuff down any more, though I think my friends are really over the burn and I'm just good at suppressing it.

"Ya no te hagas güey," Nico says, putting his glass down on a nearby table. "Tell your dad you're coming with us. This internship thing is stupid. You could get out of it if you just asked."

I shrug. The conversation is predictable. But why wouldn't it be? All our lives are basically mapped out for us, all the days ahead bleeding in with all those to come: internship, college in the States, and then back to Mexico, Dad's company, marriage, kids, success, everything

Felix walked away from. My friends may get a Eurotrip first but then their futures will look just like mine.

"Tell him you've received an offer for another internship. One that involves partying and sexy Europeans," Nico says, raising a hand up for a high five.

I ignore him and my eyes meet Isa's across the party. She gives me a slight wave and a smile that tells me maybe I'll get to fall asleep next to her tonight. It's better than tossing in bed trying to fight off memories and nameless weights.

The DJ puts on something with a beat, and the dance floor fills up, though mostly with parents. Nico and Poncho head over toward our classmates. Danny hangs back, hands in his pockets. "Nico always turns into such a bro when he drinks."

I laugh. "Yeah, have fun with that this summer."

Danny groans, "You should be there with us, if only so you have to suffer through him too." After a quiet moment, he adds, "Everything okay with you?"

"Yeah, of course," I say, eyeing the pigeon on the railing. It's grinning. "Why?"

"I dunno. Sometimes you get quiet, and I think it's gotta be about Felix. Meanwhile we're talking about stupid shit like mixed dorms in hostels or beach parties or something."

"Nah." He doesn't notice I've been making eye contact with a bird. He doesn't notice that I'm almost see-through, that I'm barely here. "Just trying to figure out what the qualifications would be for the internship that Nico described."

Danny gives a chuckle, runs a hand through his hair. "And how the hell Nico qualifies for it."

The pigeon's returning my gaze, mouthing the words *get out of here*. He always loved having mantras. This is his in death. He shows up like it's no big deal, tells me to go. Except I don't know where he wants me to go, and I'm pretty sure this feeling would follow me there anyway, so what's the point.

I turn my attention to Isa. She's on her phone at the edge of the party, smiling as she talks. Nothing much stirs within me.

Danny seems to be content with ending the conversation there, so I make my way toward Isa. I walk slowly, around the party, not through it. I take a few more hors d'oeuvres, trying to guess all their ingredients, the techniques used. I feel better when I'm in the kitchen. I can remember Felix when I'm there. I can see the way he'd hang out in the kitchen with me, teaching me how to hold a knife, how to tell when a sauce was done. I can remember our food adventures, all those that came before the Night of the Perfect Taco. Flashes from childhood: how we'd pretend to be asleep and then sneak out of bed to play video games, our family trip to Greece where we took the last photograph of the four of us together. They hurt like hell, these memories, but at least that's all they are: memories. They're grief as grief is meant to be, comforting and hard but comprehensible.

That's one plus to the summer, at least. No one will be around. Plenty of time to cook. Maybe it'll keep Felix away, make me feel less crazy.

When I get to the other side of the roof, I stand by Isa as she finishes her call. I'm glad the bird doesn't follow me. Isa hangs up and we cheek-to-cheek kiss hello. "You look great," I say.

"Gracias," she says, and we continue on in Spanish. I've always felt weird switching back and forth between English and Spanish with one person. Whatever language my first interaction with someone is, I stick to it, usually. I'm smoother in English. Funnier, I think. But with Isa it's always been Spanish, and maybe that explains the lack of stirring; maybe it's something else.

"This is amazing," she gushes. "I can't believe your parents organized it. The view is gorgeous."

Obligingly, I look at the city stretching out below, twinkling lights of street lamps and far-off neighborhoods.

"Vete de aquí, hermano," the pigeon shouts across the party. Felix always preferred Spanish too.

"My dad's into parties," I say lamely. I don't want to listen to Felix right now or fall into another predictable conversation about summer, about the future, about anything. I put my hand on Isa's shoulder and lean in for a kiss.

She accepts it but keeps her lips tight and ends it in a second or two. "I don't think I want that tonight."

"Okay," I say, stepping back. "Yeah, of course."

We stand quietly for a minute or so, at least as quietly as two people can at a party. "When do you leave for Argentina?"

"Monday," Isa says. The word barely means a thing to me. After this party, the days will bleed together, and Monday may as well be any other day. "How long's it been?" she asks.

"Since what?"

She gets that cartoonishly concerned look she sometimes gets, all eyebrows. The purple scarf she's wearing catches the breeze, unraveling itself. It looks like it's trying to escape. "I don't think you talk about your brother enough," Isa says.

The pigeon tilts its head.

"I know we were never *together*, but we spent enough time together that I should have heard his name a few times, maybe some stories about him." Isa uncurls the wayward scarf from her neck and holds it in her hand. I wish I could uncurl myself from this conversation. "I understand why it might not be with me," Isa says, her hand going up so casually to her eye that I almost miss that she's on the verge of tears. "But I hope you do talk about him with someone. Just, you know... for yourself."

"I do," I lie.

We look out at the city a little longer, elbows brushing against each other. I've always loved the expanse of the city at night, its lack of a typical skyline, its refusal to be contained to one stretch of buildings.

Then she exhales and steps away from the railing. "Okay, time for me to take advantage of your parents' partying. Any food I absolutely have to try?"

I think for a sec, happy to have the conversation turn to food. Food, I can always talk about. "The Thai bruschetta is pretty amazing."

As soon as she steps away, the pigeon flits over to me. "She's cute."

I don't respond.

He ruffles his feathers, picks at something in his wing. "Look at these people, man," Felix says, unperturbed by how I'm ignoring him. If he were still a person, I could picture him crossing his hands behind his head and leaning back. Maybe he'd click his tongue a few times in disapproval.

He's looking with his little pigeon head in the direction of the bar, where Dad and a few of the other parents are standing in a circle, holding drinks. Next to them a group of my classmates do the exact same thing. The adults sip their tequila and the kids shoot it. Add a few gray hairs, adjust their tastes so that they're from the seventies or whatever and it's basically a mirror image.

"You'll forget about cooking," Felix says, loud enough that for a moment I worry someone will hear him. "You keep going down this road, that's where you'll end up. Just like them." He bobs his head in Dad's direction. Dad, who's holding a shot of tequila, and looking like he's about to shoot it. Dad, who went to the same school as me and Felix, got a nice safe business degree—Dad, who was irate when Felix refused to follow that same path.

Dad, who hasn't even talked about Felix in months.

Felix coos and flaps his wings. If he just left me alone for a moment, it might be easier to pretend like I have my shit together.

Then Dad smiles and heads toward the DJ stand. He motions for a microphone, gestures impatiently as the DJ cuts the music and hits a few switches. His shirt is unbuttoned way farther down than any middle-aged man's shirt should be. I think he's swaying a little. Sometimes I can't stand looking at him.

"Shit," Felix the pigeon says. "He still loves his fucking speeches."

"Bienvenidos," Dad says through the speakers. He looks around for a drink, and then snaps his fingers at a passing waiter and asks for another shot of tequila. He thanks everyone for coming, cracks a joke about how this isn't a party for my graduation but a party for him not having to pay for tuition anymore. The crowd responds with alcohol-boosted laughter.

"He made the same joke when I graduated," the pigeon grumbles. Then he offers one last coo and takes off, disappearing unceremoniously into the night. For a second I feel relief. Maybe he'll stay gone.

"Hijo, I want you to look forward now," Dad goes on. "Forget about the past, about what we've lost." He pauses and looks down at the floor for a moment. He bites his lip, like he's struggling to keep back tears. "I know you miss your brother, and I miss him every day too. Life isn't fair."

The performance is impressive, but it makes me want to throw something at the stage. Dad basically wiped his hands clean of Felix long ago, and not even death has undone the forgetting. To him, Felix has been dead for years. Only for appearances will he pretend to be broken. He wants all these people to just go quiet for a moment or two, to think that he's trying to move past tragedy, instead of completely unaffected by it, like I know he is. It's what I see every day: Dad talking about work, Dad talking about my future, Dad going on like nothing's happened.

Then, after all these months, something within me clicks. An understanding. Felix has it right. Escape. Yeah, I know it's probably not a great sign that I'm thinking a pigeon is my dead brother, and I know that everything I heard Felix say was maybe not real, just my grief doing strange things to my head.

But he had that part right all along. I shouldn't be here.

As Dad keeps up the charade, talking about my future and my prospects while he's got a son in the grave, I step away from the edge of the party, cut through the crowd. Most people probably think I'm going to grab myself another drink. They don't see my hands shaking at my sides; they haven't noticed that my shadow disappeared when Felix did, that I'm not whole anymore. No one tries to stop me. Maybe they don't even see me.

It's only when I exit that I hear the murmurs start to build, and Dad's speech get derailed.

I smile the whole elevator ride down.

CHAPTER 2
MEDITERRANEAN OMELET

3 eggs
2 tablespoons butter
2 tablespoons sundried tomatoes
2 tablespoons fresh basil
1 tablespoon goat cheese
Sea salt, to taste

METHOD:

When I get home, I don't know where I'm going, but I know I'm leaving.

Mom and Dad are probably on their way home too, but they'll have to make a few explanations, give some instructions to the caterers or whatever. I have some time, but as soon as I'm in my room, I pull the suitcase from the top shelf in the closet, toss it open onto my bed. Out of habit, or maybe to distract myself from what I'm doing, I turn on the TV.

A commercial pops up: Tupperware, and then cars, cleaning products. I throw all my underwear into the suitcase, along with some socks, two pairs of jeans. I'm actually doing this? On the screen, out of the corner of my eye, I recognize the show. It's called *Today's Specials*. They profile different restaurants across the world, spend an episode with each one.

The show starts with a female chef in the kitchen at dawn, a single burner lit. The camera pans to a quiet morning in the San Juan Islands off the coast of Washington State, golden sunrise over the water, a hummingbird gorging on sugary water from a feeder. "How this is cheap real estate is beyond me," the female chef says on voice-over. They show the name of the restaurant: Provecho. Then the name of the executive chef and owner: Elise St. Croix. Something feels familiar about that, so I keep watching.

A shot of what she's making: perfectly golden omelet. Sundried tomatoes, fresh-picked basil, goat cheese. I want to step through the screen and watch her every move, so I can make it for myself. Felix and I have been watching this show for years, drooling on the couch and then scurrying to the kitchen as soon as the credits roll so we can try to recreate the dishes.

Since he died I haven't been able to watch the show at all. Especially when he shows up on the couch next to me and begs me to change the channel to it, or hijacks whatever it is I'm watching by putting himself in the screen.

They cut away, show the thirty-table restaurant. Chef Elise sits at one of the six patio tables and eats calmly, looking out at the scenery. She's in her late forties, light brown hair in a ponytail. The green of the surrounding islands pops on the screen, the morning ferry from Seattle discernible in the distance. They probably booked the restaurant solid for a month on the strength of that one image.

Then, my favorite part of the show. The kitchen comes alive. Knives coming down like they're machine-driven, flames licking at liquids in saucepans like they're trying to get a taste. The kitchen jargon that sounds like an exotic language. Onions are diced in seconds, herbs chopped and thrown into small plastic containers. A cook cracks a joke, and another one looks up from the meat he's butchering, laughing without even stopping his work.

The staff gathers around as Chef goes over the menu, like soldiers at the ready. Her white chef coat is spotless, a tasting spoon tucked into that tiny pocket in the upper sleeve. She speaks like a general in peacetime, calm but commanding. The guests arrive. Attractive servers bring out black leather menus, smiling widely, the day's specials on the tips of their tongues. Cooks begin poaching shrimp, flipping steaks with tongs.

I'm holding a stack of T-shirts in my hands, transfixed. Then I remember Felix's stack of notebooks.

He kept track of every day of his travels and would send me each filled-out journal for safekeeping. I drag my nightstand over so I can reach the top of my closet, where I've been storing them in a cardboard box. I think I know why this restaurant feels familiar to me.

The notebooks are mostly in Spanish, the rare English word marked by stray accents, as if Felix wanted to bend it to his preferred tongue. It takes all my effort not to thumb through each notebook, to not get lost in Felix's adventures. He never bothered to date them, but I always marked down what day I received them. I know the entry I'm looking for, can recall the words as if I was there too. It was about a year ago, when Felix was in Israel. He'd saved a bunch of money while living on a kibbutz for a while and had treated himself to a nice meal, at a fancy restaurant called Mul Yam.

I usually believe the best meals are to be found in home kitchens, Felix wrote. *This time, I was wrong.* Below, he'd listed restaurants he wanted to eat at in his lifetime. A few of them had been crossed out with blue or black or red ink. I don't allow myself to think of all the ones he didn't get to, but my suspicion was right. At the top of the list is Provecho.

The show comes back on. I've been watching scenes like these so often the last couple of years. Chef Elise walks down rows of planted herbs and vegetables, rallies her troops, the kitchen comes alive, mise en place, the guests arrive, twinkling lights on the patio.

It might be a simple coincidence. There are constantly reruns of this show, and there's a good chance Felix watched this same episode years ago. But it feels like so much of a sign that I look for Felix in the screen, some acknowledgment that this is his doing.

I pull my rain jacket from the closet, though I don't really know what the hell the weather will be like, just that the island is near Seattle and Seattle is rainy. I fold the jacket neatly on top of the other clothes. My heart is pounding.

I've never acted impulsively in my life. Felix got all those genes. It feels like I'm borrowing his disobedience, like I'm stealing something, acting Unlike Myself. But that doesn't keep me from putting a knee on the suitcase to force it closed.

In my parents' room, a safe is hidden behind a shoddy fortress of clothes. The combination is easy to remember; every time Mom and Dad are on the same flight, Dad sits me down with a list of instructions on what to do *just in case.* I grab a few hundred dollars, both my passports, the emergency credit card that's in my name. I use my cell phone to buy a plane ticket and then call a cab, ignoring the slew of missed notifications on the screen.

My hands are shaking and sweaty. I can't believe how easy it is to feel like I'm in control.

I use the bathroom before I go. It's when I'm washing my hands that I hear the awful sound of the front door opening. Mom's voice rings out first, fraught with worry, "Carlos?" I look at my reflection in the mirror and can almost see the back wall. All my edges are blurred. I take a deep breath, open the door.

Mom looks instantly relieved that I'm home. Dad, not so much. "What happened? Is everything okay?" She gets close, like she's inspecting me for bodily harm.

"What the hell are you doing?" Dad asks, noticing the suitcase propped up by the door. He shakes his head, and then calmly removes his suit jacket and folds it onto the little table at the entrance. "Before we get into that," he says, pointing at the luggage, "you're going to apologize for leaving like you did. That was embarrassing."

I know that this, at least, is not an unreasonable request. But I can't find the words to acknowledge it. These talks with Dad always feel like trickery, like everything he says is a trap waiting to snag me.

Mom puts a hand on Dad's forearm. She tries to whisper something, but he interrupts: "He can speak for himself. Just apologize, Carlos, and then we can talk about whatever it is you think you're doing."

I think: *I can't do this anymore.* I think: *I'm barely even here.* I say: "I have to go, Dad."

The words come out like a whimper. So, I'm not stealing all of Felix's personality traits, then. Felix never whimpered.

At least the words are out there. I wait an eternal moment for Dad to respond.

Dad sighs and, almost under his breath, says, "Great, another son who doesn't know how to apologize." Then, louder, he says, "Fine, I'll bite. Go where?"

Mom's already tearing up a little, like she knows exactly where this is heading, like she's getting déjà vu and knows already how this ends. Dad slams the wall with his open hand, repeats himself: "Where, exactly, are you going, Carlos?"

I stare Dad down, trying not to whimper again. "I have to get away from this. It's not what I want," I say. "The internship. Everything."

Dad leans back against the door, crosses his arms over his chest. "No me digas." You don't say.

For a wild moment I consider confessing, telling them about Felix, how I still see him but I feel like I'm the one who's gone. His death made ghosts of both of us and I just want it to stop. I search for more words but end up looking at the floor.

"So you're running away," Dad says. He's got a bit of a smirk on his face, like this is some argument that can be won. "Just like your brother did." He full-on smiles now, uncrosses his arms, un-leans from the door, moves out of the way. He picks up his jacket, walks past me and toward the bedrooms. "A lot of good it did him," he says.

Then the intercom buzzes; the taxi's here.

"Sorry, Mom," I say, pulling up the suitcase's handle and rolling it out the door. I don't want to acknowledge what Dad just said.

She follows behind, stepping into the elevator with me. I keep my eyes on the floor counter above, watching the numbers light up like a countdown. 15...14...13...

"He'll cut you off, like he did with Felix," Mom says. Being American, she's a little more direct than Dad. "He may not show how much he was upset by your brother leaving, but believe me, he was. You leaving too? It'll kill him."

7...6...5...

I can smell her perfume, something floral she's worn forever.

"Just tell me where you're going."

It's not Mom's fault, but I can't bring myself to say anything. I don't want to lose my nerve.

The doors ding open. Mom doesn't follow me out, but she holds her hand out and keeps the doors from closing. "I won't tell your dad. I promise."

Our doorman comes over, all smiles, to grab my suitcase. I want to just rush to the taxi, but leaving Mom is harder than storming away from Dad. "Just tell me you're coming back," she says. There's a tear in the corner of her eye, just waiting there on the precipice, and it's what I say next that will determine if it tumbles down the edge.

I look from her to the car, and I know that it's not too late to stop this and turn around. Tell them what's going on with me, open myself up to their help. "I just need to do one thing," I say, finally. "For Felix."

"One week," she says. I'm not sure if it's a plea or a question or a command. The tear, thankfully, doesn't fall. I might have stayed put if she cried.

I nod and then rush to greet the taxi at the door.

Slam the trunk, slam the door, if only the taxi driver would peel out and leave rubber trails on the asphalt.

I break free.

CHAPTER 3

AIRPLANE SANDWICH

1 pseudo-croissant roll
2 slices highly processed ham
2 slices maybe cheese
1 mustard packet
1 mayo packet

METHOD:

I have a quick layover in LA, then a red-eye to Seattle. The plane is half-empty, and I have a row to myself. But instead of laying out and getting some sleep, I stare out the window. Stars, and the moon reflected on puffy white clouds.

It's like I can feel every mile that I'm farther away from home, from Dad, from the haunted life that had set itself in stone before me. I try to think about what my parents are going through, what my friends will say, but, with my forehead against the window, it's hard to think of anything but that restaurant, waiting out there in the dark. The plane hums insistently; the screen in front of me shows a little cartoon depiction of us escaping from Mexico.

By the time we land in Seattle I'm exhausted and it hits me that I don't know where I'm staying tonight, that I have no concrete plan. I just had this destination and now I'm here. I've officially been spontaneous. It makes me feel like Felix.

I'd thought he might get left behind in Mexico with the rest of my family. I thought that was why he kept wanting me to go, to get away from him. So when he shows up at baggage claim, sitting on top of the carousel among the luggage, I'm disappointed that I'm not so easily cured.

I'll eat once at the restaurant, I think to myself, heart pounding. Eat once, honor Felix's memory. Maybe spend the whole meal just crying or something. Get it all out. Come back normal, or whole, or as close to whole as possible.

I turn my phone on finally, but I keep it on airplane mode. I'm not ready to hear from anyone in Mexico. As the sun rises, I take a cab to the Seattle piers, where the morning rays light up Puget Sound.

I buy a cup of coffee at a nearby stand, though I don't even like it. I just know that's what Felix would be doing. The heat and bitterness feel surprisingly nice, even if I'm wincing at every sip. A few minutes later the ferry boards. The trip is lovely, sun warming my face. I have to fight off sleep so that I don't miss any of the scenery. White birds fly alongside us, emerald islands all around, the Seattle skyline fading in the distance, swallowed up by the haze of the ocean.

Needle Eye Island is smaller than I'd realized. There are no taxis around, just a slew of people waiting to board the ferry bound back to Seattle. I approach the empty information booth and grab a map of the island, looking up at the greenery and then back down to get a sense of what it all looks like. Fog creeps in from the ocean, filtering the sunlight. What the hell am I doing here?

Provecho is marked on the map as a tourist destination. It seems to be within walking distance, so I set out in the direction of the restaurant. Soon I reach Main Street, a couple of blocks' worth of quaint old-school America that I'd always thought movies exaggerated, until now.

The restaurant's façade is simple: a large window facing the street, a black sign with white lettering. It's on the corner of the block, and I can see the edge of the picket fence that borders the patio.

I finger-comb my hair, wipe away some of the sweat from walking around. A car rolls by slowly, gravel pebbles bouncing behind it and rearranging themselves into the word *enjoy*, in Felix's handwriting. I wish he'd stop reminding me he's around, but I find myself grinning all big and stupid, and I realize I'm excited for the first time in months.

I walk up to the front door, salivating already at the prospect of the meal. But the door is locked, because of course it's locked. It's not even eight in the morning yet. The schedule etched on the glass says they don't open for a few hours. Well, then.

I peer into the door, cupping my hands to remove the glare. There's no one in there. I step back to my suitcase, look both ways down the street. There's hardly anyone out here with me. It almost feels like the entire island is abandoned, like I've flown directly into isolation. As if to confirm that, I look down at my feet. Still no shadow.

I take the bend around the street, wanting to see the patio I saw on TV just yesterday. The view makes me feel better immediately. Water, green islands, sailboats, puffy cartoon-like white clouds. It's a dream. I keep staring at the ocean, partially because it's impossible to look away, partially because I want to stall, give myself time to think of what the hell I'm supposed to do now.

Then I hear a door creak open, and to my left a guy in a chef coat and checkered pants appears. He moves a nearby rock over to keep the door open. His arms are tattooed to the wrist, and he's pulling a pack of cigarettes from his pocket. He doesn't notice me right away while he lights his smoke and checks his phone. It almost feels like an apparition, like he walked off the set of a cooking show.

I cough, and then the cook looks up. He's got bags under his eyes, a couple days' worth of scruff. Surprisingly young, maybe a year or two older than me, if that. Americans always look older to me, so it's hard to tell. "Not open," he says, cigarette in his mouth.

"No, I know."

The cook eyes me, the suitcase at my side. "Then what the hell do you want from me, dude?" He takes a long drag, and when I don't say anything he looks back down at his phone, exhaling a puff of smoke that dissipates quickly in the breeze coming in from the water. From the cracked door, I can hear the vague clattering of people moving about the kitchen. I want the smell of Chef Elise's food to waft out, but all I get is the cigarette.

"Sorry," I say, feeling like at least one of us is an asshole. I turn around, go back to the front entrance, where I see a girl slip a key into the door and push it open. She's wearing earphones, a baggy brown sweater, a bag slung over her shoulder. I know this is stupid and weird, but I don't have anywhere to go and can't stand the thought of wandering around the island with no place to go and no one to talk to, so I roll my suitcase over to the door. I knock on the glass.

A few seconds later the door swings open. The girl standing in front of me is pretty—late teens, dark hair, large sixties-style glasses—and for a moment I forget what the hell I'm doing here. Then, over her shoulder, I see the restaurant, exactly like it was shot in the TV show. Thirty tables, a mirror along one of the side walls to make the space feel bigger, a bar adjacent to the hostess stand for people waiting. The back wall is floor-to-ceiling windows looking out at the patio and the ensuing view.

"Sorry," I say, realizing how long it's been without me saying a word. "I wasn't staring at you. I know it probably looked like that. I was just…" I point over her shoulder, stammer, feel my mouth start to go dry. "I want to make a reservation?"

The girl chuckles. "You might officially be the earliest person to ever show up for a reservation." She holds the door open to let me in and then heads to her hostess stand. "What's with the suitcase?"

"Um. I just got here," I say.

"That's cool. From where?" She opens up a large leather-bound agenda and runs her finger down that page.

"Mexico City."

She looks up at me over the rims of her glasses, takes me in for a moment. "You came straight from Mexico City to this restaurant before dropping off your bags?"

I fiddle with my luggage tag. "When you put it that way it sounds kind of insane."

She laughs, eyebrows raised. "No, not insane. Just eager."

I wonder how I could possibly explain my arrival without sounding nuts. Revealing a single detail could unravel my whole story, and my whole story begins and ends with Felix bleeding onto the sidewalk. "I guess I couldn't wait."

She looks back down at the scheduler, biting her bottom lip as she flips a few pages back and forth. We fall into silence, and I look around as if it might all disappear at any moment. I can hear faint music coming from the kitchen. It's hard to believe that I'm standing in a place Felix never got to.

"Looks like you're going to have to wait," she says. "Earliest I have is Tuesday."

"Oh."

"Yeah, summer's busy for us. All these tourists."

A wave of disappointment washes over me, made worse by the fact that I recognize it as disappointment. This is nothing. Any sane person wouldn't bat an eye at this. So why do I feel like my whole journey has been thwarted, like I have to find a bed immediately and disappear beneath its covers?

"I mean, you could always come back and check for cancellations?" the girl says. "Those happen sometimes."

It takes me way too long to say, "Oh, okay. Sure." She takes my name for the Tuesday reservation and then I stand there for a while, not wanting to go back outside but realizing there's nothing left for us to say to each other. "Bye," I say. The girl holds a hand up as she puts her earphones back in.

"Nice meeting you!" she calls out when I'm halfway out the door.

Outside, the world looks empty again. The sun's bright and hot, and everything looks white, drained of color. I'm on an island with no place to stay, no one to go to if I need something. It sounds comically childish, but I want to call my mom. I told her I'd be gone a week; it hasn't even been twelve hours, but I don't know what else to do.

"Si sabes," a voice says.

"No, I don't," I say out loud, though I have to remember that just because I'm here on my own doesn't mean I can start talking to myself. I grab my phone and hold it to my ear.

"You know that Winston Churchill quote, right?"

"Felix, you know damn well I don't."

"'If you're going through hell, keep going,'" he says through my phone. "Not that I think you're going through hell. Far from it. This place is nice."

Yeah, okay, I think. Still kind of having a conversation with my dead brother via a cell phone that doesn't actually work. "What do I do until Tuesday?"

"Keep going," he says. "Find a place to stay. Wait for a cancellation. Explore."

It seems like a typical Felix oversimplification, but at least it's an idea. A set of instructions to follow. So that's what I do. I wander the streets until I find myself on a stretch of hotels and motels set up along the beachfront boardwalk.

I check the first few hotels (big-name chains, families of four wading in the pool, lit with joy) but there's no vacancy. Eventually, I find a room on the far end of the boardwalk, at a motel that definitely wouldn't meet my parents' approval. I unpack my suitcase, take a quick shower, emerge into this strange and sad little motel room.

What the hell am I doing here?

In the months since the Night of the Perfect Taco, solitary rooms have been the hardest to inhabit. I find myself sitting down, standing up, opening the cupboards, feeling the strangeness of having a body. I'm moments away from that now, or from seeing Felix, or burying myself under the covers for the rest of the day.

So instead, I bolt. I leave my phone behind, grab the single key for the room, exit the motel. Head out on a mission. The motel room's half kitchen has a couple of shitty saucepans, one medium-sized pot, a casserole dish, a stained wooden spoon, an ancient blender. It's a sad little space, but at least cooking will give me something to fill the days with.

"Fuck," I say when I enter the grocery store. I forget how incredible US supermarkets are, how the smell of herbs lingers in the air like a perfume. I head straight for the produce, pick up a bunch of basil, the leaves impossibly big. I take a lap around the store, taking in the ingredients. I remember going on trips to the store with Mom and Felix when I was twelve. Felix would insist on pushing the cart, running and taking his feet off the ground, letting the cart carry him down the aisles. I'd wander behind, dragging my feet to prolong the trip. I didn't know a thing about cooking back then, but I was drawn to the ingredients in a way I didn't understand yet.

I'm not sure why, but my instinct today is to go with the taste of home. Some chicken thighs, some poblano peppers, a bag of rice, Mexican crema (I'm surprised to find the real stuff, not that whipped-cream-looking shit they serve in Tex-Mex restaurants). Tortillas and Oaxaca cheese. I lose myself in the aisles, fingers trailing over heirloom tomatoes, herbs and produce and packets of exotic spices I can never find at home.

Back at my motel, I wash the vegetables, set water to boil for the sauce, roast the poblanos the way I've seen our maid Rosalba do time and time again, on the open flame of the burner. But I didn't buy tongs, so I'm doing it by hand, turning the pepper to char the skin, trying to keep my fingertips as far away from the heat as possible.

Put those aside, boil the tomatillos, clean the chicken, preheat the oven. I keep the workspace tidy, not just because the counter can hold little more than my cutting board, but because it feels good to work without clutter; it makes things easier. Felix taught me that. He taught me how to hold a knife, how to trim the fat off a thigh, how to pursue knowledge of this thing I love. I take a look around the kitchen, waiting for him to show himself, make some stupid joke. It's just the memories, though. I'll take them over worrying about Dad, and Mexico, and what my life will look like after this trip, if I'll ever feel like myself again.

I serve myself a plate, sprinkle some chopped cilantro on top. There's enough left over for at least four more people. Not wanting to eat in my sad little room, I take my plate and a chair out onto the breezeway overlooking the parking lot. It's almost two in the afternoon, the sun hot in the sky, making the emerald trees practically shimmer.

I thought maybe this would feel triumphant, a real fuck-you to Dad, to the thing in me grief has erased. But it's not quite that.

Despite his relentless presence, I miss Felix. I wish he were around to see this moment. Not hallucinatory/ghost/whatever Felix, but the real version. My brother. He would have appreciated the cheesiness of a beautiful view and a traditional Mexican dish to celebrate my escape from home. He would have been proud of me.

A young couple squeezes past me in the corridor, beach towels slung over their shoulders. "Smells good," the guy says, and for a crazy moment I want to tell them that I made way too much and that they can join me. Then of course they pass by, hand in hand, leaving me alone before I can say anything.

CHAPTER 4
PEACH CARDAMOM ROLLS

1 cup butter

1 ½ cups sugar

1 ¾ cups boiling water

1 tablespoon salt

2 teaspoons ground cardamom

.75 ounces active dry yeast

2 large eggs

1 can of peaches, drained and diced

7 cups flour

1 teaspoon vegetable oil

1 handful slightly cracked cardamom pods

½ cup powdered sugar

METHOD:

I wake up in the breezeway, more than a little disoriented. The scenery around me is jarring. The plate is by my feet, half the food spilled onto the floor. Families returning from the beach walking through the parking lot. I remember the hostess's suggestion to check back for a cancellation, so I go inside to clean up and then walk the half hour back to the heart of the town. It's all hills and trees, gently humid air alive with bugs and scents and color. I like breathing it in, this differ-ent world.

When I enter the restaurant, I'm surprised to see the same girl working at the hostess stand. It's hours later, and though it's early for dinner—even for Americans—the dining room is packed with people. Eager middle-aged couples crowd by the hostess stand, standing like people waiting to board their flights. The girl makes eye contact with me, and to my surprise she smiles with recognition.

"You're back," she says, so quickly that I wonder if we had a longer conversation than I remember. I do that classic look-behind-to-make-sure-it's-me-she's-talking-to thing. "Hoping for a cancellation?"

"Yeah," I say. "Didn't have anything better to do."

She gives me a long look, and I wonder if what I said came across weird in some way. Her glasses are perched on her head, loose strands of hair coming out from her ponytail. Something about her feels fa-miliar, but that's a stupid thought because how could it? I'm in a dif-ferent world.

"Why don't you take a seat?" she asks, eyebrows raised. For the sec-ond time today, I've been staring at her, because clearly I'm not a fully functioning human. I sit down at a nearby chair, wondering if this is just how it's going to be for me from now on. This is who I am now, the dude who stares and doesn't know how to interact with strangers.

Her phone rings, and as she picks up the receiver she tucks a pen behind her ear.

I raise my eyes up to take a look around the restaurant. Servers in black shirts carrying plates of artfully arranged food of all shapes and colors, food in all its limitless forms. Everyone in the dining room is the picture of happiness. A table of hip-looking twenty-somethings laughing as they listen to their friend's story, a woman with orange hair closing her eyes as she savors a dish's last bite. Felix seats himself next to a couple on the patio, clinks wineglasses with them. Golden light washes over everyone.

I wait. I try to settle in. It's Sunday evening. My phone is still on airplane mode, so who knows how many calls and texts have come my way over the last twelve hours or so. Right now Mexico City is a world away, an entire life away.

Every now and then, my eyes flit toward the hostess. She greets customers with a brilliant smile, leads them to their tables, rolls her eyes at the jerks when she thinks no one is watching. She answers her phone and chats with another hostess, every now and then looking at me and offering a smile.

It makes me feel a little less see-through, even though I've been sitting for nearly an hour like a weirdo, and Felix keeps running around trying to make me laugh or talk.

After a long stretch without a phone call, the hostess comes back from seating a couple and says, "You want some coffee?"

I smile, rise to my feet, though I'm not sure if I should so I kind of end up squatting. "Sure. But aren't you working?"

She laughs. "Yeah, dude. Just gonna grab some from the back. I figured since you're sticking around you might want some."

"Oh. Yeah, thanks." I'm still standing up, not sure if I should offer to help or what. "I'm Carlos," I say, holding out my hand, thanking god that I remembered no one does the whole cheek-to-cheek kiss thing here.

She shakes it. "I'm Emma. Now sit," she says. "If the phone rings, just pick it up and shriek into it, will you?"

I sit down. "You want one continuous shriek or multiple bursts of shrieking?"

"Either way, they'll complain," Emma says, maybe a little too loudly for how many customers are standing around waiting for tables. I watch her head to the back of the restaurant, and before the double doors that lead to the kitchen swing shut I can see the cook with the tattooed arms walk past, carrying a slab of meat. I think I even see Felix back there, a frying pan in hand, flames licking out at him. God, what it would be like to inhabit that world, food surrounding you.

Emma comes back out, two coffees in paper cups in hand. "One's black, one's sweetened and creamy. I don't care which I get." I grab the sweetened one, thank her, stand and then sit and then stand again.

She takes the lid off her coffee, sets it next to the phone that's been ringing so constantly that I'm pretty sure this place is booked for the next year. She blows away the steam from her cup. "So, have you always lived in Mexico?"

"Yup. Born and raised."

"Your English is really good."

"Only when I'm speaking. You should have heard me screeching at your customers a second ago. My accent's embarrassing." Whoa. Was that my second joke already? I don't think I've cracked so much as a pun since the Night of the Perfect Taco.

"You screeched?!? I said *shriek*. Shit." She takes her glasses off, rubs them clean on the hem of her sweatshirt. "If we go out of business, I'm telling the chef it's your fault."

"That probably lowers my chances of sneaking in on a cancellation, right?"

"I'd say so." Emma sips again from her coffee and then gives a chuckle. The phone rings again, and now, while she's on it, I'm not looking around the restaurant but rather opening my mouth like I'm shrieking and trying to make her laugh. I'm not sure why I am so at ease all of a sudden. Joking around in the last few months has felt like pretending, even if I'm doing it with my friends. But her laughter makes me want to try for more.

When she hangs up, she throws her coffee lid at me. A woman wrapped in a silk shawl glares at her, but Emma ignores the look. "So, is that really why you're here? You decided to take an international flight for one meal?"

For a moment I consider just telling her everything. Felix is dead and this is a link to him. We loved food together and he wrote the name of this place in a notebook once, so now I'm here. To eat on my dead brother's behalf. There's an icebreaker for you.

I do think about how good it would feel to finally tell someone that I can see him. Maybe that's all it would take to get him to leave. Instead I shrug and say yes, and Emma gives me another long look before she turns to help some customer.

I end up staying at the restaurant far longer than I planned to. I thought maybe I'd stick around an hour or two and then go exploring like Felix suggested. But the wider world doesn't call out to me. I just want to wait, watch the food go by, sit in this little corner of the world and not worry about anything else.

"You are the most patient person I've ever met," Emma says at one point. The sun's set over the horizon; the restaurant is aglow with soft lighting from scentless candles and the twinkling bulbs in the patio. "You know you have a reservation for Tuesday, right?"

"I'm kind of enjoying myself, though," I say.

"That's a little weird."

I sink into my chair, blood rushing to my cheeks. I go the next hour without saying a word. A dozen different Felixes show up. He's a server carrying one plate in each hand, thumbs off the edges, a customer checking in for a reservation. Some versions of him make a little less sense: a miniature version swimming in my coffee, telling me to relax.

Emma greets a party of six and as she walks them over to their table, I think I see her glance over her shoulder at me as she goes. She's probably noticed me staring at people, trying to suppress the urge to talk back to Felix.

At ten o'clock, the restaurant is seating its last reservations. Emma's wiping off menus with a napkin, and she jokes that I've been here so long I should have gotten paid. I try to act normal as a thought bubble sprouts out of my head and Felix shows me a flashback of the Night of the Perfect Taco: us at the stand in that one market, Felix teasing me that I should work with food.

"Yup, I'm for sure qualified to work here," I tell Emma. "I watch the Food Network."

"Don't tell anyone in the kitchen that. They keep special knives to stab people with just for that occasion."

I laugh, she laughs and we fall into a silence that lasts until I finally say good-night. "See you Tuesday," she says.

CHAPTER 5
CHERRY MOON PIES

6 ounces unsalted butter

1 cup sugar

2 teaspoons vanilla extract

1 cup flour

¼ cup graham cracker crumbs

2 teaspoons baking powder

2 teaspoons baking soda

2 teaspoons cherry extract

1 teaspoon cinnamon

¼ cup whole milk

1 pound bittersweet chocolate

2 tablespoons coconut oil

METHOD:

The next day is Monday and the restaurant is closed, so I spend the whole day roaming the aisles of the grocery store and cooking, kept company only by Felix. Every time he shows up, he undoes a little bit of the joy I'd built up yesterday.

Every now and then, I think about calling my parents. I think about Isa on her way to Buenos Aires, Danny and the rest on the way to Europe. Mostly, I just hole up inside my room and wonder whether Dad's already washed his hands of me.

On Tuesday, I wake up late, without enough energy to do anything but lie in bed. When I emerge from my room, it's practically evening, and there's a fog creeping in from the beach, more white than gray. It stretches itself across the motel parking lot and slips in between the trees across the road. The sun, well on its way to the horizon, doesn't do much to heat the day, and I have to warm my hands with my breath on my walk downtown.

Joggers rule the island at this hour, it seems. Brightly colored spandex and arm-strapped phones greet me at nearly every turn, sometimes emerging from the fog like ghosts. I walk past Provecho once or twice, knowing that it's too early for me to show for my dinner reservation. Felix shows up at my side in jogging gear, comically fluorescent. "Let's go exploring, man. You've been sitting around for almost two days. It's not healthy," he says, his fractured English making the *h* sound like a loogie being hocked up.

He leads me to the beach, which is frankly a little lame. Everyone brought their own towels and coolers and stuff, and there are no restaurants with lounge chairs and palapas set up along the beach, a staple of every Mexican beach I've been to. There should be unfettered beers and music, not the surreptitious pulls from Solo Cups I see here, the Bluetooth speakers.

"I just want to go to the restaurant," I say, watching people brush sand off their belongings, parents trying to corral their sunburnt children.

"You came all the way here. I'm excited about the meal too, but there's more to this place, don't you think?"

I don't say anything.

Eventually we head back to the restaurant. I regret it a little when I see that Emma's not at the hostess stand because I liked how it felt to talk to her the other day. But I don't regret it enough to go back out into the world. The new girl at the hostess stand gives me a strange look when I say I'll wait three hours for my reserved table, which I guess is a reasonable reaction. I watch the servers go up to the kitchen window, watch the looks on people's faces when they get their food, when they take their first bite.

Suddenly, I'm thinking about all I didn't know about Felix's life. What he ate at the Israeli restaurant, for example, the meal that made him want to come here.

"Endive salad with creamy yuzu dressing, followed by three-chili shrimp scampi," Felix cuts in. "For dessert: white chocolate gelato with fresh pomegranate and a passionfruit drizzle."

I sigh loudly, which is another tactic I've had to develop to stifle the urge to respond to him in public. Hallucination or ghost, I'm not sure whether I should strictly believe anything he says since he's died. If they're somehow his memories or just what I think his memories would sound like. Easier just to sigh.

The hours go by, surprisingly easy. I don't have to talk to anyone, don't have to interact with Dad's business partners, don't have to force jokes so that Mom and everyone else will believe I'm okay. I can just look at food, and people, and a world unlike the one I'll eventually go back to. My normal life will consume me soon enough, so for now I want to dive into this. I will honor Felix and then cast him away. Then I'll be okay.

Finally, the hostess calls my name and leads me to a table in the back, near a window looking out at the patio. If I tried, I could easily eavesdrop on half a dozen conversations around me. The hostess places a black leather menu on the table, says someone will be around shortly to take my order. I'm shocked I hadn't thought to open a menu up until this point. It reads like a dream.

When I put the menu down, Felix is sitting in front of me in a tuxedo.

He conjures up tears to his eyes. "I can't believe you brought me here. You're such a good brother."

"Shut up," I mumble, pretending to take a sip of water so no one sees my lips move.

Felix holds his hands up in surrender. "Okay, okay, we won't get emotional." He opens a menu, though there's only one on the table and it's under my elbow. "Please tell me you got the sweetbreads for us."

I look out at the patio. A full moon's reflected in the water, and the other islands in the distance are impossibly easy to see through the darkness. "I got the sweetbreads," I say, hating him for making me say it out loud, for knowing damn well that the sweetbreads are not for *us*.

He starts off on some story about his travels, and I just stare out the window until my food arrives, listening. It's easy to forget myself. Andouille-spiced sweetbreads, pork belly ceviche as appetizers, something called Duck in a Jar for my entrée, a side order of squash poutine.

The descriptions alone were a fantasy, and I was sure that there'd be no way the dishes could match up to my expectations. I was wrong.

Felix eats too. Twin plates show up when the server sets mine in front of me. Felix lays out his napkin across his lap and rubs his hands together like a cartoon villain planning his takeover.

He takes a bite of the duck breast and dips it in the sriracha au jus. "Que jalada," he moans with pleasure, scoops out some more. Except I know there's nothing there across the table from me. It's just me eating. One meal, not two.

These bites are what I'm here for, I remind myself. I try to savor them instead of diluting them with my thoughts.

For dessert: dulce de leche fondant cake with banana-cardamom gelato and orange-zest white-chocolate chips. My brother eats a spoonful as slowly as he always did when he was alive. He used to eat desserts so glacially that he could never get ice cream in cones. They'd drip down his arm, half the scoop wasted on the sidewalk.

The gelato on his plate is pooling right now, but it's a fucking lie. There is no gelato. This has been one of the best meals of my life, but it's been a solitary one. My brother isn't sitting in front of me. I'm alone in this restaurant, on this island. I came here to honor some unrealized dream of his based on a journal entry. A stupid journal entry, as if it could have told me what Felix would have done with one more day. As if he'd be here if he really could. As if this undoes anything, fixes anything.

"Hey," I hear him say. Soft clink of his spoon hitting the plate. "I would be. I am."

But I can't bear the sight of him/not him. I never wanted him to come back. I never wanted him gone.

My breath starts to come quick and shallow. I can see Felix in the reflection of the window but somehow can't see myself. The background noise of the restaurant, so manageable when I sat down, is suddenly building to a roar.

"How was everything?" My chipper server has the bill in her hand. If I hand her my credit card, sign my receipt, my little mission here is over.

I try to smile at her, but it's just not happening. To keep from revealing myself as completely out of my mind, I manage to stammer out: "Bathroom?"

She points the way, and I speed-walk to the privacy of a stall as if I'm about to be sick. Inside, I take a seat, doubling over, trying to take deep breaths but failing to. It feels like the opposite is happening, like air is being squeezed out of my lungs. My hands are gripping at my knees, but I can't even see my fingers doing it, just the little indents in the fabric where I know my fingers should be.

Without Felix, I am not myself.

Shaken, I walk over to the sink, splash some water on my face. I avoid looking at my reflection, just keep my eyes down and try to convince myself that it's all okay. When I manage to take a deep breath without it hurting, I leave the bathroom.

Right by the exit, in the little corridor between the bathrooms, I see Emma leaning against the wall. She's in her work shirt, her hair in a bun. "Hey," she says when she sees me. "You okay? I saw you rushing in there looking like you were about to pass out. Wanted to make sure we hadn't poisoned you or something." She looks over her shoulder toward the kitchen. "I probably shouldn't say that so loud."

I somehow manage a laugh. "Yeah, I'm okay." Not sure I even believe that, but what the hell else should I say?

I'm expecting her to nod, lead me back to my table, say good-bye.

Instead, she pulls her phone out of her pocket and checks the time. Then she says, "Are you done eating?" I nod. "Can you give me, like, five minutes? Then wait for me outside?"

"Um," I say. "Why?"

"I have this weird thing where if I only see someone in one location I can't ever be sure that they're a real person." She readjusts her glasses so that they're not on the bridge of her nose but out of the way, up above her forehead. Two tiny indents mark the spot where they've rested all day. "Plus, you're new to town. I like showing people around. You're free, right?"

I manage a smile. "Yeah," I say.

"Five minutes," she says. "Don't bail on me." She turns the corner. Outside, tourists walk by holding dripping ice-cream cones, changed out of their beachwear into pleated shorts and sundresses. I'm constantly on the lookout for that rising feeling of dread in my chest again, but everything seems calm within me.

Emma appears in front of me, her work shirt unbuttoned to the tank top beneath it, her bag slung over her shoulder, glasses still resting on her head.

"So, am I a real person now?" I ask, getting up.

"Yet to be determined," she says. "We're still too close to the res-taurant. Ghosts have *some* range."

"Ah, of course. I knew that." I smirk at the irony.

Emma asks if I've seen the lake yet, and I admit that I haven't even really thought about visiting it. "I saw the beach," I offer.

"Ugh to the beach." She looks at her phone for a second and then drops it into her bag. "Do you have any shattered dreams?"

"What does that mean?"

"Any huge disappointments? Life stomping down on you? Hope flittering away from you like sand spilling from the cracks between your fingers?"

I blink at her.

"Good," she says. "This lake can unshatter dreams. Guaranteed. Dip a single toe in and your hopes are restored."

She leads us away from downtown, up a street that turns into a hill. It's a full moon, and I'm amazed by how much light it provides. There's no real sidewalk, just the side of the road, grassy banks next to the shoulder. Few cars pass by us, and I'm constantly shocked by how quiet things are here.

"How does it do that?"

She gives me this excited look, eyebrows cartoonishly raised, goofy smile. "I want to keep it a secret but suck at keeping secrets, so we have to change the subject while we walk or I'm gonna ruin it."

"Okay," I say. "What about...um..." I ransack my thoughts for any-thing funny to say, anything that'll make her want to keep this walk going. I look around for clues, see that it's all moonlit shadows and trees. I finally land, somehow, on: "My brother died."

Emma meets my eyes, and I realize what a colossally poor conversation subject this is. Emma doesn't say anything, because I just held a pillow over this conversation's face and watched the breath drain out of it.

"When you said 'change the subject,' you meant to the most depressing thing I could think of, right?"

I'm not sure if I'm digging myself into a deeper hole, but Emma laughs and says, "Yeah, that was rough. But at least now I know taking you to the lake is a good call." We walk quietly for a while. "Is that why you had that little moment in the restaurant? Because he's dead?"

I turn to look at her, taken aback. "Basically," I say.

"I never had any siblings," Emma says. "I always wanted them, though. I usually pretended friends were sisters or just made them up inside my head. They'd only show up at night, when I was waiting for my parents to get home and relieve the babysitter. I'd pretend they were taking care of me instead of whichever neighbor's teen daughter was watching me.

"My parents are both chefs so they were always working a lot," she says, grabbing at a long stalk of grass and twisting it in her hands. "This was back when they were still together and we lived in New York. But they could barely handle being parents and cooks at the same time, and they sure as shit couldn't handle a marriage on top of it. Anyway, it's probably why I always have a book on me now. I need something to keep me company."

In the silence that follows, I glance over at Emma, seeing her face in the moonlight. "That's also why I'm constantly inviting people to do things with me," she jokes, not meeting my eye.

"Including near-strangers-slash-possible-ghosts that hang around your place of work."

"Exactly." Emma finds another nearly invisible break in the woods, leads us back out to the street. I can see the lights from downtown, and I'm surprised to see how high we've gone up the hill. "Wait for it," Emma says, reading my expression. "It gets so much better."

Near the top of the hill there's a scenic overlook on the side of the road, but Emma leads me across the street and into the woods again. We have to fight through brambles to reach the peak, me and this girl I don't really know.

On one side, the moon reflects off the crystalline lake that's at the near end of the island and gives the place its name. It really does look like a needle's eye. The moon looks like some fantastical orb that lives in the lake, only visible from this one spot. It's as if we're witnessing something in another dimension. To the other side there's the town, a spattering of lights that would pale in comparison to any neighborhood in Mexico City, even its most remote suburbs.

All around us, the ocean does a weak impersonation of the lake's reflection of the moon, the waves too disruptive for the water to be a mirror but still stained beautifully by the silver glow. And to the east, just beyond the silhouette of another island, the lights of Seattle are a haze on the horizon.

"How do you know about all these amazing spots?" I ask.

"My mom and I moved here right after the divorce. I had a lot of alone time," Emma says. "Gave me time to explore."

I take in the view, unable to decide in which direction I want to look. Hands on hips, still a little winded from the climb, or maybe actually struck breathless, I say, "This place is magical."

"Yeah," Emma responds. "I'm glad you think so."

She's standing only a few steps away, arms still folded across her chest, looking in the direction of Seattle. A breeze picks up, and I can see goose bumps appear on her arms.

"Look at all this, man," Felix says, appearing at my side, putting an arm over my shoulder. "I wish I could have seen this for real."

Go away, I think. Emma and I are having a nice moment here. We're quiet for long enough that my words have a chance to echo in my head. Tears come to my eyes, and I have to pretend the wind is to blame.

Emma catches on to some extent, and she reaches out and gives me a reassuring forearm touch that lasts only a second but still does what it's meant to. Then she pulls away, grabs her sweatshirt from out of her bag and slips it on as I compose myself.

Felix stands by, hands in his pockets, his gaze going from me to Emma and then out at the expanse of the island. His shirt wrinkles in the breeze, and I remember how Mom would always say the shirt was one strong gust of wind away from disintegrating. Two red bursts of blood start spreading across his chest, and though I want to look away I force myself to keep my eyes on him. I think for a second that this is it, this is when Felix leaves me. Then Felix looks down at the blood and groans. "Every time," he says, taking out one of those stain-remover pens and starting to dab furiously and futilely at the still-growing splotches.

Felix doesn't disappear; I'm still half-here.

CHAPTER 6

SEAWEED SALAD

50 grams rehydrated wakame

1 cucumber, julienned

1 stick surimi, shredded

¼ cup scallions

1 tablespoon mirin

1 tablespoon soy sauce

1 tablespoon sesame oil

1 teaspoon rice vinegar

1 teaspoon wasabi paste

METHOD:

Emma glances down at her phone. She looks indecisive for a moment and then types something. A little sound effect swoosh tells me she just sent a message. "We're gonna meet up with my friends at the lake, if that's okay?"

"Sure," I say. We stand up, brush away the loose strands of dried grass. I hope Felix stays gone, but I hope it a little more gently this time. "That's so quaintly small-town American, hanging out at the lake. What do you guys do there?"

"The usual. Bonfire, drinks if we can get them, or someone brings weed, or we play charades. Why? What do you do for fun in Mexico City?"

Sit on the couch alone watching cooking shows, have my friends drag me out to parties because they don't know how else to deal with me. "Umm, I don't know," I say. "We have these things called comidas, where everyone from school gathers at a house for tacos and a shit-show amount of drinks. It's supposed to be a lunch, but it's really just an afternoon party."

We fight through the bramble again, start to descend the hill. I still can't believe how much I can see of the woods. Each branch and leaf is lit up as if it's beneath a spotlight. This place feels like a fantasy, like any minute now we'll cross paths with a group of fairies, and Emma will simply wave hello at them, used to the sight. "Parents are just cool with that?" Emma asks.

"Whoever's hosting usually has parents out of town or something. I haven't been to one in a while." I think out loud. "That might just be a thing that's specific to my school, though. My school is kind of its own world: lots of rich kids, embassy kids, people who move every two years and have lived all over the world. I'm never really sure if my experiences are typically Mexican or not."

"Sounds like maybe not," Emma says. "But what the hell do I know?"

We break through into another clearing, with another insane view.

"So, what else do you do?" Emma says. "Like, for fun?"

"I mostly just go to movies, I guess," I say, with a chuckle wrought mostly from nerves. Then I add, "I like cooking."

"Really? How come?"

I've answered this question in my own head for years now, as if waiting to defend myself from someone's accusations. Maybe the way Dad treated Felix's love of travel helped prompt the preparation. "I love food and the joys it brings people. Cooking, to me, is an easy way to provide joy to myself and to others."

Emma cocks her eyebrow. "Good answer," she says.

"My brother may have helped me phrase it. He was much better with words than I am." I duck away from some low-hanging branches. "What about you?" I ask, thankful but not wanting to just keep coming back to my dead brother. "What do you do for fun?"

"I walk with ghosts through the woods," she says with a smile, and I laugh more than I probably should.

When we get to the lake, Emma's friends have started a bonfire. Embers float up into the night sky, and I swear to god they just keep going up and up until they stick to the night sky. There's about ten people huddled around the pit, most holding beers. I recognize a couple from the restaurant, servers and bussers who have shed their black shirts and now look younger than I would have guessed. The cook with the tattooed sleeves is here too, his perpetual cigarette tucked between two knuckles. Emma calls out a hello as they approach and then introduces me to the group.

Someone asks where I'm from, and the usual onslaught of follow-up questions ensues. The tattooed cook, Matt, brings up one of those questions I'm shocked I've been asked more than once in my life: "Did you ride a donkey to school every day?" He laughs, proud of himself, until I say that, sure, all twenty-five million Mexico City residents ride around on donkeys. The city built a second-story highway just to deal with all the donkey traffic. The group laughs, someone calls Matt a dumbass.

Emma and I both accept beers and then take a seat on a blanket. We rest our backs against the cooler, which is heavy with ice and bottles. Emma gets pulled into a conversation pretty quickly, and I want to just sit back and listen to her, watch the embers float and wait for the island to keep doing impossible things. But a girl sitting to my left ropes me into a conversation. Her name's Brandy and she very quickly tells me that she's looking forward to leaving to go to college, all the new experiences that await her. I feel like a dick for not really caring about what she's saying, for just wanting to be alone with Emma again.

"But this place is great," I say, struggling to engage.

"For a while. You left Mexico, though. So you were probably kind of sick of it, right? But if I went I'd probably be amazed by everything there." Brandy narrows her eyes, maybe a little drunk, maybe just a little like Felix, able to slip into earnestness without being self-conscious about it. "It's beautiful here. I know that. But I'm kind of blind to it now. I can't wait to get out."

I don't get the chance to think too long about what she said, because a few of Emma's other friends join in on the conversation. They're curious just because I'm not from here.

They want to know about drug lords, whether Mexicans eat burritos or if that's just Americans, all the differences between here and there, but only weird surface questions that won't actually tell them anything. In between their questions, or when Emma moves to throw another log on the fire, tosses someone else a beer, I look at her. I look at this strange place I'm in, the strangers around me, how it feels like I've been plopped in the middle of all of it. I find myself thinking: *What a world.*

Someone asks me what brought me to the island, and I feel a tightness in my chest. I look down at the beer in my hand, peel at the label. Matt barks a laugh at my awkwardness until someone smacks him and tells him to shut up again. Sound gets sucked out of the evening, and all of a sudden it's just me, feeling like a moron in front of some strangers. I'm afraid I'm about to freak out like in the restaurant again.

Emma breaks the silence with a sigh and then stands up, patting me on the shoulder as she does, rescuing me. "Wanna take a walk?"

I try to contain my smile, nod. I expect Brandy or a few others to follow along, but it's just me and her walking away from the bonfire. When we're only a few steps away, the stars, which have been hiding behind the glare of the flames, reemerge overhead. It feels like Emma's just flicking switches around me, making things beautiful.

"Sorry about my friends," Emma says. "You were getting pounced."

We walk along the edge of the lake, tiny waves lapping at our feet, though the lake as a whole seems perfectly still. "I don't mind. It's just weird being the center of attention."

"Usually when people pay attention to me," Emma says, "I'm certain they're after something. Like they're going to ask me for a donation or to sign a petition at any moment."

"Oh, that reminds me," I say, pretending to reach into my pocket for a pen. "I have this petition I need six thousand signatures for..."

"Shut up," Emma says, smacking my arm. We fall quiet, and I can make out the sounds of wildlife in the surrounding trees. Bugs, an owl, the scattering feet of critters in the leaves. "I mean it, though. I can't meet new people without giving a little side-eye to their intentions." I don't ask if I'm an exception. Emma goes on. "It's gonna sound like such a whiny thing to say, but I'm sure it's my parents' fault. You can't leave a kid so alone that she makes up imaginary friends for herself and not cause some long-lasting trust issues." She says this jokingly, but I can tell there's something tugging at her voice.

She kicks at a pebble, and we both watch it bounce toward the lake and then skip across the surface. Like, the entire surface. Hundreds of skips, the ripples visible in the moonlight. I'd say I'm losing my mind but, well, that ship's probably sailed. At least this insanity is aesthetically pleasing.

"You think parents know?" I ask. "When they've messed their kids up in certain ways?"

"Oh, I've written several manifestos to my parents about All the Ways They Messed Up."

I chuckle. I don't know where she's taking me, but I don't want this walk to stop. I want to circle the lake all night. "What's number one on the list?"

Emma thinks for a second. "Well, my mom never taught me her secret to make the perfect grilled cheese."

I gasp. "You poor thing."

"That's not even a joke. I'm exaggerating a little about her messing me up, of course. I think I turned out okay, mostly." We've made it far enough away from the bonfire so that the voices don't carry over, and it feels like it's just the two of us again. Emma's face is lit up by the moon, tiny replicas in her glasses at certain angles. "But she seriously makes the greatest grilled cheese of all time, and she's never told me her secret. I can just picture myself in college, during the prime grilled cheese days of my life, each one a slight disappointment."

"That's the saddest thing I've ever heard."

The lake has a little bay that dips into the woods, out of sight from the bonfire, and we follow the grassy shore until we're completely isolated.

"So, have you been planning to come here for a while?" Emma says, stopping at a boulder near the lake. She leans against it, starts to untie her shoes.

"No," I say, continuing my surprising trend of truth telling in her presence. "I kind of ran away. Bolted from my own high school graduation party." I look around at where we are, the little nook of lake that has us hidden from the rest of the world. "What are we doing here?"

"I'm showing you more cool island things," she says, peeling off her socks now. "This is a great night for it too. When the moon's out, it looks even better."

"What does?" I ask, following her lead and stepping out of my shoes.

"Plankton." Emma leans down and rolls up her pant legs until they're halfway up her calves. Her toenails have traces of purple polish on them, long ago chipped. She tip-toes her way to the edge of the lake, avoiding rocks and twigs. I expect her to dive right in, but she stops before she reaches the water, looks back at me.

It's really tempting to get caught in that look, so instead I tuck my socks inside my shoes, roll up my pant legs, step up to Emma's side. It's a little chilly out, and I expect the lake is colder, but there's no way I'm not doing whatever the hell Emma has in mind.

"Okay, when I say so, we're gonna take three superlong strides into the lake. Stomp as much as you can. You'll get a little wet, but, trust me, it's worth it." She moves her glasses again so that they rest atop her head. "Don't look up, don't look ahead, don't look at me, okay? You can only look down at your feet. And really stomp down. Splash as much as possible."

Emma counts down to three, and as soon as we splash into the water, it comes alive. Millions of white lights sparkle. They radiate out like a shockwave, tiny brilliant explosions like nothing I've ever seen. Emma is stomping onward, a path of light in her wake. I follow along, but I go slower, not wanting to take the next step until the last one has subsided, afraid that the magic will run out. It's like lightning underwater, like microscopic fireflies raging in sync. When the water calms back to darkness, I lean over, run my hand through the water. The lights follow suit, like it's my skin that's charged and not the water.

I hear Emma's stomping and near-maniacal laughter get closer. "What is this?" I ask, my face only a few inches away from the water. I hadn't even noticed how warm the lake is, how soaked through my jeans are. I swirl my fingers across the surface, enchanted.

"This is nature being ridiculous," Emma says. "Bioluminescent plankton. Like swimming in fireworks."

We step back to shore, sit on the muddy banks with our toes dipped into the water. Every now and then one of us will kick out to bring the lake back to life. I think back to how I lost it at the restaurant and it doesn't feel like something that really happened to me. A dream, maybe, or a story I heard someone else tell.

"Thanks for bringing me here. I needed this," I say. I raise my foot up from the water, watch electric white droplets cling to my heel. "You were right. This unshatters dreams."

"I could tell you'd appreciate it." Emma scoots closer to the lake so she can bend her knees up and still touch the water. She folds her arms around her legs, looking out at the water, a beatific smile on her face. Then she turns her head a little, rests her cheek on her knee to glance at me.

In that one glance, I know I've never been here before. I've never been in a moment like this one, never wanted a night to stretch out the way I want tonight to stretch out. If this island is as magical as it feels, it'll stop the flow of hours into a trickle. If I'm here for a reason, it's not the meal I had at Provecho.

I smile at her and she smiles back, and then I stomp my heel down in the water so that the air around us is lit up by bright droplets. Emma stomps too, hard enough that the splashes soak us both.

When we stop, I look at that spot in the lake where our feet are touching underwater. The particles of white light in the water rearrange. Felix again. Quick urge to kick him away before I think: *How many nights like this did he have? How many was he robbed of?*

"Hey, you okay?" Emma asks.

I takes my eyes off the lake, not sure how I managed to get pulled away from this. "Yeah," I say, smiling. "Really don't want tonight to end." She lays her hand on mine, and as soon as she does I really do feel okay. Like my time here isn't going to be all panic attacks and solitary cooking.

For the first time in a long time, I am okay.

CHAPTER 7
SALMON WITH ANGEL HAIR PASTA

3/4 bottle dry white wine
5 lemons (and zest)
½ cup fresh dill, roughly chopped
1 pint heavy whipping cream
4 8-ounce salmon filets
500 grams angel hair pasta
¼ cup sundried tomatoes, julienned
1 4-ounce jar capers

METHOD:

The next morning, I leave the motel at sunrise. When I said good-bye to Emma yesterday, she told me to come by the restaurant early. I'm not sure why, but I didn't really bother asking.

Fog encroaches again, but it's tinted pink by the dawn. The whole island looks like cotton candy. I linger in the parking lot awhile, see that couple who walked past me the other day packing up their car. Maybe I should be booking my flight home, but for some reason I don't want to think about it. Not after last night. Felix didn't show up again the rest of the night, and though I didn't sleep long, I slept deeply.

Before I can knock on the front door of the restaurant, Emma pokes her head from around the corner. "Come this way," she calls.

I follow behind. She's standing by the back door, keeping it propped open. "I have a surprise for you," she says with a smile.

"Me too." I hold out the coffee I bought for her on the way here.

I want a little moment reliving yesterday, some eye contact or a forearm squeeze or something. Emma takes the coffee unceremoniously and urges me inside. The short hallway we walk down is much colder than the temperature outside. It's quiet, though I can tell there's someone else here.

"Are you giving me a tour?" I ask, a little giddy at the thought. I've never been inside a professional kitchen before, and though I've had some exposure on TV, in books I've read, it's a little different than what I'd imagined.

"There'll be time for that."

I don't really know what Emma's talking about, but I'm distracted by the sights of the kitchen. We pass two huge steel doors that I imagine are home to all the ingredients from my meal yesterday. I strain to see the line, the row of cooks prepping for the day. Felix would have loved to see this. We turn a corner and come upon a door, which Emma immediately knocks on.

"Come in!"

Emma pushes the door open. Inside, at a desk facing the door, is a woman who looks surprisingly like Emma herself. She's wearing a white chef's coat, her brown hair up in a bun, bags under her eyes. Golden script on the pocket over her heart reads: Chef Elise. She looks up from a clipboard in front of her, barely taking in my presence before she starts scribbling something. "What are you doing here so early?" she asks, which feels to me like a weird way to talk to your employees.

"Meet our new dishwasher," Emma says.

Chef stops her scribbling and gives Emma a hard look. I turn to her for an explanation too, but she's busy staring Chef Elise down. I'm guessing this is some sort of joke. I'm just trying to figure out if it's at my expense or not.

Chef tosses her clipboard down onto the desk and sighs, looks at me. "Any restaurant experience?"

"I'm sorry, I'm not sure what's going on here." I turn to Emma. "You want me to work here?"

"Goddamnit, Emma, what are you bringing this kid in here for?"

Emma rolls her eyes. "You need a dishwasher, don't you?"

"That's not the point."

"Of course it is," Emma says, throwing her hands up. "You need a dishwasher, Mom. It's not the world's—" There's a loud crash, and when I turn to it Chef Elise's clipboard is on the floor and I swear I can see her nostrils flaring.

"In here, I'm your boss. You call me Chef like everyone else."

Jesus. The air in the room feels exactly the way it did when I left home. At least now I know why Emma seemed a little familiar. I'd seen Chef before, on that show. "Whatever," Emma says. "Dishwashing isn't the hardest job to learn. You need a dishwasher. He wants a job in restaurants. I'm just helping you out."

Wait, what? Where the hell did Emma get that notion? I'm so confused, which must show on my expression because when Emma sees it she gives me a little smirk. "The way you talk about cooking. You don't want to go back home, do you?"

Emma raises her eyebrows, questioning. Chef Elise has a similar look in her eyes, just a little more on the exasperated side. As I'm caught in their stares, wondering what I'm supposed to say to that, I sense another presence in the room. Of course. Felix. I try to subtly look around for him, find him in the dust swirling around in a beam of light.

"I think the girl has a point," Felix says. Only my brother could find a way to smirk when he's dust. "Why go back to the same thing? What's waiting at home for you?" At least he's in wisdom-nugget mode and not stupid-joke mode.

I think about what I said to Mom before I left. One week. It feels like a joke now. How could I have thought a week would be enough? It's enough for a meal, maybe.

My thoughts are interrupted by the squeak of Chef's chair as she rolls over to pick up her clipboard. "Fuck, Emma, look at him. He doesn't even know where he is." Great, I've been staring at a beam of light and probably moving my lips while I think up a response. Chef's about to tell me to go away and I don't know what I'd do with the rest of my day. Go back to my room, try to hold myself together by cooking things Felix and I used to. Go home. Face Dad again.

"Elias!" Chef yells out.

A Latino dude shows up at the door. "Yes, Chef." He's in a chef coat too, a towel slung over his shoulder, sweat already on his forehead. He's right around Felix's age, maybe in his midtwenties.

"Have we heard from Richie yet?"

"No, Chef. That's three days."

Chef looks back at me and then at Emma. The other cook, Elias, goes back to whatever he was doing in the kitchen. Chef leans back in her chair and then goes over to the computer on her desk and clicks a few times. Emma gives me a reassuring smile, or at least that's what I assume it's supposed to be. It's six in the morning and I think I'm in the middle of asking for a job, which was not at all in my morning plans.

Then Chef sighs and pushes herself away from her desk. "You," she says, pointing at me. "Come with me." She walks toward us, combing back a loose strand of hair. I want to explain further, say that I'm only here a short while, that I don't know what the hell is going on. Frankly, I'm a little terrified to say anything. "And you," she says, scowling at Emma. "I love you, but you're such a fucking brat."

Emma beams a smile and then I'm following Chef out the door. "Love you too, Chef," Emma calls out behind us. Felix comes along as my shadow, which is the first time I've seen my shadow in months. He's pretty bad at it. He keeps doing all these flips and leaving the confines of where a shadow should be. Given everything else that's happening, he's making it really hard for me to keep my cool.

"These are walk-ins," Chef points to the steel doors Emma and I walked past earlier, "but there'll be no reason for you to be in this part of the kitchen. You love cooking? Awesome. So does everyone else here. You don't get to do it my kitchen."

At the end of the corridor Chef points out the prep hall. There are three cooks in there: a short and stout Latino guy shoving tomatoes into some sort of chopping contraption that I've never seen before, even on cooking shows; a tall black guy stirring something in a big pot; and an older Latina looking over a sheet of paper stuck to the ticket rail above her. Chef calls out to them, says, "New dishwasher! This is…"

Caught up in the suddenness of what's happening, I'm surprised that I manage to say my name. Chef introduces them to me. Memo, Isaiah, Lourdes—I say their names a few times to myself as if I'm really planning on staying. Chef shows me where all the stations are, gives me a brief summary of what each is responsible for. Each person is introduced along with their title: Michelle and Gus are the two sous-chefs; Vee, the enormous Southern rotisseur who carries a machete-length knife in a holster at her side; Elias is the poissonnier, and he raises his eyebrows the slightest bit and goes back to whisking something.

Here is the language Felix and I used to employ as often as possible. Kitchenese, we used to call it. Any time we cooked together, we wanted to feel like we belonged, so we spoke as if we did.

Steam is billowing up into the induction hood, which is much louder than I could have ever imagined. Through the sounds of the kitchen (pots being moved, water running, knives coming down on cutting boards), things are fairly quiet. I catch a lot of Spanish being exchanged, even from the handful of staff members who aren't Latino. Most people are in chef's whites or have some other sort of coat on, as well as checkered pants or black trousers. Absolutely everyone is in these big, ugly, comfortable-looking shoes.

On the line, I'm introduced to Morris and Boris (entremetiers), who have matching loud mouths and tattoos, twins if not for their difference in race. Matt arrives in the middle of my tour, giving me a confused look, which I return, because no one here is more confused than I am. His eyes are bloodshot, as if the party continued on long after we left the lake last night.

"This is the pass," Chef says, pointing to a long station at the end of the kitchen. "This is where I am most shifts, making sure every piece of food that goes out is perfect before it continues on to the dining room floor. If I'm not here, the sous are in charge. Sometimes it's me. Sometimes it's two of us. Whoever is standing here, you don't fucking talk to, okay?"

"Yes, Chef," I say, thrilled at the way the words sound leaving my mouth. I've read the term in books, heard it offhand in cooking shows. Felix the shadow jumps and clicks his heels together. I half expect him to break out into a musical number.

I look at the pass the way an art aficionado might when entering the Louvre for the first time. I see about two dozen spots ready for plastic containers. *Mise en place*, I think to myself. I can't believe I'm here. There are a couple of containers arriving to the pass right now, oils and chopped herbs, something that looks like sesame-seed crisps.

"You're over here," Chef says, leading me away from the heart of the kitchen.

The dish station is tucked away, hidden from the rest of the kitchen by a wall, though there's another entrance that leads back to the prep area. There are multiple counters where pots and pans are already being stacked up. Isaiah walks in carrying a huge vat that's still steaming. "Comin' in hot, man," he says as he heaves it alongside the others with a deafening clang.

"Roberto's the chef plongeur, so he'll be your direct boss. You do what he says, when he says it, exactly how he says it. And that's basically true of anything anyone else tells you in here. I don't want to see you holding a knife unless you're washing it, okay? In my kitchen, you wash dishes. That's it."

I look around the little room. If I'm still, I can hear the hood roaring in the kitchen. The cooks are starting to wake up, perk up, speak up. Their voices are still soft and muffled, often overtaken by the work they're doing.

"Roberto'll be here soon, but you can get started. Don't break anything. Clean dishes go over there," Chef says. She turns to leave, but before she goes she says, "I want you to work a double today, stay until we close. Roberto will tell you when you can take a break, and when you can leave, but other than that you stay right here. Work fast, work clean and I'll let you come back."

Then Chef is gone, and I am left alone. I turn and face the sink. Felix shows up on my shoulder as a fly, rubbing his little forefeet together. "What the hell just happened?" I ask him out loud.

He buzzes around for a bit. Excitedly, I can tell. I stare at the pile of cookware, cast-iron and shiny with grease. I reach out to touch a wok, just to make sure it's real.

"Felix. I didn't ask for this."

"But you got it, brother," he says immediately. He always, always had a quick response. I don't know how he never faltered when it seems like that's all I do. "What else are you going to do?"

"Not work at this restaurant?"

"Okay, so you go home. Then what?"

I stammer for a second, because he can't really expect me to just start working here. That's not in the plan at all. I'm not, like, a huge fan of the established plan, but this is too much. This is Felixesque, and I am not Felix.

I think about what comes next: a flight back to Mexico, Dad chewing me out, the internship, all the days bleeding into one foreseeable future.

I told Mom I only had to do something for Felix. But I did that and nothing changed. Even in this room, where every surface is stainless steel and reflective, I'm fuzzy, out of focus. What if Felix wasn't leading me to this restaurant just to eat here? What if he's trying to lead me to something bigger?

Gingerly, I reach out to the faucet, turn one of the knobs. The water shoots out, removing a few loose flecks of food from the pan on top of the pile. It's a high-pressure burst, immediately hot, and there's something satisfying in its potency. A buzzer rings out, and a few seconds later I hear the back door open and Elias greet someone.

I'm not sure why, but the thought of fleeing saunters away and instead I find myself reaching for the scrubber.

CHAPTER 8
STAFF MEAL BURGERS

3 pounds ground beef, molded into 8-ounce patties
American cheese

METHOD:

The day is long.

Sometimes I can hear the laughter of people making jokes, the sound of knives coming down and orders being called out. During service there's a din of activity beyond the partition that feels like a dream. I'm not sure why I don't just leave, explain to Chef that this is all some misunderstanding. It has something to do with that din, though.

Steam from the sprayed water makes me sweat, grime gets under my fingernails. My arms are tired from lifting the pots, many of them so hot I can't even touch them at first, which makes the work pile up, which leads to people yelling at me to keep up. Anytime I have a moment to myself, I look around and I think: *Where am I?*

Roberto gives me instructions in a voice that's quiet and gruff but kind enough. He works in a blaze, often singing along to the music on the little radio he keeps in a dry corner of the room. His motions are a blur, and several times I get caught staring, trying to mimic his movements.

It doesn't take too long for Felix to make another appearance. He's in the suds at the bottom of the stainless-steel sink, he's in the steam, he's in the swirls of grease that refuse to mix with the hot water as they sluice down the drain.

"Look at you! Washing dishes and shit." His little sudsy face raises its eyebrows, smirks the way it always does. "If Mom and Dad could see you now."

"They'd go nuts," I say, forcing a chuckle. "They'd say I was taking after you too much. Slumming it."

"Is that how it feels?"

Before I can answer, Matt slams two more saucepans and three mixing bowls behind me and then goes to pick up more pots from the clean-and-dry rack. "Pick it up, dickweed. We've got sixty more covers for lunch and your clean stack is low."

I get a couple of fifteen-minute breaks throughout the day, which I use to go to the bathroom and get off my feet. I decide to go out back and call Mom to check in. I want to share this crazy new development with her, though I don't know what the hell I'm going to say. I'm standing near the patio, that insane view of ocean, trees, sky. Things are so serene here, everything still as a painting.

Mom picks up on the second ring. She gets going right away. "Carlos, honey, I know you're having fun doing whatever you're doing, but I wanted to get your flight info. There are some dinners coming up that I want to make sure you're back for."

I try to find the right words or just push out the obvious ones.

"Carlos? Are you there?"

"Yeah, sorry." Memo shows up, two heaping trash bags at his side. "Mom, I need more time here."

A long pause. I wonder if she's considering putting Dad on the phone to try to change my mind. I wonder if she regrets letting me go, if she's getting déjà vu, memories of Felix's escape. She sighs. "Okay. How long?"

How many nights like yesterday will I need before I feel okay to leave? How many nights like yesterday will I be granted? "I'm not sure," I say.

"Your dad's not going to be happy."

"I know, Mom."

She sighs again, says something in Spanish away from the mouthpiece, either to Dad or Rosalba, I can't tell. "How are you?"

I hear three loud pops. My heart spikes, and I know that when I turn around I'll see Felix on the ground. But it's just Memo knocking on the door to get back in. "I'm fine. I'm just…not ready yet," I say. I glance quickly at the screen to see what time it is. I have to get back to the sink. It's strange how quickly I see it as my obligation. "Mom, I have to go," I say, though I can't bring myself to tell her why.

They never end, these pots and pans and dishes. The end of lunch service just means my heavy work is beginning, and the exhaustion is the most physically trying thing I've ever experienced. Felix talks me through it, the most helpful he's been since he died. Stories from his travels, little words of encouragement. I also find that if I let my mind wander to Emma, it makes the repetitive motions a little easier to bear.

I revisit that glance she gave me, the way she looked splashing through the lake, how she laid her hand on mine.

At some point in the late afternoon, that guy Elias pokes his head in and says, "Staff meal."

The words are sweet relief, and I untie the apron Roberto gave me, hanging it up on the hook by the entrance. Sure, I ate here last night. But there were so many things on the menu I didn't order. The open-faced duck confit sandwich with red wine aioli, the almond-crusted salmon with zucchini puree, tempura vegetables, chipotle oil. I wonder how this works, if we get to choose whatever we want. Or maybe it's some new creation, some experimental dish that Chef tries out on the staff before adding it to the menu. To think that I might try one of her dishes before anyone else is all the reward I need for today's scrubbing, for the hot water that has splashed all over me throughout the day.

What I find instead is a sheet tray of charred burger patties, most of them covered in toxic-yellow American cheese. There's another sheet tray with toasted buns and matchstick fries. Morris and Boris are leaning against the coffee station, taking huge bites in sync. I try to hide my disappointment, follow Elias's lead and grab a plate. I'm shocked that some people are eating it just like that, munching down as quickly as possible without bothering with condiments. I'm starving too, but it's crazy to me that Chef Elise's food is at their fingertips and everyone's just letting it sit there.

There's a whole line of deli containers right in front of us, and I can't even tell what's in them, but the mere thought is making my mouth water. Whispering so that no one can laugh and/or yell at me, I ask

Elias if it's cool to use some of the mise to spruce up the burger. He shrugs. "Do your thing." It mellows the disappointment a little: pickled red jalapeños, cilantro aioli, Thai slaw.

I eat hungrily, quietly, feeling the day throughout my body. I look around the kitchen, wondering at what point they'll start thinking it's weird I showed up out of nowhere. But no one's looking at me. A few of the guys are trash-talking each other's favorite American football teams. They gossip about why the old dishwasher Richie didn't show. Just beyond the pass, by the window that leads to the dining room, a few of the servers hang around, shooting the shit, mostly keeping to themselves.

A dozen conversations all happening without me. Felix is at my side eating a burger like mine, just without the jalapeños. I look over at him as he chews nonchalantly, hungrily, licking his fingers every few bites to catch the juices that drip out. I'm almost happy he's here, that I'm not in this situation completely alone. Except now I'm trying not to act crazy in front of a whole new group of people.

Once I've inhaled my burger, I look for Emma again, but she's on her break. Then dinner approaches and I'm banished back to the sink.

When the dishes finally stop coming my way, I'm practically falling asleep on my feet. I have no idea what time it is. Aside from bedtime. Everyone in the kitchen looks the way I feel. Except instead of wanting to head off to bed, all the cooks are talking about where they're gonna get drinks. They're comparing how their nights went, laughing, tossing towels at each other as they soap down their stations. They untie their aprons, unbutton their coats, roll up their personal knives into leather carriers.

"No refires today, motherfuckers," Vee says in her southern accent, raising a meaty fist in the air. "Who's coming to The Crown to celebrate how awesome I am?"

Memo laughs, says he's in. "That bartender has been giving me the look for weeks now."

"Alright, panty-dropper," Boris says.

"Don't shit talk Memo," Chef says, appearing from her office. "This little dude is deceptively charming. Has to be, to make up for that face of his."

Everyone laughs, but I barely have the energy to listen. Then Chef is at my side, pulling me back toward my station, away from everyone. I'm terrified that she's going to make me wash more dishes. Instead, she just barks at me: "Listen, if you can't keep up, don't bother coming in."

The words nearly break me. Which is a little weird because I'm not even supposed to be here. This place doesn't mean a thing to me. I want to grab the dish towel that's hanging on a nearby hook and toss it in her face, tell her to fuck off, just go back home. This is the hardest I've worked in my life, and if this is the thanks I get, maybe it's better to make it my last day on the island.

Then one of the stains on the towels, perfectly resembling Felix's mouth, tells me: "Stay. This was just the beginning."

I want to ask him why I should even try. But I don't say anything, and it's not entirely because of the whole not talking to myself in front of-other-people thing. I meet her steadfast gaze, nod. I swallow what I really want to say. "I will do better, Chef."

She gives me a long look, and I wonder if she's just going to tell me not to bother, that I clearly don't belong here. Instead, she reaches into her back pocket and pulls out a folded piece of paper. She hands it to me.

Provecho—Back of house application.

"Fill that out, give it to Sue tomorrow morning. She's the kitchen manager." Another cold stare. I think I literally feel my skin crawling, trying to hide from her. Shit, and I thought Dad had intense looks. "You better not make me regret that," she says, pointing at the application. Then she turns and leaves.

I look down at the page. It's just paper, a few blank lines for me to fill out.

But it feels like so much more than that.

CHAPTER 9
ESCAMOLE QUESADILLAS

1 package flour tortillas
250 grams Oaxaca cheese
50 grams escamoles
1 teaspoon butter
2 cloves garlic
Serve with salsa

METHOD:

I've never been more excited for the prospect of sleep. I leave Provecho via the service entrance, ready to collapse.

Gathered outside, though, is everyone I'd thought had already taken off for the night, Emma included. She's the first to meet my eyes, and she offers a smile that seems to justify all the thoughts I've spent on her throughout the day. I approach the circle, squeeze myself in between her and Elias.

Matt's nearby, smoking as always. Memo's got a tiny black backpack on, his eyes bloodshot but smiling a big goofy grin. Morris and Boris are both looking down at their phones, speaking out loud their intentions to invite so-and-so from other restaurants around town.

"I'll see you fuckers at The Crown," Vee calls out, breaking the circle.

"Hey," I try to stage-whisper to Emma.

She widens her eyes, smiling. "Hey, yourself. I hear you've got yourself a job."

"I owe you a thanks."

"Not a big deal," she says, as if it isn't. "You seemed happy here last night."

I'm about to laugh and say that maybe that wasn't because of a desire to work in restaurants when Elias turns to me, hand outstretched. "What was your name, man?"

I shake his hand, not wanting to turn away from Emma but happy that someone's talking to me. Hardly anyone said a word to me all day, and I was starting to worry that I'm not just imagining myself disappearing, that it's really happening. "Carlos," I say.

"Where you from?"

I tell him, and he raises his eyebrows. "No shit. My family's from there." He switches over into Spanish. "How'd you end up here?"

Unconsciously, I look around for Felix. I don't see him anywhere, though. In Mexico, his appearances felt like ambushes. Here, they feel a little different. "Kind of a long story. My brother, more or less."

He nods a couple of times. The crowd around us starts to disperse, more people heading out to the bar. Elias follows them with his eyes and then looks back at me and Emma. "You guys coming?"

A minute or two ago I would have said that there was no chance in hell that I'd be up for anything except sleep, many uninterrupted hours of it. Now I hesitate and glance sideways at Emma. When she looks back at me I try to pretend I'm not so damn transparent.

"I don't know how the hell you guys have the energy to keep going,"

I say, stalling, not wanting to say yes or no until I know I won't be missing out on Emma's company. I really don't want to go to a bar right now, but for a re-creation of last night I would give up all my sleep hours for the week.

"It's 'cause we're not lame pieces of shit," Matt says, exhaling a malignant cloud of smoke.

Boris cracks up at this. "Yeah, come on, new guy. What, you're too good for us?"

I want to come up with some biting retort but instead look blankly at Matt's cigarette smoke swirling in the night air. I look at Emma, glasses perched on her head, checking a message she just got on her phone.

It feels like a whole day goes by before Matt scoffs. "If he's struggling this hard already, dude's not gonna be able to keep up anyway. He'll be gone by the end of the week."

"I'm in," Emma says, almost at the same time, putting her phone away. The group is already starting to break away, led by Matt and Boris. I know I should go home, but as soon as I see Emma turn along with them, like she's ready to leave without a good-bye, I can't help but give in.

I trail behind the group because my feet are so tired. The whole time Felix is hassling me to go to bed. It's not a long walk, though, and there's something exciting about all of this.

The Crown is a small pub with a few pool tables in the back, booths lining the wall. The cooks from Provecho are already boisterous and spread out, but otherwise the place is pretty empty. Isaiah is at the electronic jukebox in the corner, and everyone else from Provecho stands at the bar. It smells like stale smoke and spilled beer, exactly what I'd imagined a small-town bar might smell like.

I always had this idea that American bars are insanely strict with who they serve. But I know Emma is eighteen, and Matt—who is at most a couple years older than us—goes straight to the bar without blinking an eye.

"Hey, man," Elias says to me, "let me buy you a drink. As a welcome-to-the-team kind of thing."

"Sure," I say, thrilled, though any sort of booze right now will probably make me fall asleep on the floor. I'm here anyway. I might as well. I don't know how long this little adventure will last, and I'm happy not to be talking to Felix right now.

I follow Elias's lead and get a beer and a shot, and when we clink glasses it feels like I've finally stepped out from the partition between the sink and the rest of the kitchen. "Salud," Elias says.

"Salud," I return.

"You ever been here before?"

I shake my head.

"No place like it," he says. "Saved my life."

The Australian bartender pours herself a drink too, greeting everyone but me by name. Elias leaves me to go play pool before I can ask him about what he said, so I decide to join Emma because it feels like I'm supposed to.

She's raising a shot glass to the group. "May misfortune follow you the rest of your lives," she says, pausing when she notices me. "And may it never catch up." She tilts her glass in my direction and warmth bubbles in my stomach as if I'm the one who took the shot. Setting the glass down on the bar, she comes over to me, gives me an unexpected hug.

"Are you staying?" she asks. I nod, unable to hide a smile at the fact that she wants me here at the bar. Only after she steps away do I wonder if that's what she was asking.

Emma is a firefly. She glimmers, leads me to a table, bathes me in her light, flickers off and appears in another part of the bar, talking to someone else. I stare out, looking for her to reappear, sticking to myself since no one else seems interested. For maybe the first time, I want Felix's company, just because I feel like a tool sitting here all alone.

Then Emma's right back in front of me, eyes bright with joy. "Tell me everything you know about quesadillas," she says. "Are they a real thing, or just an American invention, a twist on grilled cheese sandwiches?"

"They're real," I say, shoulders hunched toward the table, like we're co-conspirators. "Sometimes they're a smaller version of what you see here, just the tortilla and cheese, and sometimes they're made with fried corn dough and stuffed with all sorts of things. Sometimes there's not even cheese in them."

Her eyes flit toward the bar, and I rack my brains for a way to interest her enough to stick around.

"Strangely enough," I say, "you're more likely to find ants on quesadillas than guac and sour cream like you do here."

Success. She raises an eyebrow. "Shut up, I don't believe you."

"It's true," I say. "They're called escamoles. Usually they're fried in butter and garlic and eaten with omelets or tacos. Technically ant larvae, but yeah."

She wrinkles her nose. "Are they good?"

"They're okay."

"I want you to make them for me one day," she says. Standing up, she announces she's not drunk enough, and then she flickers off, disappears somewhere in the bar, leaving me alone to fight off sleep.

Every time she looks over in my direction, there's this shot of adrenaline that beats the exhaustion away, that tells me last night was not a fluke. Then Emma clinks glasses with someone and flickers off, shines her light over by the pool table. Disappointment stirs within me.

My head falls back to rest against the wall for just a moment and I'm instantly asleep. I'm not sure how much time passes. Despite the noise of the pool cues and Isaiah's upbeat musical selections, what wakes me up is the feel of something tickling my forehead. I wave my hand to swat it away, and in the ensuing sounds of laughter my eyes snap open.

Matt is in front of me, a big grin on his face and a permanent marker in his hand. At his side, Boris is doubled over, cackling. "Welcome to the team!" Matt says with a sneer.

I wipe at my forehead, and through the dark of the bar I see the faintest trace of black on my fingertips. I rub again, suddenly aware of the slight weight of ink, how it's already drying. Matt and Boris let loose with another round of exaggerated laughter. Elias appears at their side, assessing the situation. I'm sure he's about to tell them off, since he's been nice to me, and he comes off as more mature. But he just cracks a grin and shakes his head and then tells me I might want to go wash up.

In the bathroom mirror, I stare at the crude drawing of a penis that now takes up the entirety of my forehead, hoping for the love of god that Emma didn't see it. And that it'll wash off. A couple pumps of soap and some vigorous scrubbing do nothing. The whole time I'm thinking how immature and stupid and unoriginal Matt is. I'm trying to ignore the faintness of my reflection.

I push open the bathroom door, flushed with embarrassment. Disoriented, I look around the dark bar for the exit. My eyes land on Emma, arms around the neck of some faceless, shapeless wad of flesh. My stomach drops, the recognition of the act undeniable.

I find the exit, and speed toward it, one hand cupping my forehead. I hear Matt calling out behind me, "It's just a joke, you wuss!"

What a world, I think, but this time in Dad's voice, mocking me. I should have listened to Felix and gone to bed tonight. I shouldn't worry about Emma, get caught up with a girl who was probably just trying to be friendly last night. I should go home.

It takes me two blocks to realize I've been speed-walking in the opposite direction of my motel. "Hijo de la chingada," I yell.

My shadow laughs. "I never hear you say that," Felix says.

"Not now," I beg, hands shoved in my pockets, head down.

"'Not now' what?"

I look up and see Emma, eyes glazed and distant and happy. Her cheeks are flushed, and she's got a beer bottle in her hand.

"Huh?"

"You said, 'not now,'" she says, taking a step closer to me. "Was that to me? I can let you…" She gestures down the road.

"No, no," I say. "It was…" I trail off, knowing I have nothing sane with which to finish the thought. Emma is a near stranger. She showed me some cool spots around the island; we had a nice night. I have no right to feel hurt. But there it is anyway. "I don't know what it was."

Emma chuckles, which leads to a hiccup. "You know what sounds good right now?"

"Industrial-grade soap?" I say, reaching for my forehead. "Bed."

"Quesadillas. Do you know where we can get some at this time of night? Ants optional."

My mind flashes to the fridge in the motel, the package of tortillas and cheese inside. It flashes to her making out with someone at the bar, and I know I should keep this latter image in mind. Then Emma sways a little, stumbles a few steps. "You okay?"

"Yup," she says. "Just a quesadilla deficiency." She smiles, face glowing with booze and warmth and whatever else.

I look over her shoulder, down the road that leads to what, this week, I'm calling home. Aside from the faint thumping of music coming from the bar, the night is dead quiet. We're on a small two-lane road in the middle of the woods, and from here it'd be impossible to tell that anyone lives on this island at all. Emma's looking at me expectantly, and I remember what she did for me last night, how she noticed my panic attack and showed me something that made me feel better than I have in months. I didn't have to pretend. Whatever hasty romantic notions were thwarted at the bar, I know that much was true.

"I could probably make some at my place. But…" I try to convey what I'm thinking. That she's a little drunk and I'm a little out of my mind. Hard to do in just a hand gesture. "Maybe I should help you get home instead?" I say.

Emma rolls her eyes. "Your place. Quesadillas. Lead the way."

After a twenty-minute walk, I push open the door to my motel room. Emma steps in, sets her bag down on the floor, says nothing.

Not knowing what else to do, I head to the kitchen. "Sorry this place sucks. If you use the bathroom, ignore all the stains. I'm pretty sure none of them are blood." Goddamn, jokes again.

I open the fridge, pull out the flour tortillas, pour the tomatillo salsa I made the other day into a bowl, light the flame on the stove and set my saucepan on top of it. There's such comfort in these things, things I know how to do.

Instead of plopping herself down on the edge of the bed, like I expect, Emma takes a seat on the edge of the counter, watching me work. I try to focus on the cilantro I'm chopping when her leg and my arm are inches away from each other, make sure my fingers are curled away from the blade.

"Hey, Carlos?"

"Yeah," I say, not looking up.

"You still have a penis on your forehead." She chuckles and then rests her head back against the cabinet, closing her eyes. "I didn't get drunk enough," she says.

All day, I've been hoping for a repetition of last night. I'm not sure this is what I was envisioning. "Sorry I don't have anything to offer." Then, before I know what my mouth is doing, I ask, "So, who was that guy?"

"What guy?" Emma asks.

"You were..." I flip the tortillas I'm warming on the pan. "That guy."

"Oh," she says, shrugging, looking one-hundred-percent more interested in me pulling stuff out of the fridge than in the conversation. "Some guy. Drunken makeouts are fun."

"He's not, like, a boyfriend?"

Emma laughs. "God, no. Some tourist."

My knuckles against the blade are a kind of security blanket right now, something to keep my mind off this strange nervousness that's settled into my stomach.

When I look up, Emma's got her eyes on me, her legs swinging slightly so that the heels of her sneakers hit the cupboard by her feet. The arrhythmic beat fills the motel room, and I can't even hear my thoughts over it.

I'm afraid she'll bring up the fact that she caught me talking to myself. The thumping of her shoes feels like that countdown music on Final Jeopardy and I have to say something or a buzzer will go off and someone will take away ten thousand dollars from me. So I ask her if she knows what she wants to do with her life, because that's a question everyone lobs at everyone else, right?

She opens her eyes, tilts her head toward me with a look that says: *Really?* "No idea. I've got time to figure that out. Probably a few more drunken makeouts before I need to really decide."

I force a chuckle. Wipe the knife blade, put it on its block. Petty jealousy in the pit of my stomach, and I think that maybe it's replacing some of the other pain I've been living with but that it's pain either way. "What about school? Do you have that figured out yet?"

"Yeah, to an extent." Emma reaches over to the plate of cheese I sliced into thin strips since there's no grater, scoops a pinch into her mouth, chews with pleasure. "I know I'm going to University of Washington in the fall. Not much more than that. Go around looking for imaginary friends, I guess." She laughs. I fold the cheese into the tortillas, press down with the back of the fork so the cheese will melt the two sides together. A little square slips out of the pocket, sizzles as soon as it hits the pan. I let it brown for a second before I scrape it off with the edge of the fork, and offer it to Emma. She uses her finger to grab the burnt cheese off the fork, slip it into her mouth, gives a gentle sigh. "You? You have it all planned out, right? The glamour of the kitchen. I could see it in your eyes yesterday. I just wanted to help, you know..." She flicks both wrists forward, as if she brushing flies away from her food. "Push things along."

"I don't know if *planned out* really applies to me. I have no idea what I'm doing," I say, and then try to chuckle when I realize that's exactly right. I have no idea what I'm doing. Maybe what she saw in my eyes yesterday was only psychosis. "I don't know why I stayed to work today," I admit. "My brother used to tell me I should work in kitchens. But I never really thought it was an option."

"Well, it sure is now."

"Yeah, did I mention how weird that was?" I laugh. "I'm only supposed to be here a week." I slide the fork under each quesadilla and lift them off the pan, placing them on a small plate. I try to appreciate this moment and not cling to anything else. Just this.

She takes the plate and looks me in the eyes, swaying a little but not breaking eye contact. "You should stay longer," she says, taking her glasses off and resting them on her lap. I want to say something smooth and flirty, but nothing comes to mind. "You are the nicest dickhead I've ever met," she says, barely acknowledging her own joke before she takes a large bite of the quesadilla.

I laugh and take a bite of my own, thinking maybe this is where the night changes. After this we'll go out into the breezeway, chat until the sun rises, her head resting on my shoulder. It'll be one of those nights where secrets spill out and bind you closer to another person.

But Emma takes a few bites and then leans her head back against the wall, falling asleep before we can say anything else to each other. So I go to the bathroom and scrub at my forehead with soap and a sponge that barely works. When the water and suds start to drip down my neck and onto my shirt, I realize that I still smell like dirty dishes and grease, so I hop in the shower, trying not to be lulled to sleep by the warm water. Condensation on the tiles forms into Felix's face, and I immediately smack the wall, wiping the droplets away. I keep my eyes closed the rest of the shower, breathing slowly, trying to think of nothing but water.

When I come back out, Emma's gone. Our empty plates are pushed to the side, half-inch-wide trails left in the salsa, perfect fingers running through the spilled leftovers. I stand for a long time looking at the space she occupied, wishing she hadn't left me alone.

CHAPTER 10
GRILLED CHICKEN KEBABS

3 pounds chicken breasts, cut into 1-inch cubes

1 red bell pepper

1 green bell pepper

1 red onion

1 cup mushrooms

FOR THE MARINADE:

1 bunch parsley

1 bunch cilantro

1 shallot

3 tablespoons dried oregano

½ cup vegetable oil

¼ cup red wine vinegar

3 cloves garlic

1 tablespoon red pepper flakes

METHOD:

Ah, coffee.

Now I get it. Why the whole world reaches for this first thing in the morning.

It's six in the morning, and the kitchen is preparing for another brunch. Everyone's quiet as they arrive, bloodshot eyes, sleep still creaking their joints. Without coffee I'd be a zombie. Felix, fucking class clown that he is, walks through the kitchen as an actual zombie, hands out in front of him, groaning.

I bought a second coffee for Emma at a nearby bakery, figuring she'd need it after last night. But she's not in, so I offer it to Elias instead. "Did you get enough sleep last night?" he asks.

I laugh, a little confused. "We got off work, like, five hours ago." Last night when I set my alarm, I was sure I was doing the math wrong, no one could possibly survive off this little sleep and go work around flames and blades. I can't imagine this exhaustion being a part of your daily life.

That thought makes me wonder why I'm here. Why I bothered getting out of bed to come back. Why I'm not on the way to Mexico. Instead, I filled out that application and gave it to Sue first thing this morning, imagining the look on Dad's face if he saw me doing it. I didn't want to picture the look on Mom's face.

Elias smiles wide, a smile that reminds me of Felix when he was being a smartass. "Welcome to the restaurant world." I get giddy at the words and start thinking that this island really is magic; that's the only explanation for how I've managed to find myself here so quickly. Then, keeping that same smile, Elias says, "Don't fuck anything up today. If the dishwashers fall behind, we all do, and I do not feel like falling behind." The giddiness dissipates a little.

I go to my station to check in with Roberto, but nothing's piled up yet, so I get to go back out in the kitchen, watch it slowly come to life. Lourdes comes in carrying a huge vat of something, which she puts on a burner. A few cooks gather around her station, talking about last night. Vee has a distinctly rum-like smell to her. Memo stayed past the bar's closing, so there's conjecturing as to whether or not he and the bartender, Lisa, went home together. Isaiah bets Gus three prep-sheet items that Memo was successful. I'm happy to feel invisible, as long as no one brings up the whole penis-on-my-forehead thing.

"Ya está," Lourdes says, taking the lid off her vat. "Quién quiere?"

The whole kitchen clamors to try to get the first cup. It smells like cinnamon, and I try to get a glimpse of what it is. "Qué es?" I ask Memo.

"You shitting me, man?" Boris says, laughing. "Yo, Matt, check it out. The kid from Mexico City doesn't know what atole is."

Fuck.

"I know what it is," I say, trying to save face. "I just couldn't see." I know what atole is, of course…but I've never actually had it. Just one of those things I've somehow missed out on, like a phrase you've misheard most your life until you're embarrassingly corrected in public. I used to think it was *nip it in the butt.* So, kind of the same thing?

Whenever my family goes out to eat, it's usually fancier restaurants— an Argentine steak house, a French bistro, one of those classic return-home tacos. Mom likes to eat healthy, and so she's taught Rosalba to make recipes off the internet, dishes with quinoa and kale and coconut oil subbed in for butter. Felix was the biggest proponent of traditional Mexican dishes, taking me to restaurants and markets our parents wouldn't set foot in, begging Rosalba to bust out anything in her repertoire. And there's so many dishes in our cuisine that it's not crazy to think that I might have missed out on this one cinnamon-y beverage, ubiquitous though it may be.

There's no way I'm offering any of this up as an excuse, though.

"Hey, dickhead, are you lying about being Mexican?" Matt says, letting Lourdes scoop him some. I barely hear what he says afterward, his word choice stinging more than it should. I had to scrub my forehead so hard that it still kind of hurts. "Do you know what mole is? Salsa? Have you heard of salsa?"

"Ya, déjenlo en paz," Lourdes says, handing me a Styrofoam cup and offering a smile.

"I could tell you were a rich boy," Matt says. "Didn't you come in here for a meal the other night?" He snaps his fingers in recognition, not waiting for me to respond. "You did. And now, what, you're slummin' it with us common folk?"

I want to protest, want to ask him why he's got it in for me. Instead I shrink. I'm surprised no one reacts, because I catch a reflection of myself in a nearby soup ladle, and I look like that computer-generated tiny version of Chris Evans in *Captain America* before he gets turned into a superhero. I take another sip of coffee for strength, wait for an ally to show themselves. Zombie Felix creeps up behind Matt and starts gnawing on his skull. Which I guess is a sweet, protective gesture.

"Fuckin' rich people," Matt adds. "They always forget their country's food. That's a sin."

Sous-Chef Melissa pokes her head into the prep kitchen, takes stock of the situation. "Fun times in here? You guys done all your shit for the day, then? Ready for service?"

There's a chorus of "No, Chef. Sorry, Chef." The congregation scatters. Boris bumps into me and tells me to get the fuck out of the way. I take my atole straight to the sink, try to take out my frustration with my scrubber. I don't understand how the hell there's suddenly such a large pile for me to work through when everyone's been standing around.

The exhaustion sets in almost immediately, especially when I think about how long the day will be. I don't understand why I'm doing this to myself, but at no point do I actually get the urge to hang up my apron and go.

If I have a spare moment, Roberto has me go out and help clean, since cleanliness reigns supreme in kitchens. I grab a dishrag and wipe away drops of sauce and oil, take out garbage. Avoiding Matt and Boris, I go around each station, asking if I can take a cutting board, if they need more rags, any pans. Chef comes in, makes eye contact, gives me maybe the slightest of nods. Felix is in the air, ready to mock her solemnness, but somehow I keep my brother from fully taking shape (whichever shape he was planning on taking).

By the time I'm finished, the kitchen is deserted, the induction hood off, making everything eerily silent, peaceful. I'm even more exhausted than I was last night, and the scene feels even more surreal, the way a recurring dream is stranger because of its slight familiarity.

Despite the tiredness, I find myself hoping everyone isn't gone. That they're up to something, lingering by the exit planning another night out. That I can tag along, not return to that motel room. I get the feeling Emma hasn't left without a good-bye.

Sure enough, there's the same group as last night hanging outside. I stand at the periphery, hoping for someone to notice I'm there and step aside to make room. The restaurant's closed tomorrow for a holiday, and despite the long hours we've all pulled, no one wants to pass up the opportunity to party all night and sleep the day away. Matt suggests a late-night barbecue at his place, and everyone chimes in with their approval. They disperse to pick up beer and things to grill. Matt doesn't even look at me, much less offer me an invite, banishing me to a night in that motel room, with nothing to do but try to beat back panic attacks, trying to figure out why I'm still seeing Felix, why I've started looking forward to his company.

Then Emma appears at my side, work shirt unbuttoned, a baby-blue tank top underneath. She smells like lavender and lemongrass, like a morning spent in bed, drifting off into pleasant dreams. "Thanks for those quesadillas last night. They saved my life." She bites her lip in that way that's probably already settling itself deep into the folds of my brain. I'm going to start missing her in little moments of the day, I can tell. "Walk with me?"

I look over at the group making their way down the street. "I don't think Matt wants me there."

"Matt's an attention whore. The more people are there the better he'll feel. Plus, he's really an okay guy once you get to know him." Emma nods her head in the group's direction. "Come on, walk with me. Please?"

I can't find it in me to resist that. We turn down the street away from the restaurant, and I let Emma lead the way. We walk along the shoulder, grass at our feet, fireflies flickering at the edge of the woods. Emma sheds her work shirt and folds it into her bag.

"So," she says, crossing her arms, "I vaguely remember falling asleep on your counter last night. Did I do that mid-conversation?"

"More impressive: you did it mid-quesadilla."

She laughs, makes a face. "Oh man, sorry. That's lame."

"And dangerous. You have no idea how many people die choking on their own quesadillas when they're drunk. There are PSAs in movie theaters in Mexico about it."

Emma smacks my arm. "Shut up." She laughs again. Every time she does I get the feeling that a little part of me is coming back; my skin becomes less translucent. Since the Night of the Perfect Taco, I haven't really been able to make anyone laugh. Dad even pointed it out a few times. "You used to be funny," he said once, as if he couldn't think of any possible reason why I may have lost my sense of humor.

I try to forget about Dad. "Did you feel okay today?"

"Yeah, I wasn't really that drunk," she says, shrugging. She's kicking at pebbles, a quirk that I find oddly charming, maybe because in Mexico City it would be a pointless endeavor. The cracked and crowded sidewalks would make you lose track after a kick or two, but here Emma kicks the same gray pebble for a mile. We walk for twenty minutes or so, following the sounds of the staff ahead of us, the wind blowing in such a way that it carries their conversations to us.

Matt's house is on the opposite side of the lake, in a part of the island that I haven't been to yet. It's a fairly small house with a huge backyard, surrounded by trees. By the time we arrive, there's about twenty people sipping on beers. Half are from the kitchen, the other half the bonfire crowd from the other night, kids around me and Emma's age, still in high school.

Emma leads us directly to the non-restaurant crew. There's about ten of them standing in a circle around the back porch, a couple more seated on the stairs. Brandy says hi, and Emma introduces me to the rest of the crowd. I wonder briefly if one of the guys (Reggie, Paul, Ben) was at the bar last night, if one might be the Faceless Wad of Flesh. I try to suppress the jealousy, set my mind on just making Emma laugh, chasing after that feeling.

Emma appears at my side with a beer almost as soon as I notice that she stepped away. "If you get drunk tonight, it's now my turn to make you something to eat," she says. "Preferably cheesy and salsa-y and not so insect-y."

I immediately start chugging the beer, and her laugh unravels a knot that's been in my stomach all day.

I stand in the circle, laughing occasionally, sipping on a beer just to keep myself busy. I try to contribute to the conversation, but it comes out as a stupid joke. I think maybe, in my exhaustion, I got confused and made the joke in Spanish so I repeat what I said. They all stare at me like I'm insane. Emma too.

So I slip away toward the grill.

Isaiah's working on getting the coals started, while Elias and Matt sit on nearby patio furniture, putting dishes together on the glass table. Elias is skewering vegetables and pieces of marinated chicken, and Matt is concocting a sauce in a stainless-steel bowl. I wish I would have stopped by the store or the motel room so I could contribute something, or at least have something to do. I ask if I can help, but no one really needs it, or no one hears me ask.

Back and forth I go, trying to make myself a part of either group.

Kitchens or the island, I don't have enough experiences to talk about so I've got barely a toe in each little pool. The night pushes on, a chill coming in from the ocean.

As the temperature drops, dew forms on grass and fogs up the sliding glass door that leads into the house. Felix shows himself there, waving goofily, and since there's no one else for me to go to (Emma, occasionally looking over, smiling, is deep in a one-on-one with Brandy), I pull up a chair next to the door, sit down with a plate of food on my lap. It's like I'm a shadow, visible but easy to miss.

There's a surprising amount of detail in the cloudy window. Felix's stubble is visible, the exact way he would put his arms behind his head when relaxing. The gunshot's not there, but I can tell he's wearing that shirt again. "It hasn't been a bad week, huh?"

"I guess not."

The little particles of condensation that are acting as Felix try to reach out to smack me on the arm, with obviously no results. "Relax. What, you want to be best friends with everyone already? These things take time. New experiences are lonely. You should have seen how it went for me sometimes."

I bring a chicken skewer up to my mouth to hide the fact that my lips are moving. "Really?"

"Really. When I was in that kibbutz in Israel I sometimes went days without talking to anyone."

"That's pretty shocking, since you never shut up."

"Funny," Felix says. He reaches out on the glass, makes three snowballs out of the fog, starts juggling. "If you think loneliness goes away because you've effectively started your adult life, you should think again."

I take a bite, chew purposefully, trying to pick out the flavors in the marinade. Almost like a chimichurri, lots of herbs. Elias and Memo are smoking cigars; Emma's friends are passing around a joint. Paper plates with crumbs and sauce puddles are strewn around the yard, on tables and chairs and at people's feet. Clouds overhead cover up the moon and stars that I am growing accustomed to seeing every day. I must be covered by a cloud too, because I'm speaking freely to a door and no one seems to notice.

Felix splits the balls he's juggling into four and then five and then ten. I fight the urge to reach out and wipe away the condensation from the glass. I don't want to be alone again. Out of the corner of my eye, I see Felix chuck a ball at me. I flinch, and then I have to pretend that I'm swatting away a mosquito in case anyone's watching.

"I can't believe you fell for that," Felix laughs. "On so many levels."

"Shut up," I say.

He does for a sec. Emma looks over in my direction. Her glasses are slightly smudged, her cheeks rosy and her hair in a messy bun. She doesn't wave me over, but she does smile, and I smile back, happy for the acknowledgment.

"Hey, Carlos?" Felix says.

"Yeah?"

"I'm bored to death."

I want to roll my eyes but keep it to myself in case anyone's looking. I get up to make myself another plate of food, even though I'm too tired to be hungry. Another chicken skewer, some roasted veggies, Argentinian choripán.

I attempt mingling one more time. Matt, Morris and Boris are smoking those flavored mini-cigar things, chairs gathered in a semi-circle, facing the rest of the party. I'm maybe twenty feet away, already losing my nerve, when all three of them stop their conversation and just watch me approach. I take an immediate turn toward Emma's group, and I can hear them burst into laughter.

Emma smiles at me when I approach, and Reggie steps aside to make room for me. They're talking about some show that I haven't seen the newest season of, since I've been watching nothing but the Food Network. It takes me all of three minutes before I butt in with another stupid joke, and the looks I get make me long to be ignored again. I urge my body to get back to that whole disappearing thing. After making an excuse about needing a beer, I go rejoin Felix by the glass door.

"Hey, I thought it was funny," he says with a wink.

"No, you didn't."

"Okay, no, but I give you points for trying."

I look back up at the party, and Emma's talking one-on-one with one of the servers, a dude with eyes so blue I don't believe them. I look down at my beer, fiddle with the tab.

Back when he was alive, Felix had a knack for providing comfort. When our uncle committed suicide, Felix sat with Mom on the couch all night, holding her hand and a box of tissues and letting her cry into his shoulder. He was fifteen. Whatever the reason Felix is still here, I guess I prefer this iteration of him rather than really losing him, like Mom and Dad and the rest of the world have.

"Tell me more about that last trip you were on," I say. "You never got to."

He smiles, gets up from his chair (image of a chair, hallucination of a chair on Matt's sliding glass door, whatever). "Why don't I show you?"

Felix steps off the glass, turns into a little cloud of barely visible condensation, lays himself down on the ground, where the drops of dew on the grass start to bounce around. They join together to get heavier and force a given blade down, or they scurry away and let a single particle rise to the top to reflect the lights coming from the house behind me. Before my eyes, a cityscape appears on the grass.

He tells me about crossing from Laotian villages into Vietnam. He reminds me that he usually didn't prefer big cities—as great as some of them were, none could ever compare to Mexico City—but Hanoi was different. The drops of water rearrange again. A streetside café, tiny tables, chairs facing out, two electric fans pointed at the customers. Scooters parked everywhere, zooming past, honking often. "Everyone's awake early, drinking strong, cold coffee," Felix says. "The smell of meaty, spicy soups in the air. Government announcements coming from the speakers up on the street posts, interrupted by constant motorbikes. It's loud and everyone's in a rush, sure. But I knew looking at Hanoi what people mean when they describe a city as a living thing."

I stay a little longer than I probably should, especially since I'm on the fringe of the party and not really in it. I don't get drunk; Emma doesn't take me anywhere to eat something cheesy. I think I see her arm linked through the blue-eyed server's right before I leave. I've known her for a week. Why do my insides stir as if I'm mourning?

I tell myself I should be sleeping anyway. I should be talking to real people. I say this to Felix on the walk home, and for once he listens, lets me go on. It is a welcome consolation, talking to Felix like this. The magic he can conjure up. It keeps me from wishing for other things.

CHAPTER 11
ATOLE

5 cups water
½ cup masa
2 cinnamon sticks
5 tablespoons piloncillo
1 tablespoon vanilla extract

METHOD:

The next morning I wake up knowing that if I linger in bed it'll be one of those suffocating days where I can't think about anything other than Felix and death. So I skip the shower and get dressed and bolt out the door toward the boardwalk. It helps to walk and watch people go about their lives. Tourists, most of them, here for a brief spell before they return to wherever it is they came from.

When I try to think about getting back on a ferry out of here, I think of the lake as Emma showed it to me. I think of the way light works here, as if it's filtered by a cinematographer. I think of the sounds of the kitchen.

Then a pang of guilt hits me that I haven't called Mom again, so I find a quiet place to sit. I'm on a bench within view of the lake, which is shimmering with an array of blues that feels impossible within such a small body of water. Birds flitter from tree to tree around me, red-winged blackbirds, cardinals and one that's small and yellow and chirps relentlessly.

Mom answers within a couple rings. "Hey, honey," she says. She asks how I am. I say I'm good, with a cheerfulness that is probably too forced. I can sense the next question on the tip of her tongue, begging to leap out. "Have you booked your flight back yet?"

I hesitate, wondering if I'm really going to say what I want to.

"Mom, I don't think I'll be back this week."

Instant silence. If it was Dad instead of Mom, I'd be wondering if he hung up. But Mom wouldn't do that. I've just tripped upon one of those things that steal the words from a parent.

"When, Carlos?"

"I don't know," I say, and those simple words are as satisfying as if I've confessed to something much bigger. I almost feel like Felix will disappear on these words alone. Like he led me here not for the meal but to stay gone from the life waiting for me in Mexico.

A cool breeze blows by, soothing the heat from the sun on my skin. "I got a job, Mom."

On her end, Mom laughs. "A job? What are you talking about?" She pauses, waiting for me to explain myself. When a few seconds go by, she realizes I'm not going to elaborate. "You said a week." Her voice falters.

"I know." I'm so aware of the smell of saltwater, of the waves crashing gentle and steady a few blocks away. I'm aware, too, that Mom probably had a similar talk with Felix once. That at one point he stopped promising he'd be back and just chased after what he wanted. "I'm sorry, but I want to give this a shot."

She's about to cry, I can tell. She's about to ask me what about her, or what about college, or what about a bunch of other things I don't know the answer to. This, though, I feel sure about.

A week goes by. The sink I stand in front of for hours at a time becomes more and more familiar. The station is comfortable, even. I can reach for a new rag without taking my eyes off the pan in my hands. There's a certain pleasure in figuring out the most efficient way to stack plates, in running pots and pans to the cooks before they come in to bitch about not having enough.

When I run dishes to the waitstaff, I'll often manage to take a detour to see Emma. If I say something that makes her laugh, or if she starts talking to me, I find that I work that much faster when I get back. If she's short with her words, or if I don't see her all day, or if Matt's got it in for me, the day doubles in length.

The work itself doesn't get any easier, but I learn little things that make the job go by faster. I buy comfortable shoes that are mostly rubber and won't get soaked throughout my shift. I get a stack of shirts at a thrift store that I won't mind staining. I learn to bring a change of clothes, so that I won't smell like garbage if people are going out after shift, or if Emma and I take a walk to the lake, which happens once, early in the week.

It's just the two of us. She shows me more secret passageways through the woods until the trees clear to reveal a large, moonlit meadow. We stop at the edge. Emma's looking at me expectantly, and at first I'm not sure what I'm supposed to see. I see tall, unkempt grass surrounded by trees. Then, like my eyes are playing tricks on me, fluorescent green lights flash on and off in the field, some of them rising up like bubbles in a pot of boiling water, some shooting across and lighting up the ground below them.

"Whoa."

"Pretty, right?" Emma says, turning her neck slowly from me to the meadow.

"I almost never see fireflies."

"I did some research, and they're not even supposed to exist west of Kansas. I have no idea why there's so many of them here."

We walk through the field together, and in the blinking green lights I see Emma's hand inches from my own, I see the curves and dips of her face in profile and I wonder how it is that I can find the space between things beautiful.

Emma stops for a second and reaches into the waist-high grass, her hand disappearing in the dark. She pulls it back out to reveal a berry I have never seen before, not in the smorgasbord of rainbow-colored fruit at American grocery stores and definitely not anywhere in Mexico. It is the size of a child's fist, and the skin is prickly, like a lychee's.

"When I was a kid, if I was mad at my mom, I'd hide out here for the day, picking out berries," Emma says. "I had no way of knowing if they were poisonous, but I'd feast on them anyway." She digs her thumb into the skin to reveal a pulpy white interior. She takes a bite out of it and then hands it to me. It's sweet and tangy and would be great in a vinaigrette, as a sauce, maybe along with some roasted duck. "I don't even think anyone else knows about these, because I've never seen them anywhere else. I'm sure she'd put it on her menu if she found out about them, but I like keeping this one thing to myself."

We grab them by the handful, take them with us down the hill toward the lake. Sitting on the shore, gentle waves lapping at our ankles, we peel the berries one by one. A day or two ago, I thought of Emma as pretty. Tonight, her profile outlined by a full moon, she looks beautiful to me. I wish I could drive the thought away, but there it is anyway. The water—or something else about these nights—really does feel like it can cure hopelessness.

Now it's Sunday morning again, pre-brunch. I haven't seen Emma the last couple of nights because of late shifts and the fact that she has other things to do, a life beyond me. I try to ignore a longing for her so intense and specific that it's like a food craving that won't go away. I try to forget it and focus on the kitchen, where I feel sane.

The workload has not piled up yet. Roberto is not even around, which means I have shown up earlier than asked for again. Station to station I go, checking to see how I can help, if anyone wants to talk, if anyone *will* talk. Lourdes arrives, and I rush to help her bring the vat of atole to her stovetop. Matt walks by and hits my ass with the flat end of a wooden spoon, which stings like hell and makes him laugh way more than it should.

A sudden yell rings out through the kitchen. No one's playing music yet, and the hood always feels quieter at this time of day, like it, too, needs time to wake up, so the words are clear. "Fuck, Gus!" It's Chef. Heads turn. "You've got to be kidding me. You can't do this right now."

There's the sound of the office door slamming open. Gus walks down the corridor, past the prep kitchen. He's got his leather knife roll tucked under his armpit. Lourdes keeps her head down, gets started zesting lemons. I can't help but gawk. Memo and Isaiah set their knives down on their cutting boards too, twin cocked eyebrows. Chef comes storming after Gus. "At least give me two weeks. You owe me that much."

I simultaneously want to stay out of it and follow every word that's said, so when the prep cooks file out, pretend to go to the walk-in freezers to grab something so that *they* can listen in, I follow behind.

"Sorry, Chef. But it's not my problem. The new place doesn't open up for a few weeks, but they're having some issues right now and the owner needs me there." He grabs something else from his station and then heads over to the lockers. "I'll see if Boris can finish out his two weeks, but I gotta go."

"What the fuck. You're taking Boris with you?"

It feels like everyone's eyes meet at the same time, like we're watching some soap opera and registering each other's reactions live. Chef crosses her arms in front of her chest, uncannily similar to what Emma does when she's broaching certain conversation topics that she's shy about. "It's the middle of summer, man. We're slammed every day. Don't you have any fucking loyalty? I can't do this right now two cooks down. Give me time to find a replacement. That's all I ask."

Gus checks his phone. "I really gotta go." He walks right past Chef, answers a phone call on his way out. There's this terrifying moment where it feels like Chef's gonna catch everyone staring and start throwing knives. But then everyone kind of has the same thought, and we scatter to our stations, knowing already that shit's gonna be heavy today.

When I see that the kitchen is starting to come alive into that pre-service dance, I disappear behind my partition, ready to work my ass off. In some ways, the busiest times are the best. My mind is free to wander, but it doesn't wander to the Night of the Perfect Taco, the question of Whether I'll Always Be this Way.

Often it goes to new dishes, strange combinations of flavors. Lately, though I wouldn't admit it to anyone, much less Emma, I plan out dates. I don't let my mind skip ahead to a predictably sexy ending but rather linger on the details of each step. Meeting her at her door, the exact way I'd greet her. A kiss on the cheek, my lips on her skin. A picnic on that hill she loves, fireflies illuminating our grilled cheese sandwiches (roasted vegetables inside, three artisanal cheeses, thyme butter).

Today, I grant us an early kiss in the fantasy, and goose bumps shoot down my arms even as the hot water and the scrubbing fibers grate my fingertips through the gloves down to unrecognizable smoothness. I didn't know there could be such pleasure in just the imagining of someone's company.

CHAPTER 12

MEXIMAC 'N' CHEESE

2 cloves garlic

1 white onion

1 habanero pepper

200 grams bacon

1 cup grated Monterey Jack cheese

1 cup grated Manchego cheese

1 cup grated Chihuahua cheese

½ cup dark beer

¼ cup buttermilk

500 grams macaroni noodles

METHOD:

When I step outside, I'm briefly replenished by the gorgeousness of the weather, another nonsensical full moon. It'd be a perfect night to swim in the lake, but Emma's not waiting for me outside the restaurant, and, without her, the urge to go there is muted.

I start heading home instead, try to remember what's left in my fridge. I'm not sure I even have the energy to cook anything, but it's become a habit I enjoy after my shifts, one that helps me fall asleep with ease. I'll probably need it to push Emma out of my thoughts.

I hear steps coming behind me, and at first I assume that it's Felix.

I turn over my shoulder and see that it's actually Elias, half jogging to catch up with me. "Hey, man," Elias says. "Crazy day."

"Hasta la madre," I say.

"You up for some pool? I need a drink and everyone's going to this guy's party I don't feel like going to."

I picture going to my motel, looking up YouTube videos of cooks poaching eggs or dudes who can wash dishes with machine-like speed. A shower, more fantasies. Falling asleep with my phone on my chest.

So we go to The Crown. It's a quiet night and there's an open pool table. I get quarters from the change machine in the corner while Elias pays for beers. It feels like such a Felixian place that I scan the crowd looking for him. A couple of old townies are at the adjacent pool table, playing without exchanging a word. A thin woman with frizzy hair is half off her bar stool, talking loudly to the guy next to her, who looks desperate to escape the conversation. Felix loved places like this, windows into the lives of others.

Elias comes back and shoots first; the pool balls separate with a crack. "So, how're you liking the job?"

I take a moment to think about it while I line up a shot. The sore muscles, the wandering thoughts, being the bottom of a totem pole with no ladder in sight. "I'm loving it," I say, and I don't think it's a lie.

"No shit." Elias drinks from his beer, a long first gulp that's pretty standard after a hellish shift like we just went through. "I fucking hated dishwashing."

"You did it too?"

"A year. It sucks." We take a few quiet turns. The internet-equipped jukebox is playing something distinctly not-bar-like, something slow and mopey, which would never fly in Mexico City, where every establishment likes to blast pop and dance music.

"Shit, man," Elias says after a while, "you're not gonna say congrats?"

I look at him askance.

He looks up midshot, smiling wide. "You didn't hear? Chef promoted me to sous."

"Whoa, that's awesome." I walk over with my beer, and we clink glasses. He takes a tough shot between two other balls, but since the world's on his side today he nails it.

He runs a hand through his hair, walks around to the other side of the table to line up another shot.

"So, what's your story anyway? You just showed up like a hero in one of those old Westerns. The stranger no one knows. If I've learned anything from those movies, you're either here with some sort of a plan, or you're running from something."

"A little of both, I guess."

Elias laughs, one loud burst. "That's exactly what those dudes would say." I screw up my first shot pretty bad, grimace like I was expecting it to go in. Elias takes his time getting back up, savoring his beer. "You cook?"

I nod, excited that the truth is easy on this one.

"Work in restaurants before?"

I shake my head, bow it in shame.

Another crack of a perfectly hit ball. "Picked a damn good place to start," Elias says with a grin. "I hear you've been working your ass off too."

"Just trying to keep up," I say, scratching the back of my neck.

Elias walks around the table. "Good, humility. Kitchens need that. Lots of dudes come in thinking they're the shit, thinking they deserve to be on the line. No one likes to say they're struggling when they are."

I take small sips of the beer, which is some American microbrew that's way stronger than what I'm used to, the flavors big and bold. Elias kicks my ass and then racks up again. Lisa the bartender comes by with another round, and since the bar's mostly empty, she hangs out next to us for a bit. Her accent reminds me, like everything else, of Felix, those six months he spent in Brisbane, somehow starting a construction company before shrugging it all off and moving on. Sometimes I'm comforted by the thought of all the things Felix got to do in his life, and sometimes the thought of all he could have done with a normal lifespan comes crashing down on me.

"This is Carlos," Elias tells Lisa. "From my hometown, just started at the restaurant."

"Welcome," she says. "How the hell did you find yourself here?"

"I have no idea," I say, trying to shake away morbid thoughts.

Lisa laughs. I turn to Elias. "How'd *you* end up here?"

"Shit, that's a long story." He takes a sip from his beer, puts it down. "I hopped around the restaurant scene in LA and San Fran for a bit. Then a buddy of mine was opening up a taco place in Seattle, asked me to come with him. We didn't stay open long 'cause we had no business running a restaurant, but our food was good. Chef found me there and saved my ass by dragging me onto the ferry with her when that place closed down."

"Saved you from what?" I ask.

"I was up to my neck in debt and drugs, man. My buddy and I spent most of the investment money on speed and blow, trying to chase after some romanticized vision of being rock star chefs. We idolized Marco Pierre White, wanted to do all the crazy shit that went out of style when people figured out it was a stupid way to run a business. It didn't go so well. The shape I was in when Chef found me—I would have never worked in a kitchen again." He trails off, and I think I hear a note of fear in his voice, which makes me wonder just how bad it got.

The squeak of a stool being pushed back makes us both turn away from the conversation. The skinny woman at the bar drops a twenty on the counter and then stumbles out the door. A warm breeze pushes in from outside; dozens of stars are visible in just that brief opening, surreal and comforting.

I turn back to Elias. I want to hear everything about his journey to Provecho. I wanna know all the steps involved, what his life has looked like since. But he's looking around the bar, losing interest, so I leave it for another time. We spend the next hour just talking about food: the best things we've ever eaten, the best things we've ever cooked. I haven't talked with anyone like this since Felix died.

At around two in the morning, I get a text message from Emma, a picture of her shrieking at the camera.

Would you like to make a reservation? I text back, smiling at my phone.

Eww. Terrible joke, she responds. What are you up to?

I tell her, a little proud that I can answer with something truthful, that I'm not just passed out in a motel room, begging for sleep to save me from my thoughts. You?

The same thing I do every night, Carlos.

Trying to take over the world? I write, sure she's making a *Pinky and the Brain* reference, this old cartoon that Felix got me into.

Her response isn't immediate this time. Elias is at the bar getting us one more round. Aside from a lone couple necking in a corner booth, we're the last ones left in here. Nope, scrolling through the internet to feel less lonely. Talking to you.

I hope I'm helping, I write.

Sleep is tugging at me, begging for bed. I'm pretty sure I'll never be well-rested again. But there's a momentum to things here that I can't break, and instead I sink the three ball, take a long drink from my beer. Lisa is starting to close up the bar, and she keeps the door propped open as she takes out the trash. More stars are visible than before, as if they're coming out just for me.

Back at you, she writes, and that's our good-night for the evening.

CHAPTER 13

BANH MI TORTAS

25 bolillos

7 ½ pounds flank steak

6 stalks lemongrass

16 ounces pinto beans, soaked overnight

7 carrots, grated

7 cucumbers, sliced

4 jalapeños, sliced

3 bunches of cilantro, roughly chopped

METHOD:

Two days later, when I try to buy my morning coffee, my credit card gets declined. I'm guessing Dad wasn't too thrilled when Mom told him I was staying longer. I'm honestly surprised it's taken him this long to try to force me back home. There's a moment of panic, which subsides strangely easily once Anne, the nose-ringed girl who usually works mornings at the bakery near Provecho, just tells me not to worry about paying, that I can get her back next time.

I remember how Felix used to talk about money, how even when he didn't have much he was okay letting it slip away. He was always so candid about it too, confessing to sleeping on park benches and eating nothing but rice, like he wanted to rub his lifestyle in Dad's face.

The memory calms me down a little, but I can't quite shrug it off the way Felix clearly could. A part of me is clawing at all the awful things that could happen, all the terrible possibilities hidden among the world that could destroy my precarious position of independence. At least I paid for my room another week in advance. Plus, I'll be getting a paycheck soon. My very first paycheck, and it'll have a restaurant's name on it. Not Dad's company. There's something thrilling about that.

Though I now have access to that employees' entrance, I still prefer to knock on the glass and wait for Emma to appear. The moment she greets me carries me through the day, late into my shift when my muscles ache and no one has yet to say a word to me.

"You are the best," Emma says, taking the cup I brought her and holding the door open for me.

"Not really. Yours spilled and I didn't want to get another one, so I just kind of scooped it all back in there. Got most of it! Hope you like asphalt-y coffee."

"You kidding? It's my favorite."

It's a more relaxed morning. Midweek, we still get booked solid, but service only starts at lunch, so the early hours are slower. Plus, it seems Chef's out of town, leaving Michelle and Elias in charge. Memo's playing banda music nice and loud, and he's not the only one who knows all the words. Isaiah's singing along too, the words clumsy as they come out, all the r's slipping instead of rolling. Matt yells at him to turn "that mariachi shit" off, but even he's in a good mood. When I come by offering to take out his garbage for him, he even looks away from his prep sheet and says, "Sure. Thanks, man."

Then he dumps out a whole gallon container of sauce into the bag so that it'll leak, smirking at me as he does it. Baby steps, I guess.

The pleasantness in the air makes it easier to work, and I speed through my stack faster than I have all week, even though Roberto is again working cold foods and I'm on my own. Scrub a pot, load the washer with dishes, stack saucepans according to size. I carry glasses over to the server station, mugs to the coffee station, garbage to the dump. I walk past the hostess station, where Emma is on the phone, and I make a face like I'm shrieking to make her laugh.

When I walk past the office, Elias calls out to me from inside. "Hey, man. You busy?"

"Nope," I say, leaning into the doorway. I almost do a little dance while I say this. It might be the first time that I'm completely caught up on everything in the middle of the day. It won't last long, but I want to bask for a moment. Felix always told me to celebrate small victories.

Elias looks away from the computer monitor where he's checking who knows what. He's got a pen in his hand that he twirls a few times. "You up for making staff meal?"

I freeze. Of course I've imagined this happening before. The fantasies while I scrub dishes are not reserved for Emma alone. But then I think of Chef's warning not to touch a knife unless I'm washing it. "Um," I say. Suddenly, my fantasies—which always end in culinary triumph—feel like a joke. I've never cooked for more than five people. My knife skills compared to everyone else's are sad, like I chop in slow motion.

Emma shows up at the doorway, smiling at me as she turns to Elias. "Hey, just so you know, Sylvia called in. She's sick or something."

Elias groans, looks at his computer, clicks around. "Call Bill, see if he can come in. If not, try Linda." Then he turns back to me. "So, what do you say, man? I'll take you into the walk-ins, show you what you can use. The rest is up to you."

Emma quirks an eyebrow.

"Come on, man."

"I'm not qualified, am I?"

"Okay, now's not the time for humility, man," Elias says, chewing on the back of a pen. "Everyone's slammed. You told me you can cook. Just grill up some burgers or something."

"I can't believe you're hesitating," Emma says, nudging me with her elbow. I break out into a smile, but I can't bring myself to look at either of them.

"Look, man, we're still short, and you're caught up on your work. Even if I thought you couldn't put cereal in a bowl, I might put you in charge of staff meal."

"Dooooo iiiiiit," Emma says, now grabbing me by the shoulders and shaking.

Maybe I shouldn't be surprised that her touch undoes the doubt within me.

When I look up, Elias smiles like he knows he's won, gets up from the office chair. "Follow me."

The opening of the steel door will be a moment I remember for the rest of my life, I'm sure of it. It's not necessarily because the walk-in resembles all the ones I've seen on TV (every kind of produce lines the shelves, crates of fruit, plastic-covered containers of sauces and marinades and herbs). It's not Elias gesturing me in or even Emma at my back, hand on my shoulder, giggling on my behalf. I will remember this moment because it so clearly feels like I belong here.

On my left are all the sauces used in the set menu, each carefully labeled with a name and a date, although most are riddled with spelling errors. In the back are lowboy freezers loaded with all sorts of meat, almost every cut of beef or pork that I can recognize and plenty that I don't. This is like the cracked-out version of roaming the supermarket aisles waiting for inspiration.

Elias points me to some flank steak that we have to get rid of soon, a few dozen Mexican style bolillo bread rolls. "You're pretty much free to use the pantry and the veggies. Grab stuff from the front, 'cause it's older. You can use my old station. Ready to serve in an hour or so, before we open. If you don't know how to use something, ask me. But don't really 'cause I'm busy." He grins.

I'm squatting to take a look at some cooked pinto beans in Tupperware. There's lemongrass nearby, and I think of Felix's demonstration of Vietnam the other day in the grass. I start to get ideas. "Thanks," I say.

"Like a kid in a toy store," Elias says, and though I can hear him and Emma laughing as they head out, I barely register the noise.

A few minutes later I set the meat down on a cutting board in Elias's old station. Matt hovers over my shoulder and says, "What the fuck you think you're doing?"

"Staff meal," I say, hoping he doesn't go overboard with giving me shit, that he'll take it easy. Inside I'm cowering, un-Felix-like, just hoping he'll leave me alone. "Elias asked me to, since I'm caught up."

Matt gives me a little side-eye, but then a pot starts to bubble over and he curses under his breath while he rushes to it. Isaiah cocks an eyebrow, tells me that if I need help with any of the equipment to ask first before I fuck anything up. It's a nice gesture, I guess, though the tone implies he wants to throw something at me.

Never before have I bothered to exactly portion my meals, but never before have I cooked in a kitchen like this one. It's the first time since I got here that I'm cooking for anyone other than myself, and I want to make sure I'm not messing anything up.

That's exactly what I do, though. I try to make the guajillo aioli from scratch, wasting ten minutes and five eggs before I realize I used the egg whites instead of the yolk and have to throw it all away. The veggies for the sandwiches are sliced unevenly, I overcook the steak and leave lumps of garlic in the bean puree. It's almost forty minutes after Elias told me to have something ready when I pull out the last of the bolillos from the broiler where they've been toasting. I assemble the sandwiches, cut them into halves, wish to become completely invisible. People are gonna tear me apart.

Elias is in the expedite station, meeting with the front of house manager. I stand nearby, not wanting to interrupt. When Isaiah sees me standing there for a while, he calls over. "Hey, man, if those are done, just play the music."

"Right," I say. I'm convinced Chef is going to barge in and fire me.

That Elias himself will throw me out and tell me never to set foot in a kitchen again.

Felix appears for the first time all day. He's a white, transparent, Casper-style cartoon ghost, floating around like a kid's last-minute Halloween costume. "I can't believe the emotion you're going for right now is worry. If I were you, I'd be dancing. You just cooked in a professional kitchen, brother."

I give him a look.

"You're right. I've seen you dance. Please, continue worrying."

I hang around the window where the sandwiches are sitting under the heat lamp, not sure what the hell else I'm supposed to do. People don't abandon their stations right away to come eat; they still have prep sheets to go through, slack to pick up from us being understaffed. Elias shows up pretty quickly. "What do we have here?"

"Banh mi tortas."

He raises his eyebrows at me. "Nice." Then he takes a big bite, wipes at some bean pâté that's on the side of his mouth. He nods while chewing, bites again. I can barely stomach half a sandwich myself while I wait for people to trickle in and lay their reactions on me. "Not bad," Elias says, and it doesn't sound like a compliment to me. I disappear back into my station, for once happy at being cast away to a corner of the kitchen that proves I don't belong here.

Every now and then, I pause, dry my hands, take another bite of my sandwich, taste buds hyperactive to what could have gone wrong (underseasoned meat? Too much cilantro? Awful all around?). I keep looking over my shoulder, anticipating Matt coming in to tell me I'm a joke. But no one says a thing.

When I leave that night, I feel like crawling into bed. I'm slightly buzzed from sleep deprivation and sick with the disappointment of screwing up a simple meal. Sure, no one gave me shit, but they weren't quite licking their lips either.

I'm on my way home when I see Emma stumbling across the road near The Crown, heading into a stretch of woods. I know the girl finds pathways where they don't exist, but her gait implies a stupor, a lack of control, and I call after her. She looks over her shoulder at me and pauses while I catch up.

Moonlight filters through the space between the trees. She turns her back to me until I'm there, and when I get there, she whips around and says, "My dad's an asshole."

"Mine too," I say.

She laughs and surprises me by falling against me, cheek against my chest. I almost fall backward but gain my footing. Then I realize my T-shirt's getting warm and damp.

"He always does this shit. Cancels at the last minute. Cancels right when I get my stupid hopes up, like the one parental instinct he got is a sense of when I've just started feeling good about him." She sighs against my chest, pushes back and reveals tear-streaked cheeks and red eyes and dilated pupils.

A beat goes by, and then she says, "Fuck," and she leans back into my chest for an hour or three or fifteen minutes, I'm not sure. I want to keep her safe from whatever's hurting her.

Insects buzz around us with a pleasant hum, like the island's trying to comfort Emma. She steps back again and blinks, looking at me as if she's realized I'm here, as if she's just realized anything is here.

"Carlos?"

"It's me. You're okay."

"Where are we?"

"The woods," I say. "Right near The Crown. I saw you stumbling."

She bites her lips, wipes at the pain all over her face. Some of it smears onto her sweater; some stays put. "I don't know why I feel this bad," she says.

I imagine it has something to do with dilated pupils and shitty fathers, but instead I put a hand on her shoulder to steady her and say, "Let me help."

She hiccups, nearly falls asleep on her feet. It's a struggle to get her home, partially because of her slurred, half-mumbled directions. We finally manage, and as we climb the stairs to her room, I'm thankful Chef isn't around to potentially surprise us in this awkward situation. There's a few posters on Emma's wall, a video game console in the corner, several bookshelves crowded with haphazardly arranged novels.

Emma slips into bed and starts snoring almost immediately, shoes still on. I make sure she's on her side, slide a trash bin next to the bed. I keep her bathroom door open, in case the urge is immediate. I sneak downstairs to get her a glass of water.

I help her tilt her head up a little and gulp down enough water to maybe make a difference. She goes right back to snoring, curled up atop her colorful, striped bedspread, knees to her chest. There's a whiteboard in the corner of the room, smudged nearly black from shitty erasers. I think about all I could say to her, and instead write: *I hope you don't feel awful when you read this. If you're ever lonely, you can call me.* I sign my name and head home, sleep soundly.

At the end of the next day, I hang up my apron and wash my hands. The mood, as it always is this time of night, is one of survival. I have to wait for everyone else to survive before I'm gone, though, so I'm usually among the last to leave. Only a few people are left. Elias and Michelle are having some sort of meeting about the menu.

"Good job today, baby," Elias calls out. People call each other all sorts of weird things in the kitchen, I've found. Almost everyone has multiple nicknames for each other. I've got "Fake-xican" and "baby," I guess.

Vee is pulling up the black rubber mats that run throughout every station; a few ovens are on their cleaning cycles or slow-cooking something overnight. Other than that, the kitchen is a glimmering polish of stainless-steel cleanliness. The floors are mopped; the roaring hood is off.

"Thanks, Chef," I say to Elias. "See you tomorrow." I push the door open, noticing that what was debilitating exhaustion a week ago now feels like the status quo. Something I can survive.

"Of course you can," Felix says, following behind. I don't respond yet, because I have all night with him. Lately, I haven't been dreading his arrivals. I'm starting to think that this whole thing has nothing to do with getting rid of him.

When I turn the corner, I spot Emma sitting on the bench in front of the restaurant, reading a book, tilting it so it catches the light of the street lamp. She's got earbuds in, one leg tucked beneath her.

"Just forget it," Felix says, because he knows what I'm thinking. "She seems like she's a mess, like she just wants to toy with you. Focus on the kitchen. That's going well."

I wave a hand in his direction and am honestly surprised when he flitters away like smoke.

I know maybe Emma doesn't give me as much thought as I give her, that she likes making out drunkenly at bars and having it mean nothing, that she's leaving the island soon. But I also know that I want to surround myself with her. I slip a flannel shirt on over my gross, smelly T-shirt and then plop down next to her on the bench.

Emma jumps a little, gives me one of our shared, silent-shriek looks. She reads for a second or so, still listening to music. I check my phone for the first time since the morning but don't really care enough to delve into the notifications. Emma slips a bookmark into the pages and pulls out her earphones. "Hey. Thanks for yesterday."

A strong breeze blows by, makes the streetlights sway slightly. The shadows shift on Emma's face and her eyes brighten; something I can't point to makes me ache and yearn that we had something more. She looks up and then back at me, combs her hair behind her ear.

"Don't mention it," I say. "You looked the way I feel sometimes."

Secrets slip out of me when I'm with her. She smiles at me, and I can't help but reciprocate. We do that at each other like idiots for a second. For once, I'm okay with the awkwardness hanging around.

Firefly meadow and the lake? I want to ask, but the words don't come.

A mile away, waves crash on the shore with such force that they send out a fine mist that shimmers beneath the streetlights, coating me and Emma. We're quiet for long enough that it feels inevitable that eventually I will muster the courage to say what I want. Then Emma says good-night, and she gets up from the bench.

On the walk to my motel room, Mom calls, but I'm in no mood to talk, so I let it go to voice mail and then check the message she leaves.

"Carlos," she says, imbuing my name with too much emotion, the way only a mom can. The moon should be a waning crescent by now, but it's still full. Somehow, it still allows the surrounding stars to stand out, and it's almost more beautiful than it was last week.

"When do you think you're coming back?" Mom asks, her recorded voice fraught with worry. "Your dad and I miss you. We're worried about you, and there's some paperwork for school that you still need to fill out."

I think of Emma reading on the bench. The way she was focused on her book, how the orange glow of the street lamp made it look like she was in a photograph. Light doesn't behave like that anywhere else that I've been. Everything here is ethereal.

Yeah, I've noticed the absence of my family. I've noticed how many of my meals are solitary, even at the restaurant, with people around. How I rarely talk to living people. But anytime I think about my parents, it's not Mom's care that I remember, it's Dad's good-bye: *So you're running away. Just like your brother did. A lot of good it did him.*

I don't call Mom back.

CHAPTER 14
MILKSHAKES

Some milk
A lot of chocolate ice cream

METHOD:

It's four in the morning and I'm hiking up the hilly street to meet up with Emma.

I'd been lying in bed, looking up videos on how to arroser fish, sleep eluding me. Then my phone started to buzz. I'd assumed it was Mom again, even with the time difference. I'd thought maybe something had gone wrong. Then I saw Emma's name on the screen.

"Turns out I'm lonely," she said when I answered. "Wanna go on a date?"

My room lit up, a cloud passing by to uncover the moon or something. "When?"

"Now," she said and then paused. "I have kind of a crazy idea for a date that I've been meaning to try out but haven't had the chance to yet. Because you were in Mexico before."

"Right, my bad," I said, sitting up in bed, certain she'd be able to hear my smile through the signal. "So, what's your idea?"

Now I'm the only person on the island who's awake, except for maybe some of the fishermen heading out to open water or some of my kitchen mates heading back home from the bar.

After a whole lifetime of being told four a.m. is dangerous, especially on foot, it is freeing to feel such peace. Safe among the trees and the moonlight, I don't keep my cell phone in one hand, ready to call for help, the way I always did in Mexico when leaving a party, conditioned to fear the city even though I was in neighborhoods where things rarely happened.

Fireflies have been accompanying me the entire walk, and when they take Felix's form, I'm happy that the situation leads us to talking about dating. We never really had the chance to before.

"Just be yourself," he says, another platitude that offers no real advice unless it's completely earnest.

"Did anyone think you were smooth," I ask, "or could they see through your bullshit?"

"Hey, man, I did okay."

I want to ask him about girls he loved, but the past tense kills me, so I just let him rattle on with his advice-column wisdom until I knock on Emma's door. The fireflies he's made up of flitter away. A few seconds later she answers wearing brightly colored elephant pajama shorts and a loose-fitting Sharon Van Etten tank top.

"Hi," I say because I don't want to say what I'm actually thinking, that this is weird and lovely and I'm a puddle of nerves and she looks fantastic and how the hell has life led me here. "You look great."

"No, damn it!" she says. "This is a reverse date. You'd say that at the beginning, and that's not now. Now's the end."

"Right. Sorry." I put my hand on the door frame and then look down at myself wondering if I'm even sane enough to be on a date right now. "Should I be in pajamas?"

Emma laughs, grabs my hand. "Okay, so maybe this isn't as smooth as I was envisioning. But this next part might help."

"What's the next part?"

"Well, assuming the date went well, which I am…"

"I like that assumption."

"Then, we kiss good-night." Emma says, biting her lip.

I take a moment to process this information. I might need a whole new brain to wrap around that statement. "We start the date with a kiss?"

"No, we're ending it with a kiss." She steps closer, puts her free hand around my waist so that I can feel how much warmer it is inside her house than in the cool air I've been walking around in. "Instead of worrying about the kiss all date, we'll get it out of the way now, so that we're not nervous. Like in that movie."

"What movie?"

"Doesn't matter," she says, pressing even closer, giving my hand a squeeze. "You ready? We're going to say good-night now." Over her shoulder, through a window, I can see the beginning of a sunrise softly erase away the night.

"Good night, Carlos. Thanks for a great date."

"Good night, Emma."

Our first kiss unfolds the way first kisses usually do: with equal measures of clumsiness and slobber and awe. It is phenomenal and not in sync and the slight part of me that is worried about the latter is completely overshadowed by the joy of the former. I feel transported, but, instead of to some other place, I'm transported more fully to the exact place where I am. To the taste of her lips, the feel of her body against mine, the quiet of the world around us. Emma pulls away from me, her cheeks and lips flushed red. More of that whole smiling-at-each-other-like-idiots thing. "Shit," she says. "I'm still nervous."

"Me too," I laugh, but her hands are in mine and I can feel myself start to relax already. "What's next?"

"Well, now we go to sleep."

I laugh, though only because I don't know what muscles to use for a more appropriate reaction (i.e., making my head explode).

Emma leads us to the living room. "The way I see it, after our date we both want the night to keep going, and so I invite you over to watch a movie and some cuddles, but we end up falling asleep." She stands in front of the couch, powers on the TV but nothing else, so that the screen is showing a *no signal* message. Then she turns around, suddenly hesitant, wringing her hands, biting her lip. "Is this too weird? Was this a bad idea?"

Emboldened, thinking this is far from a bad idea, I close the slight gap between us and we kiss again.

It turns out that, while attempting to sleep near each other early in a first date provides a glorious amount of touching and comfort and arousal, it does not make for a conducive sleeping environment. Emma and I end up doing more giggling than anything, our hands clasped together beneath a thin plaid blanket.

"Carlos, are you asleep?"

"Of course I'm asleep," I respond, eyes tightly shut.

"Okay, good. Because if we don't fall asleep, then we can't do the other parts of the date." I fake a snore, nuzzle a little closer, don't even envision what these other parts of the date might be. Emma throws an arm across my chest, matches the snore, and within moments we're laughing again.

Who knows how long this goes on for, jokes interrupted by rare moments of quiet, where I think maybe one of us is about to really fall asleep, and I'm surprised by how benign my thoughts are in the silence. Then Emma turns on the video game console to find a movie on Netflix. Before hitting Play, Emma runs out to the kitchen to make us some popcorn and grab some drinks. On the couch, I run a hand through my hair in disbelief.

Emma comes back, settles herself against my chest with the oversized bowl on her lap. She picks up the remote control, cranes her head back so her lips are grazing my jawbone. Through the sheer curtains, I can see the sun poke its red head over the ocean.

Throughout the movie, we alternate between raucous laughter ("Why is he wearing snakes on his wrists? That makes no sense!") and a silence more comfortable than I could have ever imagined. Outside people begin their days. Garage doors grind open, car engines turn on, children freed by summer squeal as they run outside to play.

When the credits roll, I ask Emma, "Can I kiss you again?"

And she responds wordlessly.

At the diner downtown, while a mix of local fishermen and tourist families have eggs and bacon, Emma and I dine on burgers and milkshakes. It is distinctly and satisfyingly American. I consider how, despite my passport, I have never really felt American. The one thing about Dad's plan that felt right all along was me staying in Mexico. Now, though, I'm not so sure. Slanted sunbeams streak across the table through the blinds, lighting up Emma's skin.

I didn't think to pack a swimsuit when I was making my escape to the island, so we go into one of those convenient beach-goods stores on the boardwalk and buy me the cheapest, ugliest pair of swim trunks we can find, along with a beach towel depicting a kitten eating a cobra in space. Since Emma's offended that I didn't bring a book with me either, we go to the used bookstore and I pick out a paperback by Italo Calvino, who I've never heard about but sounds intriguing.

By the time we get down to the lake, the tiredness of a long week and our early meet up is sinking in. We set the towel down on a tree-shaded stretch of grass and strip down to our swimwear. We read for a few minutes, but before too long the heat has me dropping my book on my face, so I push it aside, turn so that I'm facing Emma, doze off.

I wake up briefly and see Emma's in the same position as me, her face inches away, eyes serenely closed. Somewhere in the distance, people are splashing around in the lake. It seems like we're miles away from anyone else, worlds away. I maneuver myself half an inch closer, amazed at the slight distance between us.

Again I wake up, and this time I'm alone. The air is a little chillier;

the sun has dipped beneath the peak of the island's hill. I sit up, rubbing the sleep from my eyes, wondering where the hell Emma's gone, instantly nervous that the date is over.

"You're cute when you sleep," Emma calls out from the lake, which is turning pink with the sunset. She's only a few feet in, lying facedown in the shallow water, hands propping her head up.

"Are you saying I'm not at other times?"

She shrugs. "At least now you know."

I run into the lake, which is so warm that I can't help splashing past Emma until I'm fully submerged. Then I turn back around, just as she's swimming into my arms.

Night falls, and we're standing back in front of Emma's door. Her hair's still wet, dripping onto the faded welcome mat on her porch. I swear I can still see bioluminescence clinging to her; each drop that falls looks like tiny contained fireworks. We're both grinning like fools.

"So, how do we start this date?" I ask.

"I had planned for an awkward hug," Emma says. "But I really want to kiss you again."

"Bold start," I say.

Emma shrugs, tilts her head toward mine. "I'm okay with that."

CHAPTER 15

TOM YUM POZOLE

6 uajillo, pasilla, arbol chili peppers, toasted and rehydrated

5 cloves garlic

1 onion

5 stalks lemongrass

2 tablespoons galangal

3 kaffir lime leaves

50 grams fresh ginger

3 16-ounce cans hominy

10 cups chicken stock

10 cups water

8 pounds pork loin

8 tablespoons lime juice

8 tablespoons fish sauce

4 tablespoons oregano

METHOD:

On Tuesday morning, Chef Elise returns, and I attack my dishes with the vigor that only the happy can muster. Though all the cooks are busy replenishing mise containers, bubbling stocks and sauces meant to last the week, I'm ahead of the incoming tide of pots and pans. It's like magic how quickly I go through the work, how much better I am at this than when I arrived a few weeks ago. I don't know how much Mom and Dad would share in the feeling, but pride surges within me when I finish a stack. More than anything, I am happy that the sight of Felix—when he invariably shows—cannot undo this.

Roberto takes a coffee break, and I go around emptying people's bins for them. I see Chef in the office, making phone calls, checking off items on a clipboard. Typical teasing from Matt, who seems to be the only person in the kitchen who can always see me.

Elias intercepts me near the pass. "Hey, man, how do you feel about making staff meal again?"

Though the kitchen is at its typical roar, and Chef's on the phone in her office, I instinctively lower my voice. "Don't you remember? Chef told me to stay away from the food. I'll help someone else or something, but..."

"What, the mysterious hero is scared?" Elias cuts me off. "Chef's loaded with paperwork and shit back there. If you're handling your stuff and not messing with other people, no one cares what you do. You could teach yourself how to salsa dance if you wanted to."

"She's not going to, like, fire me or stab me or something? I didn't exactly kill it last time."

Elias rolls his eyes. "Cut the shit, man. You got time to cook or should I find someone else?"

I look back at Chef's office. I've been hoping every day for another chance to cook, redeem myself. Felix appears in her doorway. "If you don't say yes, I will haunt you in increasingly annoying ways." I nod quietly, and Elias leads me to the walk-ins again.

I've got a few hours before it has to be ready, and the first thing my mind goes to is pozole, the rich aromas that'll fill the kitchen. Felix and I used to make it at home sometimes, weekend mornings when he was hungover. We'd hang out in the kitchen the whole day, taste-testing, letting the broth simmer itself delicious. It's the meal my friends always ask me to make for them. Dad too.

It's relatively easy to make, so I won't screw up, but I can find a way to mix it up too. Maybe keep the Mexican-Asian fusion theme going. I grab an assorted handful of dried chilies from the pantry, some lemongrass, a jar of galangal, kaffir lime leaves.

After the chilies are toasted, the prep work is pretty easy. Just throw most of the stuff into a stockpot and let it simmer for a few hours while I disappear behind my partition, safe from Chef's wrath. I relive kisses with Emma as the suds and steam surround me. Every time I come by to deliver dishes or pots to the line, I check on my creation, give it a stir, taste with a clean spoon and then carry it back to the sink with me to dispose of the evidence.

At around noon, the soup tastes exactly like I'd envisioned. It tastes so good that I'm actually a little sad that Felix can't ever try it. When Elias comes by to ask if I'm almost done cooking, I get Roberto to cover me and then set up a tray of garnishes so that people can do what they want to it (an oregano–nam prik pao mix, limes, radishes). "Everything's good to go," I say. "Don't tell Chef it was me, though."

Elias takes a spoonful, blows on it gingerly and then swallows, shakes his head. "Fuck, man. Those sandwiches the other day were alright for staff meal. But I could tell you had something."

I turn the music up to make the announcement. I serve myself a bowl first and then hang around to see people's reactions. Lourdes is pouring herself a bowl when Chef turns up, among the first to do so. She leans over Lourdes's shoulder, comments about the smell, offering her compliments. I beam so hard I'm surprised the whole kitchen doesn't burst into flames.

"No fui yo, Chef," Lourdes says.

I keep my eyes down, slurping at the broth and the hominy. Elias is leaning against the wall, smirking at me with his eyebrows raised.

"No? Who the hell else makes pozole here? It's different than usual. Ginger, lemongrass. This is nice."

I try to beg Elias not to do what he's thinking of doing. The look on his face is such a Felix look that I'm afraid I'm hallucinating. Every time Felix was about to piss Dad off, he'd get that same smirk. For the first time, I wonder if Felix can inhabit the living. "Everyone was slammed, Chef. So I told the new guy to whip something up. Told me he could cook. I kind of agree."

"The dishwasher," Chef says, as if I'm nameless.

I imagine her firing me on the spot or maybe emptying the stockpot into the sink. I picture a finger pointed at the exit, maybe me even getting shoved out. Fuck, what if she actually stabs me?

She doesn't visibly react, though. She serves herself a ladleful and sips at the broth thoughtfully. Her eyes are locked onto mine, and I'm pretty sure she's killed someone like this, that the only reason the expression *if looks could kill* still exists is because not enough people have witnessed the fact that her looks *can*. Lourdes and Memo chat obliviously about their families while Chef finishes the bowl quietly.

She doesn't take her eyes off me the entire time. Eight insane minutes of prolonged eye contact. My head might actually explode.

"Not enough balance here," she says, finally. "It's all spice." She sets the bowl down on the counter and crosses her arms over her chest, still burning holes with her stare.

"Yes, Chef," I whisper, though I'm not sure I say it audibly enough for her to hear. I want to turn my head away because I can't ever remember being this uncomfortable, not even at Felix's funeral when we were burying my brother, but I could see him dancing through the crowd. My stomach drops as I realize that I've disobeyed her orders, that she could easily send me packing back to Mexico.

"Come with me," Chef says.

I walk through the kitchen already feeling nostalgic for it. Its roars of activity and noise, its unique language, Kitchenese in English and Spanish, its bursts of curse words and laughter. Flurries of food and fire.

In her office, Chef gestures for me to sit and then closes the door behind me. She sits down behind her desk, leaning back, hands folded over her stomach. Again, just a quiet stare. There's a wall calendar covered in red-inked handwriting, a few Post-its. There's a pen holder on the corner of the desk, a couple clipboards hanging up on the wall, not a trace of clutter. A wall clock ticks loudly.

Fuck, I don't want to go back to Mexico.

"So," she says, after an eternity. "You cook."

I straighten out a little, clear my throat. I'm not sure what approach she's taking here, but at least it isn't instant berating. "Yes, Chef. I'm sorry, I know you told me not to, but…" I start to stammer an explanation, but she shuts me up with a raised hand.

"Culinary school?"

I shake my head. The way she asks, it makes it sound so obvious. Why didn't I even think about that before?

She doesn't nod, doesn't smile.

Through the door, I can hear Sue, the kitchen manager, call out, "Six open menus!" Dinner's starting up. I'm technically off the clock now, but I wish I'd signed up for another double. I want more time here, and I'm afraid all that will be undone when Chef says the words that cast me away.

"You have your own knife?"

I furrow my brow. If Emma were here, she'd probably joke about Chef wanting to stab me with it.

"No, Chef."

"Go buy one."

Chef Elise is still looking at me, and she hasn't blinked in months. I nod. Finally, she swivels her chair away from me, turns to the computer. "You're going to start coming in early. Bring a knife," she says, clicking the mouse a few times. "You're still a dishwasher, but you can take over staff meals, as long as you're caught up." She gives me a look while I try to contain my smile. "Don't get all fucking giddy about it. No one wants that job."

"Yes, Chef," I say, though Felix has shown up behind me and is literally pulling the corners of my mouth up into a smile. I dip my head so that Chef won't see. She clicks around on the computer a little more, while Felix does a little dance. I almost feel like joining in.

Then Chef looks back at me. "What are you waiting for, a hug good-bye? Go away. I'll see you at six."

I scramble to my feet. "Yes, Chef. Sorry, Chef. Thank you." I close the office door behind me, bringing Felix along. The empty hallway looks like it's not lit up by fluorescent light bulbs, but by the Needle Eye sun, a constant golden-hour hue. I can't resist it: I join my brother in a celebratory jig.

CHAPTER 16

CARROT CAKE

2 cups flour
3 large eggs
12 ounces grated carrots
2 cups sugar
½ cup softened butter
¾ cup vegetable oil
1 teaspoon baking powder
1 teaspoon baking soda
¼ teaspoon ground allspice
1 teaspoon ground cinnamon
2 teaspoons vanilla extract
1 cup chopped pecans
Pinch of salt

METHOD:

When I step outside the restaurant, I've got the whole evening ahead to myself. Usually, my free hours fill me with a nameless dread, a weight that presses down on me and brings me no joy.

But tonight the empty hours feel full of possibilities. I could explore the island by myself until Emma gets off the late shift (which she should be arriving for at any moment). I could cook us a seven-course meal. I could get on a ferry and go check out Seattle. I stand on the corner, where I can turn one way and see the ocean (sun still a few hours away from setting, sailboats floating on golden waters) and turn the other and see Main Street (tourists lining up for dinner, smiling families everywhere).

A block or so away from the restaurant there's one of those super-white-middle-class French-named stores that sells everything from melon ballers to fondue sets. Stuff I've only ever seen on cooking shows. I marvel at all the little kitchen gadgets that I would never be able to find in Mexico. An ice-cream maker. A vegetable spiralizer. A pepper corer. I know Felix would scoff at the opulence, but I still want every single ridiculous tool. I picture how I might use them. A cross between chiles rellenos and jalapeño poppers, maybe, using a corer and that deep fat fryer over there. I'd serve two on a plate, stuffed with corn, Oaxaca cheese and cilantro, arranged carefully over a sea of red salsa. If I made this dish, Felix could never have it. The realization threatens to stop my giddiness cold, so I step away before the thought can fully land.

I go over to the knives, wondering why I don't know more about picking them out. There's a whole row of stainless-steel chef's knives, and I pick out one called a gyuto, just because I think I've heard the name before. It's a stupid purchase considering how much money I've run through already, but I leave the store feeling like I'm King Arthur with Excalibur in my hand.

As I make my way back to Provecho to wait for Emma, I can picture her walking with her earphones in, kicking pebbles, taking shortcuts only she knows through the woods, secret pathways that part just for her. It's like I can feel her the closer she gets, a warmth emanating from her that could reach me from halfway across the island. When I see her turn onto Main Street I feel like my skin is actually glowing with joy.

She breaks out into a smile when she sees me, and I have to play it cool to keep myself from running through the crowd and into her arms.

"Hey," she says.

I want to tell her the news right away, but instead I take her by the hand to the back of the restaurant, and I kiss her the way I've been wanting to all day. *What a world*, I think, slipping my fingers through her hair.

Even the slamming of the side door does little to interrupt that thought, until it's followed by a throat clearing. Emma and I pull away from each other, and I see Emma's cheeks redden and her glasses fully cloud. It makes me want to kiss her again, but something in her expression makes me turn around.

Chef's got a full garbage bag dangling at her side, stone-faced.

"Hi, Mom," Emma says, pulling her glasses off to wipe them clean.

Chef nods a hello, and I realize this is awkward, but it does nothing to beat away the joy pumping through my veins. Behind Chef, low, fast-moving clouds blow by, clearing the horizon for an upcoming sunset as if by design.

"Carlos, I forgot to tell you something," Chef says. "Follow me." She chucks the trash bag into the Dumpster and then disappears back inside the restaurant.

Confused, I look back at Emma, who's cleaning her glasses with the hem of her shirt. She smiles at me, tells me she'll call when she gets off work.

Chef is waiting for me in her office, leaning back against her desk with her arms crossed in front of her chest. "If you want to stay at this restaurant and work your way up, you stop seeing her."

The lights dim; the temperature drops.

"Emma?" I ask, stupidly, once I make sense of what she's said.

"You can't have both," Chef says. She doesn't sound angry, only like she's delivering very specific instructions, like this is just a meeting with the waitstaff about how to explain a new dish. "I'm not going to prohibit you from seeing her, because she gets to decide for herself who she dates. But if you choose to continue to see her, you can't work here."

I'm frozen in the doorway. I can hear that magical clatter of the kitchen prepping for service, people getting fired up for another night booked solid. But it feels like white noise right now. Like all the sounds are getting sucked up by the induction hood.

I want Chef to explain further, want her to provide some sort of logic that will make this easier to understand. She uncrosses her arms and then grabs the apron that's hanging from a hook behind the door, tying it around her back. "Did I make myself clear?"

I have no idea what I want to say, dozens of questions and complaints are on the tip of my tongue, but instead I stammer out another "Yes, Chef."

"If I see you still chasing after her, you're out," Chef says and then leaves without another word.

I exit the restaurant in a daze. I amble through downtown and the boardwalk, getting in people's way. I cross streets without looking and hear honks for the first time since I got to the island. Wind rustles the trees wherever I go, and once I get to the more isolated sections of Needle Eye, I can hear Felix in the swishing of the leaves.

I let my brother whistle to himself for a while. I desperately want to regain the bliss I felt outside the restaurant, right before Chef decided to blow it all to hell.

Night falls late in this part of the world, but it happens at the exact wrong time, when I'm snaking my way through the woods, trying to find the places Emma has taken me to. I struggle through nonexistent paths, brambles clawing at my arms. The moon disappears behind sudden clouds, and though the typical night chill has swept in, I sweat myself into a stupor trying to find the hill that looks out at the island. I use my phone's flashlight, keeping my eye on the battery draining away a percentage point at a time, struggling to get a signal. I keep imagining it buzzing in my hand, messages from Emma that I won't know how to answer.

Eventually, just by heading up any slope I see, I do make it to the top of that hill. Provecho's white light stands out against the other shops in the tiny Main Street stretch. All over the island I can see the tiny flares of backyard campfires, people enjoying the night, the company of others. Devoid of the moon's glow, the lake looks like a pit of darkness.

"Why are you getting so flustered?" Felix says, using the wind and the leaves to speak.

I find a big rock to sit down on. I wipe the sweat from my forehead, check my phone again to see if Emma's called or texted yet. "You know why," I say after a while.

The wind dies down a little, so Felix quits the charades and shows up as himself. He scoots me over a little and takes a seat next to me. He takes a deep breath, which kind of pisses me off, because what reason does a ghost have to sigh?

"Okay, I get it," Felix says. "It sucks. Emma's a cool girl. But these things don't always last. She's leaving anyway. This makes things less complicated, no?"

I pick up a pebble, chuck it in the direction of the lake. There's no way it hits anything but the side of the hill below, but I swear I hear a splash. "I've never had anything like this before, Felix."

"I understand."

"And don't give me any of that pseudo-inspirational bullshit."

Felix actually laughs. "Me? What would I say?"

"'Don't be sad it's over. Be glad it happened.' That kind of thing."

Felix stands up, reaching down for some pebbles. He chuckles again. "Just 'cause it's trite doesn't mean it's bad advice." He throws all the pebbles at once, and a few moments later I clearly hear them splash, each carrying a different tone.

"It's stupid," I say. "I don't want it to be over." I check the time, imagine what's going on in the restaurant. The last few tables are being seated right around now, which means Emma's shift will be over in a bit. The sink is probably buried right now, the steam from hot water making the station feel muggier than a swamp.

"Would you rather be done with the kitchen?" Felix grabs another handful of pebbles, throws them one at a time. It's almost a song when they land, and Felix smiles, not necessarily at me, just at the world he no longer inhabits.

I don't bother responding to the question, which is clearly a trap. The phrase *can't have your cake and eat it too* pops into my mind, and I wonder why the fuck everyone thinks it makes sense. How do you have cake without eating it? I'd blame my lack of understanding on being foreign, but there's no quirk of language or culture here. It's a stupid saying.

Burying my head in my hands, I feel like shouting. I can't believe there's parents around that still do this kind of shit. Why does the world not want me to be better already?

Felix is tossing more and more pebbles into the lake, trying to get a melody right. "Cielito Lindo," the song which starts off advising people to sing and not cry.

"So, what," I say, looking up, "I just give her up? Just like that? When things are going so well?"

Felix pauses for a bit, turning around to look at me. The scruff on his face is the same length it was that day, and the light in his eyes has never really gone away. He bounces another handful of pebbles in his hand, thinking.

"I know it's hard to turn away from something that brings you joy. And in most scenarios, I wouldn't tell you to. You know that. I'd be pushing you toward whatever makes you happy whether you liked it or not." I feel a text message buzz in my pocket. "You didn't come here to meet a girl," Felix says, shrugging. He turns back and times out the pebble throws so that a few seconds later the song comes floating toward them. "If Chef says you can't have both, whatever her reasons are, you have to make a decision."

I look in the direction of Provecho. Emma's probably sitting on the bench in front waiting for my response before she decides which direction to go. I would rather be frozen in indecision, just stay up on this hill and pretend everything's okay. Even if Felix is still around and nothing all that much has changed.

I try to picture what I would do if I left the kitchen to stay with Emma. How long until I ran out of money from my one measly paycheck, until I'd be forced to call my dad, come back home with my tail tucked between my legs? What will choosing Emma matter then?

I pull my phone out of my pocket, read the message I knew was from Emma. I'm off! What're you up to?

I have to take a deep breath. I'm feeling queasy and just want to throw the phone into the lake too.

Kind of exhausted. Rain check?

I hate myself for sending it, but I have no idea what else I could possibly say. Felix joins me back on the rock, putting an arm around me. We sit there for a while, not saying much, just staring out quietly at the island below.

If I get fired from the kitchen, I have to go home.

But without Emma, is this place worth sticking around for? Even now, the view of the island doesn't compare with my memory of when

I was here with her. It's beautiful, sure. But it's lacking something, as if the colors are muted. The lighting isn't what I know this place is capable of.

I get a text message wishing me sweet dreams, and the colors mute a little more.

CHAPTER 17

CUBAN LECHÓN ASADO

50-pound pig

5 heads of garlic

4 cups orange juice

2 cups lime juice

1 cup sherry

½ cup pineapple juice

4 tablespoons oregano

3 teaspoons ground cumin

6 bay leaves

2 tablespoons black peppercorns

2 tablespoons kosher salt

5 tablespoons olive oil

METHOD:

Morning comes, and I have not managed to push Emma out of my thoughts. The sun's barely coming up when I arrive at the side door to meet with Chef. It's a mostly clear day, which causes the dawn to paint the sky instead of clouds.

I hold my gyuto at my side, flat against my leg. I knock twice, hard. Chef appears in a moment, moves aside wordlessly. I hate her for taking Emma away from me and have half a mind to throw a fit. But a) I'm not exactly the throwing-fits type, and b) Felix reads my thoughts and makes an announcement over the kitchen speakers: "You're about to get private lessons from an incredible chef. You sure you want to throw that away?"

Swallowing my anger, I follow her into one of the walk-ins, where Sue is counting tomatoes while holding a clipboard. "You got this for a few minutes?" Chef says, and Sue nods. Then Chef reaches for a white onion, and heads back out to the prep kitchen. She sets the onion down on the counter.

"Do you know how to chop an onion?"

I feel my eyebrows furrow. "Yes, Chef. Of course."

"Show me."

I hesitate but then think to myself, *Clearly this is a test.* I pull my new knife out from its plastic sheath, set it on a cutting board next to the onion. I wish I didn't have to use it for the first time under these circumstances. It feels so right in my hand, like it was designed specifically for my grip. But Chef's got her diamond-cutting gaze on me and I'm trying hard not to throw the onion across the room at her.

I step over to the sink, wash my hands thoroughly. A wave of insecurity hits me, as if every time I cut an onion in the past I was doing it wrong, Chef knows this, and this is all just a way to mock me. She's just standing there, staring, arms folded. I take a deep breath, try to adopt a Felixesque ease. I'm standing in Chef Elise's kitchen, about to receive her tutelage. I should be thankful.

It's all muscle memory, really. I remember the day Felix taught me how to do this. I was thirteen; he was a couple months away from leaving home. Mom hovered behind us, trying to convince Felix that I was too young to hold a blade. He'd laughed mirthfully, as if Mom was a kid who'd said something naïve and ridiculous. I cut the onion in half, peel off the skin, keep the root intact. Nine or ten slits vertically, making sure the knife's tip doesn't go all the way to the other end. Then I turn the onion swiftly and start making horizontal cuts, using my off hand to move the onion toward the blade and curling my fingers away to avoid mishaps, using my knuckles to keep the knife straight.

The smell of the onion threatens to tear me up, but in a matter of seconds the first half is in a neat pile at the edge of the cutting board. I repeat the steps well before my eyes start to sting. Every little piece of onion is even like it's supposed to be. I run my finger along the blade to free a few pieces, but aside from that nothing is off the cutting board, not an ounce of onion was wasted.

I grab a clean dishrag, wipe my knife clean and set it down. I turn back to look at Chef, defiant, proud.

But she's no longer standing beside me. Confused, I call out, "Chef?"

When there's no answer, I wait for a full three minutes. Maybe this is part of the test. She still doesn't show, so I wander around and find her in the walk-in with Sue. "Chef?" I say, knocking on the steel door frame. "I'm done with that onion."

She glances at me over her clipboard, like she's forgotten I was there at all. "Your knife still has its fucking price sticker on it," she says. "Don't waste my time if you're not gonna show up prepared. Go clean your knife, test it out. We'll try again tomorrow."

Shame creeps down my spine, and I practically scurry away from Chef toward my dish station. I peel the sticker away, roll it into a ball, throw it in the trash, even though there's no satisfying way to chuck a tiny sticker when you're pissed. I step over to the sink, wash the gyuto with searing water, set it to dry on a towel. My thoughts land on Emma and I instantly feel like my insides have been hollowed out.

It's still three hours until the actual shifts start. At first I try to wait quietly, but the inactivity makes it feel like the world is pressing down on me. I can't believe I forgot to take the fucking price sticker off. I can't believe Chef will fire me if I just stay close to Emma. I can't believe the quickness with which things go to shit.

I go outside and take a seat on the floor with my back against the wall. I look through my messages with Emma. In those messages, I sound like myself. Like the version of me from before Felix died. I sound like a normal person who does not see ghosts, does not flee his hometown in the pursuit of a meal. I have to close my eyes and take a few breaths to keep a sudden nausea at bay.

A few minutes later a pickup truck pulls up. Chef Elise comes out to greet the driver, holding a clipboard. I rise to my feet and offer to help. Chef barely acknowledges me until it's time to haul in an entire pig for tomorrow's special roast. Through my outrage, I manage to feel curiosity about how she'll prepare it, an eagerness to see her mind at work. Food, my ultimate sedative.

Luckily, Chef has me hold the pig's legs as she picks out all the ingredients that will go into the marinade. Apple cider vinegar, orange juice, lemons, onions, garlic, chili peppers, whole sprigs of thyme. Then, because of course he would, Felix turns the pig's head to look at me. "Hey, man," he says.

I roll my eyes, think, *Unless you've got some brilliant pig-brining recipes, not now, man.* If Chef is going to be picky about stickers, she certainly won't take my talking to spirits in stride. I want his help, but it's not the most convenient timing.

"You really think I would be here if you didn't need me now?" Felix says as he gets lowered into the bin he'll be brining in. He probably has a point. "So, what's this about? What's on your mind?"

I don't want to say, but of course Felix is in my thoughts, so he knows right away. "You don't want to do this without her."

"Here, pour this," Chef says, handing me a large bottle of orange juice. "Don't splash. Make sure you don't miss any spots." She and Sue step out, leaving me alone with the pig.

I twist open the lid, checking to make sure no one's around. I lean close as I pour the juice and whisper, "I don't have anyone else here who gives a shit about me. Nothing else makes me happy." I empty the bottle out slowly, letting the sound of the liquid sloshing into the bin drown out my voice. "Look, I know I didn't come here for the girl. But she's here, you know? I can't just ignore that."

Felix looks up at me, drops of juice clinging to his little pig eyelashes. "She's leaving in the fall anyway, man. She doesn't want to stay on this island, and you do. She's into drunken makeouts, and you're thinking about way more than that. It's doomed. Why risk a chance like this over her?"

"Because it's not meaningless," I say. I don't know why he's so adamant about this, why he doesn't get it. "I need someone other than you in my life."

Felix blinks once, sighs and then turns his neck forward again, becomes dead again. I guess I won the argument?

When Chef returns and excuses me, I take the back door as if I'm leaving until shift starts, but I come back around and knock on the front door. Emma of course has no idea about my inner turmoil since last night. To her, nothing has changed. She greets me with a hug that makes me feel like going against Chef on the spot.

"Hey," she says, her breath on my neck.

I end the hug quickly. "Hey." I take a small step back, just in case Chef is watching.

She smiles, rests her elbows on the stand. "You should have come over last night. We would have made out a bunch."

"I wish I would have," I say. Behind me a middle-aged couple comes in, which is probably a good cue to leave. I smile at her, tell her I have to get to the sink. Halfway out the door, I look back at Emma, wondering if I should bring up what her mom said. But just thinking about it makes me mad, and I'd much rather focus on having her here in front of me.

The rest of the day goes by pretty quickly. For staff meal, I make tikka masala chicken tacos, topped off with a chai yogurt sauce. The masala sauce is way too watery, and the chai yogurt curdles, which I guess isn't that bad because my grip slips and I end up spilling half the saucepan on the floor. Elias throws a dishrag toward me. "What's with you, man?"

I shrug, kneel to sop up the mess. Felix's face forms in the spill, and it's the stupidest thing in the world that I can't bring myself to wipe it away. I'm frozen there for a minute, holding the rag an inch above the floor while everyone's legs maneuver around me. It's like I'm suddenly afraid that wishing him away will finally work, now that I don't really want it to anymore.

I finally muster the energy, clean up and then remake the sauce, serve a dish I am in no way proud of. People line up to eat and there is no joy on their faces. Drained, I take a break outside, wait for the island's beauty to replenish me.

The beauty of Needle Eye feels muted, especially if I think about Chef keeping me away from Emma. A couple of minutes after I step outside, Elias comes out and asks me if I need a place to stay.

"What do you mean?" I ask.

"Well, with Boris gone, we've got a spare room at our place," Elias says. "Easier you than some stranger. It's yours if you want it."

It's like every time I think my stay here is done, something happens that insists I belong here. So, maybe Chef's warning makes things a little murkier than they were yesterday. Maybe I'm not suddenly an incredible chef. But I don't want this to be a temporary escape, some experiment in joy before returning to the life Dad wanted for me. I want to be here.

My motel room is paid for through the week, but Elias tells me I'm free to move in whenever I want and just pay rent once I get my first check.

I spend the rest of my break looking through my emails on my phone, searching for the acceptance letter I got from the University of Chicago. I find it and click through the links until I get to the admissions page and figure out how to contact the school. If Dad hasn't completely lost his shit yet, this'll probably do the trick.

I send an email asking what I need to do to withdraw from school.

By the end of my shift, I have been up for nearly eighteen hours. My body is calling out for sleep, and my thoughts are muddled. The six hours in between now and my next training session won't be nearly enough to recuperate, especially when I'm itching to see Emma and make it up to her for bailing yesterday. We meet outside a coffee shop to avoid discovery, and when I kiss her cheek, the comfort of her skin makes me want to fall asleep in the warm nook of her neck. How could I ever deny myself this? I lay my head on her shoulder and pretend to snore.

"Long day?" Emma asks with a laugh.

"Tell me the truth. Restaurant people have discovered a way to live more than twenty-four hours in a day, right?"

"Duh, it's drugs," Emma says. "If I learned anything from my dad, it's that."

I laugh but don't pull my head away. "Shut up, that's not true."

"Oh, sweet, naïve Carlos. Chefs are fucked-up people. My dad had cocaine parties at home when I was eight or nine."

My first reaction is horror, an anger that anyone would put Emma in that position. Or any kid, for that matter. "Jesus. What was it like growing up with that?"

"Cozy," Emma says and gives a single laugh, the sway of which goes from her body to mine. "It wasn't all that bad, really. Just some crazy moments. They both became much better parents after they split up. Even if they still won't teach me their secrets to a perfect grilled cheese."

I force a laugh, and a thought flashes through my head that Dad has his parenting flaws too, but I'm not sure whether he'd count as a bad parent. I don't want to think about Dad, though. I want to just stay by Emma's side, talk to her.

"Wanna go to the lake?" she asks.

I groan. "I should sleep."

"No, you shouldn't," she says, and I agree, because how am I supposed to do anything else? I'm whole when I'm with her.

Amazing that the hike through the woods can get any better. But the world has its surprises, and with Emma's hand in mine the night becomes Technicolor. Fireflies light the way to the meadow, where we pick up fistfuls of berries as a midnight snack.

I want to tell her about Chef's stipulation, but I don't want to accept that it's really happened. That I might lose her or the kitchen. The words are stuck in the pit of my stomach, and nothing gets them out, so I decide to smother them, to keep them in there until they're no longer true.

We get to the lake, slip our toes into the water, shoot electricity out across the surface. We lie on our backs, face each other. In an instant we're pressed together, kissing like we are drunk, kissing like it'll make us glow. The way she kisses, it's as if this is the only way I can breathe, through her. She kisses a spot just below my ear that makes goose bumps shoot down my arms, presses herself close to me. She kisses like she's proving to the world that we're alive.

The next morning, one and a half onions into the training session, I nick my finger. Chef Elise throws a dish towel at my face. "Stop bleeding all over my fucking kitchen," she mutters as she walks away. Instead of wrapping the towel tightly around the bleeding tip, I let a few drops escape onto the counter, stain the perfect, shimmering steel.

I stand at my sink, listen to the kitchen come alive, try not to slam dishes into shards. I run the water so hot that steam surrounds me like the island's thick morning fog. In this cloud, I can hide.

Later that night, Elias comes with me to the motel to help me carry my suitcase and the assorted kitchen utensils I've bought during my three weeks on Needle Eye. The house is on the other side of the island, a little closer to where Emma lives. I'm already picturing the best route to get to the lake, trying to remember the shortcuts she's shown me. It takes me a while to recognize it as Matt's house.

"Home sweet home," Elias says, opening the door.

Inside, Matt is on the couch, playing video games with a kid I remember meeting at the barbecue, another one of Emma's friends.

"Hey, man," Elias says. "What are you guys up to?"

"Day off." He does some button mashing on the controller and then notices me and kind of nods but doesn't say hi. "What's the Fake-xican doing here?"

"Moving in," Elias says. We pass in front of the TV, eliciting some yelling complaints. Elias shows me the kitchen, which, unlike the rest of the house, is perfectly neat. The downstairs bathroom is a mess, tissues overflowing from the trash bin. A dirty sock lies on the windowsill, and it looks like it hasn't been moved in weeks. "Sorry," Elias mutters. "It's the price I pay for living with fuckin' eighteen-year-olds, no offense. I'm still up to my ass in debt, so I can't afford to live alone, and other roommates are never quite as understanding about having people over for drinks at two a.m. once a shift lets out."

We go upstairs, where my room is. There's a mattress on the floor, pushed up to the corner. A dresser with its drawers still open. A few clothes hangers are piled on the floor, evidence of a speedy departure, as if Boris was afraid that Chef would show up any second to chase him away. It's nothing like my room in Mexico, with its TV and video game systems, its view of the hills and high-rises of my neighborhood. No Rosalba will come by to tidy up every morning.

I drop my bag down on the floor, giving Felix a clandestine smile when he shows up in the corner. Back downstairs, Elias slips into the kitchen to grab himself a beer, which is almost the only thing available in the fridge, apart from some bagels, deli meat and a few bottles of hot sauce.

We settle down on the couch next to Matt and the other kid, Rob, watch them shoot each other up for a bit. "I see you've been going in early," Matt says after a while. "Chef got you shining her shoes or something?" He chuckles at himself.

"Just some training," I say, though his reaction makes me regret saying anything.

Matt pauses his game, eyes wide. "Training? With Chef? What the hell?" He looks at Elias and then back at me. "You just fucking got here."

"It's none of your business," Elias says, taking a drink from his beer. "It's her restaurant."

Matt doesn't turn his attention back to the screen, though. He leans forward, eyes glued on me. "What makes you so special, huh?"

"I wouldn't be jealous," I say. "So far she's just found different ways to call me a moron."

Matt ignores me, points a finger at Elias. "What the hell is Chef thinking, man? This kid is nobody."

Elias raises his hands up, palms out. "You wanna ask her, be my guest. Let me know in advance so I can be there to watch her tear your head off."

Matt's nostrils flare. "I worked my ass off to get here. We all did. I don't like little rich shits who get things handed to them."

I feel myself wanting to diffuse the situation, calm things down. I think about telling him about Felix, that I'm out of my mind, just so he doesn't think my life is perfect. *I spend half my time in the kitchen trying to remember not to talk to the wall*, I want to say.

But none of it comes out. Instead I just stare back at Matt mutely, like an asshole.

"Jeez, man, relax," Elias says. "Just 'cause he's getting a little extra attention doesn't mean anyone's gonna chase you out of the kitchen. This isn't fuckin' *Chopped*."

This elicits a chuckle from Rob, who tells Matt that he's going to start the game again. Matt keeps staring at me for a second and then turns his attention back to the TV. "Whatever," he mumbles, before he resumes button mashing. "You earn your place in a kitchen is all I'm saying."

Elias and I sit down and watch them play for a while. I get quiet as the three of them start shooting the shit casually. I'm guessing I'm the only one who sees Felix on the screen, trying to dodge bullets. He's not that good at it.

Felix winks at me from the screen when he respawns. If I were back home, with Danny and Poncho, I'd probably laugh at this. But here I feel the need to suppress the laugh, not give Matt any reason to snap at me again. I sit there on the couch quietly, trying not to be weird, wishing everything came as easily as it does with Emma. I watch Felix die again and again. The joke gets old pretty quickly.

CHAPTER 18
FRENCH ONION SOUP

4 onions, sliced (not chopped)
½ cup butter
2 garlic cloves
½ bottle red wine
2 quarts beef broth
2 bay leaves
2 thyme sprigs
1 loaf baguette
¼ pound gruyere cheese

METHOD:

On my fourth day of training with Chef, I'm still chopping onions. She sticks around a little longer this time, observing. Matt shows up early and circles like a vulture. When I get through all four onions that she brought out, I wipe the tears from my eyes, hoping we'll move on to something else. "Too slow," Chef says, and she brings out a whole bag of them.

I sigh and get ready to chop, willing myself not to just let muscle memory do its thing but to focus on speed, on technique. Curl my fingers away from the knife, rest my knuckles against the blade, chop. About three onions in Chef yanks the cutting board away from me, almost making me cut off a finger. Onions scatter to the ground. "You have no idea what you're doing," she says, and she leaves me to clean up the mess.

Seeking solace from the shame, I find Emma's name in my phone. I think maybe I should just leave the kitchen and focus on the joy she provides. Felix whispers in my ear that she's leaving the island, that I'm putting the kitchen at risk. I cast the thought away.

Underwater fireworks tonight? I write. I'll buy some snorkel gear.

It feels like stolen joy, sending this message. Stolen from beneath Chef's nose, Matt's threats, Dad's dismissal, Felix's death. In the moments between my lessons with Chef and my shift beginning, a nameless weight threatens to beat me down. It's the one I've been trying to keep at bay for months. But before I had no way to deal with it other than the kitchen, and now Emma's response keeps it at bay: See you tonight.

Day five, I chop. Blade sharpened, fingers curled away, wrist flicking as quickly as possible. *Thwack, thwack, thwack,* the knife slices through onions as if asking for a harder task. Felix stands behind me, trying to encourage me. "Too sloppy," Chef says. "These have to be even, every time. Look at this," she says, grabbing a pinch of onion and holding it under my nose. "Does that look even to you?"

I can barely see the onion, it's so far up my nose. All I get is that sting of its smell, and I pretend that's the only reason my eyes water. "No, Chef," I say.

My phone buzzes a few minutes later and I dry my hands to pick it up. Do you think both of us could fit under my hostess stand?

Probably, I text back, knowing I'm smiling just as wide, and if Chef bothered to stick around she'd know right away what it means. I'm really good at folding myself. Why do you ask?

Not making out with you gets hard at work.

I get a sinking feeling in my stomach. A nagging voice within me tells me to just let Emma know what's going on, be honest, ask her if we can sneak around instead of hiding this from her. Except I don't think I can handle this one good thing turning hard, don't want to think about anything but the joy in front of me.

Day six. *Thwack, thwack, thwack.* Last night Emma came over and we wore snorkel gear as I chopped my way through onion after onion, protecting each other from teary eyes, though I'm not so sure my eyes are affected anymore. There are now at least a dozen gallon bags full of chopped onion piled into the freezer at home. Matt asked what the hell we were doing, but when Emma's around he's a little more civil. All the more reason to spend my days with her.

"Not fast enough," Chef says. "You're wasting my time and my fucking onions. Bring your own tomorrow."

I swear there's a hint of a smile on her face as she says this. I'm becoming increasingly convinced that she's just a sadist. That these morning sessions are nothing but a way for her to torture me. "Don't be dramatic," Felix says. "She's just demanding." I bite my tongue.

Day seven. I wait in front of the cutting board until Chef's at my side. The longer she keeps me waiting, the more I notice that my shadow's still gone, that my fingers are see-through. Nameless weights and ghosts build up, Felix as more than a memory.

I'm determined not to let anything she says get me down today, though. I think of Emma, think of the joys of the island. Chef finally shows up and gives me a little nod, and I pick up the knife exactly the way I know I should. I make sure the board is on a wet towel to keep it from moving, make sure the blade is sharp, make sure everything is in its right place. Then I let my fingers take over.

The onion is chopped into perfectly even pieces in a flash. It's getting to be like I'm breathing this. I wipe my knife, put it down, step away to allow Chef to inspect the pile. There is no way she'll have a complaint now. This was perfect.

"Jesus Christ, Carlos, a six-year-old would have learned how to do this by now."

I'm ready to explode, tell her about Emma and be done with her bullshit, when one of the remaining onions takes the shape of Felix's face. "She's a lot like Dad, huh? He was always a stickler." I have to take a few deep breaths, clutching the counter, before I'll allow myself to say anything to Chef.

By the time I look away from the onion, she's gone. I grip my knife, ready to slam something into bits. What's left of the onions by my cutting board gets cut so quickly it's almost like the onions fall apart on their own, not wanting to be subjected to my rage.

I go outside for a breather before shift begins. I run into Emma, and the mere sight of her makes me feel a little lighter. Without thinking much, I reach for her hand.

She smiles at me and then maybe notices the look on my face. "Everything okay?" she asks.

I want to just pull her close and nuzzle my face into her neck. I want to take us both beneath her hostess stand, pressed as close as possible, stifling our laughter so that the rest of the restaurant—the rest of the world—won't hear us.

Then I remember where we are and I have to let Emma's fingers go so that our hands drop away. I mouth, *Sorry, later* at her and then go around the corner to take a seat at one of the patio tables.

The view of the island stretches out in front. Azure sky, perfectly white clouds, hills that could be colored by crayons. The water's so reflective it's almost metallic, and it turns the whole world into a mirror image. It's funny how I've already grown to take it for granted. I'm still blown away by it, of course, but I would have imagined the amazement to stick around every moment of the day. Now it's almost like any other thought, there for a moment before something else takes its place. Chef's going to find out I'm seeing Emma. Or she'll realize I'm not actually a cook at all. I can't be taught. I'm just a runaway, a rich kid playing out a fantasy because he couldn't handle having a dead brother.

I look at my phone to try to take my mind off things. There's an email from Danny, asking me how things are going, saying he heard a rumor that I'm in Alaska, hunting grizzly bears. Doesn't really sound like you, but you've been pretty AWOL on social media so who the fuck knows.

There are a few messages from Mom too. Three "how are you"s in a row, which I keep forgetting to answer. It doesn't really help me feel any better right now. I send an enthusiastic response, hoping it'll help Mom feel better and maybe hurt Dad a little, show him I'm doing great.

I tuck my phone away. It's a hot day out, no fog at all, sweat already forming on my forehead. The kitchen's going to be sweltering. People are going to be on edge and they'll notice the moment I screw something up, which I probably will at staff meal.

"What the hell am I doing here?" I say, hunched over, eyes on the floor, assuming Felix will make himself known.

"I was gonna ask," someone says, but it's not Felix. I look up. Elias has a coffee mug in his hand, and he's pulling out the chair next to me. "What's up, man?"

Oh, you know. It's been six months since my brother died and I still see him everywhere. I've been on this island for less than a month, I'm falling in love with a girl who's on her way out the door and I'm apprenticed to the Soup Nazi of onion cutting.

I shrug, squint at the strong morning sun. I can't say anything.

Elias actually gives a chuckle, as if he can tell all of this is going through my head. "Welcome to the restaurant world, man. Just 'cause it's fun doesn't mean it won't stress you the fuck out." He takes a sip from his coffee, puts his feet up on the chair in front of him. I'm still not sure what to say. That weight is pressing down on my chest, and it feels like I'm moments away from another panic attack.

"Let me guess," Elias says. "Chef is getting to your head a little bit?"

I find it in me to nod.

He chuckles again. "Yeah, she'll do that." He reaches over and gives me a friendly smack on the arm. "Don't worry about her, man. She's tough, but she wouldn't be taking time out of her day just to fuck with you."

"Really? 'Cause that's exactly what it feels like," I say. I look back over my shoulder, into the dining room. The only thing I can see is my own reflection in the windows. Emma might be in there, smiling at me, or Chef and Matt might be scowling, hoping for me to have a breakdown. There's a bad feeling in my stomach, and I try to settle it by looking out at the beauty of my new home. "I'm not getting anywhere with these stupid onions. She's either an asshole or I'm so bad at this that she's afraid to let me touch anything else. Maybe I'm not ready."

Elias full-on laughs now. "Relax, baby. How do you think I got to where I am?" He drinks again and then puts the mug down on the table and crosses his arms behind his head. I think he's seeing this as a pleasant, quiet moment before the madness of service starts. I wish I could be in the same mind-set. "Listen, man, you're going to be okay. I've tasted your food. You've got some skills. But these things take time. They take struggles, you know?

"It wasn't that long ago that I was in Seattle, watching the business I started fail, all my money in it fuckin' burning away with each supply order we put in or, worse, each late night partying." He sighs and reaches for his coffee again.

"Right now you're at the bottom, and people are gonna give you shit. Trust me, I've been there. Everyone in this kitchen who's more experienced than you has been there too. You think Chef made it easy on me?" Behind us, the patio door slides open and Michelle, the other sous-chef, asks him if he has a minute.

He stands up. "You're doing fine, man. No one climbs without struggling."

As soon as he disappears inside, a cloud over the horizon turns itself into Felix. It points in the direction of the restaurant. "That dude's trying to steal my role. Tell him I've got the market cornered on inspirational pep talks."

What Elias said didn't magically solve my issues, but I find it in me to laugh, which is an improvement from a second ago. "You wouldn't have said it like that."

"Damn straight, I would have said it better." He flips himself upside down, does a handstand-walk across the horizon. Then he does a little somersault and stands upright again. "But he's right, you know. It's not all just going to magically happen all at once. Or has no one ever told you that?" He puts his hands on his hips for a second, chewing on his lip. "Shit, actually, no one really does tell you that, now that I think about it."

Felix shrugs the thought away. "You're fine. Trust me. You're young. You're alive. Give it time."

"I'm fine? I'm talking to a fucking cloud," I say. That nameless weight is creeping back in, and I want to run from it. "I miss you, man. I miss Mom and Dad. Sure, I've got Emma, but Chef could find out about that at any moment, and..." I trail off when I hear someone coming out onto the patio. It's Matt, smacking a cigarette pack with the palm of his hand. He smirks at me when we make eye contact, and he lights his cigarette, still staring at me. I turn back to the view.

"You think I never had that?" Felix says, ignoring the fact that Matt almost certainly just saw me talking to myself. He climbs out of the sky, turns into a flesh-and-bone version of himself and takes a seat next to me. I keep my eyes on the horizon. I don't want to deal with being insane right now; I've got other shit on my mind. "Happiness is not easy," Felix says, and I think I know what's coming next. The line sounds rehearsed, part of a larger speech that Felix probably tinkered with and repeated throughout his travels, pitching it at younger backpackers he'd run into at hostels, in bars. It still comes out sounding sincere. "But it's possible."

Felix scoots his chair into my line of sight, not letting me pout. "You're going to be okay," he says, smiling before he disappears.

CHAPTER 19

PIBIL EGGS BENEDICT

1 English muffin

2 slow-poached eggs

4 ounces pulled pork, cochinita pibil-style

A pinch of chopped cilantro

FOR THE HABANERO HOLLANDAISE:

2 habanero chilies, deveined and seeded

3 egg yolks

1 tablespoon lemon juice

¼ teaspoon Dijon mustard

½ cup butter

METHOD:

When I make my way back into the kitchen, the staff is gathering around Chef. She's standing in the pass, waiting for everyone to show up. Sue's at her side, ready to take notes. I slip in between Elias and Memo, playing it cool, like I didn't just have a breakdown outside.

Once everyone's around, mostly quiet thanks to the morning calm, Chef adopts a slightly militaristic stance. Anytime she speaks I'm sure she's about to fire me, belittle me, make a spectacle of my inadequacies.

"Alright, guys, today's gonna be a shit show. We've got more covers than we've had all summer." She picks up a clipboard. "We've got a ten-top and a twelve-top coming in right as we open, so we're gonna get our asses kicked from the get-go."

There's a few groans at this but a few high fives and whoops too. Elias leans toward Memo and whispers, "Listo?"

"Siempre, papi," Memo says with a grin.

She looks down at her notes, and there's a building excitement in the air. Someone in the back is sharpening a knife, the metallic clang of it reverberating through the murmurs in the crowd like a war drum. "You're gonna need some energy if you're pulling a double today, which is every single one of you, right?"

A few laughs and some more "Yes, Chef"s.

"So, Memo, why don't you make a shitload of scrambled eggs for everyone? We should have some of those sausages from last week's special left over so fry up whatever's left of them. Roberto, Carlos, these guys are gonna be running through pans, and you know how many fucking glasses the brunch crowd uses up, so we need you guys on top of your game. Help them keep their stations clear when you can, and we'll keep your beer glasses full when this is all done."

Someone claps a hand to my shoulder, and I can't help but get caught up in the rumble of excitement building up in the kitchen. My mind stops drifting to nameless worries, focuses on the present. Chef runs through the specials and then she dismisses us by saying, "Have fun out there," and everyone flurries into motion. Burners flicker on, the hood starts to roar, knives come down on cutting boards, thumping like the beat of a war drum. What a world.

Just like that, all else fades, disappears to irrelevance. I collect some pans from the prep kitchen, depositing them at my sink and then running back out for more. I take out a few bags of trash, and I hear the whirr of the first order ticket coming out from the printers at each station. Chef's voice calls out over all the chatter in the kitchen, "Ordering! Three veggie omelets, three pulled pork bennys, four special bennys..."

All the cooks respond with a well-coordinated, "Yes, Chef!" They make little comments to each other, coordinate their respective components so that everything hits the plate at the same time.

I heave the trash into the Dumpster outside and get back into the kitchen before the side door even shuts. I might not be holding a knife, I might be the lowest guy in the pecking order, I might always be out of my mind. But I'm a part of this kitchen now. I belong here. I don't even pause to watch the first orders being cooked. I've got a job to do.

Every dirtied dish that comes my way I take pride in, as if it's an onion that Chef has asked me to chop. This is the thing I've done more than any since I got to the island, probably, more than sleeping, more than cooking, and I'm good at it now. These struggles will lead elsewhere.

I run through a tray of coffee mugs and champagne flutes smudged with lipstick and the pulpy remainders of the fresh oranges used in the mimosas. Roberto and I communicate two or three words at a time, always in Spanish. "Sartenes primero?"

"Sí."

"Ve a ver," Roberto says, our shorthand way to see if anyone needs help.

I glance through the stations, trying to spot anything that might need tending to. A plate that's been set aside and might get in a cook's way, a mug of coffee someone was sipping on and doesn't have time to bring to the dish station. If two cooks are talking, I do not interrupt, knowing they might be trying to time their respective duties. If I do have to step into a station to remove a dish towel or clear out their trash for them, I announce myself in Kitchenese. "Behind," I say. "Coming through, hot!" if I'm rounding a corner and carrying pans. Forget English, forget Spanish—this is the language I was born to speak.

Chefs call all the activity that takes place during service "the dance." And now that I'm closer to it than I ever have been before, I know exactly why. There's a liveliness to the kitchen, constant movement that feels both primal and yet measured, like a frantic waltz. If I have enough time to study any one person, that's exactly what it looks like. Vee, for example: how she will test the doneness of a piece of meat on the grill by pressing into it, flip the steaks that need it, take a half step to the right to check the broiler, pivot backward to double-check her ticket, half spin back to the grill. You could set her movements to music.

Chef is standing at the pass, expediting, adding sprigs of rosemary and drizzles of chipotle oil. She calls out a new order, and the entire line sets into choreographed motion. I think of being in class, not that long ago, how our teachers were rarely treated with this much deference.

Approaching Matt's station to grab a hotel pan that's just kind of sitting there, I call out, "Behind," making sure Matt can hear me. I see him give a little nod and then turn back to the portion of veggies he's sautéing.

I use a damp towel in case it's still hot, but just as I lift it up, Matt takes a step back, his elbow coming down on my forearm. The pan slams against the counter with a clatter and then goes flying down at the ground. Browned bits of potatoes and rosemary splatter against the stainless-steel cupboards at our legs, which we both jump away from to avoid getting burned.

"Watch it, asshole!" Matt yells.

Taken aback, I'm frozen for a second. Heads turn in our direction. Chef and Elias are both at the pass, staring up at us.

"Chef, you watching this shit? I thought you told this guy to stay in the back washing dishes."

"Goddamnit, Carlos," Chef yells. "Didn't you hear that whole fucking speech I gave today? You pick the busiest day of the year to start running into people?" I open my mouth to complain, to point out that look in Matt's eyes. "Why the hell should I let you run around if this is how you handle it? Breaking pans and shit. You gonna pay for a new one?" Vee slides a plated half rack of ribs through the window, calls out the table number and returns to her station. Chef grabs it and continues to berate me while dusting the plate with curry powder. "Are you gonna get your shit together or are you gonna make me regret letting you set a single fucking toe in my kitchen?"

"Yes, Chef," I mumble, kneeling down to pick up the pan, face reddening in shame and anger. I look up at Matt, who's red-faced and muttering as he turns his attention back to his sauté pan. I wish I could toss this pan at him, wish he knew how much he might be undoing.

"It wasn't Carlos's fault, Chef," Elias says. "I heard him call out 'behind.' This little shit just did that on purpose."

There isn't really a DJ-scratch moment, because the kitchen would fall apart if things ground to a halt. But there's a definite sense that people are turning their attention back on the altercation. No one's talking; there's only the roar of the hood, food sizzling, the dull hum of the noise from the dining room.

I stand up, the pan warm in my hands.

"You don't know shit," Matt starts to say, but Chef shuts him up with a glare.

"Is that true?" she asks, looking at me.

I feel everyone's eyes on me, especially Matt's. I shift uncomfortably. "Maybe he didn't hear me," I say, finally.

"Because you didn't say a word, you fucking amateur!" Matt yells.

Chef gives Elias a glance. "I heard it, Chef," he says. "And I'm back here." He shrugs and then passes a couple of plates over to the window to the server station, dinging the bell and calling out, "Table six."

With that, everyone resumes their work, but I can tell their ears are still cocked to hear what Chef will say.

Matt starts to complain, but Chef shuts him up again by raising her hand. Even if it *was* a misunderstanding, he was such an unequivocal asshole that I'm happy to see Chef exert her power. She looks at me, the rage now gone from her eyes. "Get back to the sink," she says simply, and that's all the apology I get. Then she turns back to Matt. "You're telling me he's the amateur? You should know better, prick." She doesn't bother waiting for a response, just turns her attention to the food again, yelling, "No more bullshit, everyone. Get back to work."

When the night is done, I push the door open and am greeted by a wave of fresh, warm air and a sky twinkling with stars.

"Okay, no more onions," a voice says behind me. I spin around and see Chef leaning against the wall, having a cigarette. She's got a leather jacket on, her hair up in a tight bun. She smokes slowly, and I get the feeling that she doesn't really like people knowing she smokes. Her face is half-hidden in the shadows, and it makes her look like a villain in a noir film, like I'd be right to be scared of her. "Tomorrow, it's omelets," she says. "Bring the eggs." She exhales and turns around to lock the door and then leaves without another word.

I swear I see the stars rearranging into Felix's smug grin for a second and then my phone buzzes in my hand, distracting me. Lake? Me, Brandy and a few others are on the way now.

Hell yes, I respond.

I can't picture a better way to celebrate the mini-promotion, and though it's a beautiful night for a slow stroll, my strides are quick and purposeful. I check my phone and see an email from Mom, something forwarded from the University of Chicago, a bunch of question marks added into the subject line. It makes me laugh nervously, and I decide I can put that off until later.

Breaking through the clearing that leads to the stretch of beach Emma likes, I see a few plastic lounge chairs lined up. They're set up in that bay where the bioluminescent plankton is brightest, and I can see their toes lighting up in the water. Before approaching, I take a moment to appreciate all of it. I can pick out Emma's laugh in the voices, which are carrying over on a warm breeze, the same one that's causing little ripples in the water and making it look like the stars reflected on the surface are dancing. Felix is so right. I'm young. I'm alive. I'm going to be okay. Look at this world. How could I not be okay?

I get closer to the group, the sound of my footsteps alerting them to my presence. They all say hi, Brandy enthusiastically, the two guys there, Paul and Reggie, less so, since we've never really talked. I wish this were Mexico, just for the excuse to lean into Emma and kiss her cheek hello, feel her skin on my lips. Instead I lay a hand on her shoulder, seat myself on the rocky shore by her feet.

We end up playing a game called Turn of Phrase, which is basically a mix of Cards Against Humanity, Pictionary and charades. I've always been kind of bad at charades; I can never translate the movie or whatever into actable motions quickly enough and always end up standing there awkwardly gesturing lamely with my hands and looking frustrated.

Tonight, though, the normalcy of the evening makes me dive into the game completely. When it's my first turn to act, I draw the card and stand in front of everyone, and I don't feel like they can see right through me. I have to act out the phrase *not a single fuck was given*, which would normally cause me to just stand there giggling and shrugging until time was up. But instead I wag a finger and thrust my hips and pass out imaginary items to everyone. It takes Emma only about twenty seconds to get it, and we hug in celebration. I'm so into the game I even forget about my exhaustion.

When I'm not acting, I find myself reaching out to Emma. In small ways, mostly, light touches that individually would probably be innocent and friendly but cumulatively speak to something more. At least I mean them to. I'm not sure how Emma sees it.

The game ends and the others jump into the lake. We lag behind, my hand reaching for hers. Crazy how I can tangibly reach for joy this way. Just be near her and I'm better. Emma bites her lip, looks at me seriously. "What was that about today? In the restaurant."

I should say something true. I should tell her about her mom's caveat. I should tell her that I had to go have a talk with my dead brother because sometimes I feel like I'm made of hay and that the wind could carry me away back to Mexico or else just scatter me into oblivion. "I had a phone call coming in," I say. She studies my face for a moment, and I offer such a fake smile that I'm shocked she doesn't see through my bullshit right away. Eventually she turns away, apparently believing me.

I don't want to be the guy who lies to the people he loves. But I don't want to make what we have about anything other than joy, don't want it to unravel because of such a small thing. Emma splashes into the lake; an aura of electricity surrounds her. Her friends laugh nearby, and she swims over toward them, the glowing water harder to see in the distance. So I follow.

The night's so warm, the water just as nice. I think: *What a world.* All of this feels unearned, sudden. It feels like it can be undone. I know everything can be, all too well. I splash over to Emma, catch my reflection in the water, whole despite the ripples. We float on our backs, looking up at so many stars it feels like the Milky Way is bearing witness to us.

CHAPTER 20

CHICKEN SKEWERS AL PASTOR

6 pounds chicken breasts
3 red bell peppers
3 green bell peppers
3 red onions

FOR THE ADOBO:

2 cups orange juice
1 cup white vinegar
1 cup guajillo peppers, rehydrated
1 head of garlic
6 chipotle peppers, rehydrated
2 tablespoons oregano
2 tablespoons cumin

METHOD:

On my tenth day of training with Chef, I'm making another omelet. I rushed the first one and it fell apart before I could plate it, making Chef snort derisively and put me back on onions for the day. The second one looked good to me, but Chef stopped at the first bite, reached for the nearby ramekin of salt and dumped it over my head. I'd been so focused on the cooking time that I forgot to season.

This one, though, looks perfect. Not a tinge of brown, perfectly shaped and fluffy. I garnish it with a sprig of parsley on top. Even if she finds some fault in it, I hope she eats the whole thing, I'm so sick of eating eggs. Aside from the staff meals, it's all I've eaten the last three days. I cook them back at the house constantly, for anyone that wants one. I beg them to.

Matt says the omelets are awful, but he eats them anyway. He's toned down his insults in the kitchen when Chef's around, but he still blames me for the other day. At work he simply doesn't talk to me, including when he drops off hot pans, so I reach for them and burn myself. At home it's a constant barrage of insults, most of them involving the word "crazy," which tells me he for sure heard me talking to the clouds that one day. Worst of all, when he saw Emma come over the first time he smirked and said, "I see what's going on now. Chef playing favorites with the son-in-law. Smart move, rich boy." It felt like I'd roped a noose around my neck and given Matt the other end.

Now Chef is examining the omelet, lifting it up with her fork to inspect the bottom. She lets it drop with a sneer, and pushes the plate back toward me. Her eyebrow's raised. "You expect me to eat that? That's not how you make an omelet." Then she grabs the parsley sprig and pops it into her mouth. "Don't waste a garnish on shitty food."

When she's gone, I pull out a squirt bottle of hot sauce I made at home, write out "fuck off" on top of the omelet. I've been buying ingredients out of pocket, bringing them for the staff meals in the hopes that it'll impress someone. I had to stop buying Emma coffee in the mornings, partly because it looks too suspicious, partly because I'm running out of money. My first paycheck disappeared into rent and onions. I take a few bites of the omelet before pouring on the sauce, trying to figure out what's wrong with it, why Chef pushed it away. The eggs are still runny, or I over-seasoned or, in the few seconds it took me to transfer the omelet to a plate, it lost all its warmth and I just served Chef a cold omelet.

I have no idea what's wrong with it.

On my break, I take my phone outside. The messages from Mom have started to pile up, and my guilt has reached a breaking point. Today I realized when I think of my parents now, the first thing that comes to mind is no longer Dad's parting words. There's enough of a distance to it all finally, and I don't even care that Dad cut off the credit card. Mostly.

Instead I just want to share things with my parents, tell them about everything. About Emma, about Chef, about how I've actually been cooking in the kitchen. I want them to know what's going on here, want them to know I'm okay.

Taking a seat on a wooden crate outside, I scroll until I find Mom's number and then dial, actually looking forward to the phone call.

"Carlos?"

"Hi, Mom. Sorry it's taken me a while."

There's some background noise as she steps away from a conversation, maybe leaves whatever restaurant she's having lunch at to talk outside. "It's okay. I just missed your voice."

"Voices aren't a thing people miss, Mom."

"I miss you, you idiot, that's what I'm saying." She sighs, and then there's the sound of someone honking nearby. Just one honk at first, but then it's answered by a choir of other cars, as if people think whoever acted first really had a good idea going and needs some support. Strangely enough it makes me miss Mexico City.

"How are you?" she asks.

"I'm great," I say, somewhat struck by guilt by how quickly I say that, and how long Mom is quiet for. "How are you guys?"

Another pause. This is why I don't like phone calls. You shouldn't be able to tell through a pause in a phone call that the mood is about to shift, but you can, and there's nothing to do but to sit there and just wait for it to fucking happen. I sit back down on the crate and wait.

"It's your dad," she says after a while, and I'm preparing my retort for whatever Dad's complaint is when she adds, "he's not doing well."

I feel my stomach drop. I lean my head back against the wall, closing my eyes to the sun. "What's wrong?" Felix appears in front of me, the afternoon sun dropping behind him, flaring over his shoulder. He's more silhouette than person.

"He's been getting tired easily, stressed. He says it's work but I'm worried about him. His blood pressure has been high."

I breathe easy. "I guess he's gotta take it easy on the quesadillas then," I say with a forced chuckle. At first, I want to complain to Mom for making it sound so scary at the start. But I can kind of see what she's trying to do. With a son in the grave, it's probably hard not to want the other one near you, where you can keep him safe.

"What's this about dropping out of school, Carlos?" she asks, just as Lourdes opens up the back door, and motions for me to come back inside. "How long is this going to go on for?"

I hesitate. Does she really want to make me say the words out loud?

Then the side door opens up and Lourdes pokes her head out, looking around. "Roberto te necesita," she says.

I nod at her.

"Mom, I have to go." I get up, brush myself off. "You don't have to worry about me. I'm doing great here. You could even come visit in a while, maybe." A pause on the other end again, no sounds of traffic, though. I wish there were, because I think I can hear her stifling a cry, maybe moving the mouth piece away. And for some reason, even though I don't know for sure whether Mom is stifling a cry or just ordering the check or something, I feel like I'm suddenly having to suppress a cry too.

"Send my love to Dad," I say, and hang up before my voice can break.

CHAPTER 21
PLAIN OMELET

3 eggs
Who the fuck knows?

METHOD:

Alright, so, I don't know what an omelet is supposed to taste like. That's the only conclusion I can draw as Chef pushes away another plate. The omelet I just served her is so perfectly yellow that it's the first image you'd see if you looked up the word online. It's so fluffy that a cloud just passing by felt threatened and scurried away. An egg in the fridge just wrote a blog post about how it aspires to be an omelet just like this one when it passes into the afterlife.

Felix's face appears on the omelet, takes a big bite out of itself, shrugs to the best of an omelet's shrugging capability. "I don't know, man. I taste pretty good to me."

Since the other day, Felix hasn't been showing up as often. It makes me feel a little saner when he's not around, especially when Emma's around. He gives me space with her, which I'm happy about, even if, more than once, I expect him to chime in with a comment and his absence feels like the whole world has been muted. I expect him to try to guide me toward doing the right thing with Emma, convince me to be up-front with her. But he offers no advice there.

Matt, on the other hand, seems supernaturally ubiquitous, appearing at every turn at work and already on the couch at home when I arrive. He accuses me of bribing Chef for the lessons, of having cartel family members threaten her into letting me work in the kitchen. "You're a moron," I say.

"A moron who knows how to make an omelet and works on the line," Matt says and smirks back. At work, he's constantly doing that towel-whipping thing that only assholes in locker rooms on TV do. To be fair, a lot of the other cooks do it too, but he seems to take special pleasure in snapping at my arms and in the stinging red welts that show off his good aim.

As Chef disappears to her office again, throwing another insult my way, I sigh and spoon some salsa on the side of the plate. I chew carefully, trying to find the flaw, begging the omelet's faults to speak to me.

"Seriously, no idea," Felix says.

I finish the omelet, clean up after myself. I go outside to wait for my shift to start, walk a few blocks away, looking to intercept Emma before she arrives to take reservations. Cup of coffee in hand, scanning the street for her, I realize how quickly I've gotten used to this. The early mornings, coffee, watching these tourists jogging toward the boardwalk, the soreness of my body. Just being here, not in the grips of my life in Mexico.

Emma appears from around the corner, her work shirt folded over her forearm. When she spots me, she pulls her earphones out, wraps the cord around her phone. We kiss hello, and I'm in awe that she's part of my day. That I've found this place at all.

"I think you've conditioned me to think of you every time I taste coffee," she says.

"Yup, that's been the plan all along."

"I guess if that's as scheme-y and evil as you get, I can live with it." She smiles and takes a sip of my coffee. A knot of guilt forms in my stomach. I look around for some wispy version of Felix to give me that nudge I need, to push me toward action. That's when I see Matt and Elias round the corner. Matt spots me at the same time, and he shouts out halfway down the block, "Hey there, lovebirds."

I wince, looking around to make sure no one heard him. Elias rolls his eyes. "Why are you always such a tool, man?"

"What?" Matt says. "I'm just congratulating my friend Emma and our roomie here on their budding romance. Is that so wrong?"

"Don't be a dick," Emma says. I know it's directed at Matt, but I can't help but feel I've put myself in the words' path.

"Come on, man," Elias says. "Leave them alone."

"Is this a secret or something?" He smirks at me, and I know right away. He's practically waving it in front of my face. Chef doesn't know about me and Emma and he could tell her at any moment. If he feels I'm getting too far ahead in the kitchen, if he's getting sick of seeing me around, if he just feels like it.

I'm gripping my coffee cup, envisioning throwing it in Matt's face. Emma picks at something on her bag's strap, looks at the ground. No one says anything for a second, until a silver-haired couple walks through our little semi-circle on the sidewalk.

"Sheesh, fine," Matt says, raising his hands up. "I'm late anyway."

He gives me one last smirk, and then he and Elias head off in the direction of the restaurant, leaving me and Emma alone.

"Is it a secret?" Emma says, biting her lip. It looks like maybe she's already thinking that I'm not worth it, that the drunken makeouts were more fun.

I try to regain my footing, try to sense if the world feels the way it did on the Night of the Perfect Taco, like things were about to irrevocably change. I feel like an asshole for even comparing this to my brother's death. I take a deep breath, preparing for the confession.

"Your mom," I say, squinting in the morning sun. I feel like I should be memorizing Emma's features, clutching as tightly as I can to her memory. "When she said she wanted to start giving me lessons, she also said I couldn't keep working at the restaurant if I dated you."

Emma's jaw sets. "She said that?"

"Yeah."

Emma raises an eyebrow. "And you're still seeing me."

"Well, yeah." A family walks past us, the dad accidentally bumping my shoulder as he chases after a golden-haired toddler who's giggling as she waddles down the sidewalk. I don't want to picture my days without Emma.

"But you want to stop?" Emma asks.

I meet her eyes, furrowing my brow. "What? No! Hell no. I can't stay away from you." This makes her smile, and the effect is like the first taste of something sweet, like thirst quenched. But she suppresses the smile, still making up her mind how she feels about this. "Isn't that obvious?"

She shrugs, not amused. "So, what are you saying?"

"Just that maybe we can't make out at work anymore." I look up hopefully at her. She moves her glasses to the top of her head, and I know she does it all the time, almost a tic, but there's something I adore about it. "I'm sorry I didn't tell you before."

Emma crosses her arms in front of her chest. She's quiet for a second, either upset or just absorbing the information. I guess I don't know her well enough to be able to tell. We walk in silence for a little while, until I hear her mutter, "She's such an asshole." I'm not sure if it's meant for me or just for herself.

"So, what? You want to sneak around?" Her jaw is still set. I can practically see her weighing her options, all the other joys available to her, easier ones.

"Is that okay?"

Emma sighs. She kicks a pebble hard, so that it bounces off the sidewalk and onto the street, still rolling along when I lose sight of it. "Sure. Whatever."

We don't say another word until we reach the restaurant and head to separate entrances with nothing more than a parting smile.

When I get to my station, Elias is in there waiting for me. "Hey, man, sorry about Matt. I swear he's not always that bad. You just bring it out of him."

"Great," I say, laughing. "I only have to see him every second of the day."

"Yeah, about that. You busy tonight? I think it'd make shit at the house a lot less dramatic if we all hang out a bit, unwind. Gonna tell people to spread the word, get a good scene going."

The news of a party spreads fast in the kitchen. Elias doesn't so much ask our roommates' permission as announce the fact that a party will be happening, and the words bounce around the kitchen like living things.

I try to get a read on Chef all day, to see if Matt's given anything away. I know deep down that she would not be the kind to react subtly if she found out I was going directly against her orders, but I still fret about it the whole day. By the time shift is over, it feels like the whole restaurant is coming over to our place, including Chef. I'm gonna have to stay away from Emma.

Earlier, I had swung by the hostess stand to tell her to meet me down the block so we could at least walk to the party together. Now I sneak away from the crowd, pretending to make a phone call so I can wait for her. I look forward to slipping my hand into hers, to stealing a few quiet moments with her among the fireflies and moonlit woods. But ten minutes later she still hasn't shown. Downtown is too small a place to lose someone in, so I figure she got caught up in a group of people leaving and couldn't think of an excuse to slip away.

I can hear the convoy of loud-mouthed cooks a few blocks ahead of me. I think about jogging a little to catch up to everyone, but then I notice my shadow is doing things it's not supposed to. "You're still hanging around, huh?"

"You think I'd leave you alone?" It's not even a full moon and still the light is stronger than the spare streetlights. This place is so ridiculous.

"You don't think I'm doing fine here on my own?" I ask.

"That's not what I said," Felix says. "I'm actually pretty proud of you, Carlos."

God, why do those words feel so great, even coming from a ghost? It's hard to remember that I wanted him gone so badly a few weeks ago.

I keep walking up the street, following the voices up ahead. Felix follows at my side, though the light dictates he should be shifting with each passing lamppost. "I miss parties," he says, when we get closer and can hear the sound from the house reverberating down the block. "I miss that level of drunkenness where you're just curious to know everyone. Death doesn't have that."

I sigh and look up at the sky. It's too beautiful here to rage at his death. How can a night sky like this exist in a world full of grief? A couple of shooting stars streak across the sky, and I suppress my rage with wonder.

"Why would you say something like that?" I ask, not sure if the question is directed at Felix or myself. "You can stop reminding me you're dead. It's not like I've forgotten."

Behind me I hear someone call out, "Again, man? What the hell is wrong with you?" Mierda. It's Matt, carrying a case of beer, clearly overhearing my one-sided conversation.

I turn away from him, not wanting to deal with his shit. He calls out a couple of times in between fits of laughter, but I half jog the rest of the way up the block, ignoring him.

At the house, the party's already underway. I spot Emma immediately, my eyes flitting toward her as if there is a beacon shining from her. She doesn't spot me right away, but Chef is here already too, and I don't want to go say hi while obviously beaming, so I go grab a beer instead.

Isaiah and Morris are hanging out by the cooler, and I just kind of stick around, listening to their conversation, simultaneously trying to figure out how to break into it like a normal human being and trying not to completely hone in on Emma. She's at the far end of the backyard, near a couple of strung-up hammocks. I text her that she looks great, but she must not be looking at her phone, because she doesn't respond. My beer is gone already, its label peeled to shreds. I go get another one.

I look around, thrilled by the fact that this is where I live now. All these people are, technically, at my house. Most are out in the backyard, though I can see a few people through the kitchen window and hanging out on the couches. Food, of course, lingers in the air, as if it's a cloud that's followed us here, cartoon-like. A charcoal bite to the backyard, the heat of the oven emanating from inside. Back home, my friends approved of my cooking, insofar as it got them fed. Dad approves of hobbies, to an extent. Felix was into cuisine as a representation of culture, as a fuck-you to Dad, as a symbol for me.

But these are my people.

I walk around aimlessly for a while, grab another beer. It doesn't take too long before I start feeling these quick drinks, and suddenly I know exactly the frame of mind Felix was talking about. I'm curious about everyone. Instead of getting lost in my own head, with the knee-deep muck that exists there, I come out into this surreal but present world. Isaiah and Morris are having a conversation about what Jackie Chan's post-acting career might have been, which suddenly feels like the funniest thing in the world.

"After your body breaks down, how do you put those skills to use, you know?" Isaiah says, excitedly. "He wasn't a phenomenal actor or anything. Just had his karate moves and some charm. He hasn't been in movies in a while, so what's he been up to? You think he's working at an insurance company or something? Just kind of scampering around the cubicles delivering memos?" He makes a frantic motion with his hands; I have no idea what he's going for.

I laugh along, until I realize I don't really know who they're talking about. I text Emma, I'm in the middle of a conversation about Jackie Chan, and it's hilarious, but I don't, exactly, know who Jackie Chan is. Was he an actor?

I see her check her phone and smile, shaking her head. Her response comes through a few moments later, a little buzz of joy. Prime Minister of Japan in the '90s.

Wow. I am completely lost.

Don't worry, I've got your back.

After a while, feeling like I can't help but look at Emma if she's nearby and I'm gonna get myself in trouble, I go into the kitchen. Vee's there, and I realize I've never really had a conversation with her. I feel the urge to remedy that immediately. I want to know how she got into cooking, how she made her way to Provecho, what she likes most about working in kitchens. If she feels weird being interviewed by a semi-drunk kid like me, she doesn't show it. She tells me about how she grew up in North Dakota, bored as hell. How she applied to be a line cook at a diner just for kicks and eventually saved up enough money to go cook somewhere else. She met Chef Elise in New York, at some catering gig ten years ago.

I notice Matt on the couch, passing a joint to Emma's friend Reggie as they play video games. Emboldened, remembering Elias's words about Matt not being all bad, I grab a six-pack from the fridge and bring it over to the living room. "Anyone need a beer?"

Matt mumbles a thanks and cracks one open, eyes me with the suspicion usually reserved for murderers. I plop down on the couch, watching the gameplay for a while. After a few moments, Reggie gets up to go use the bathroom and passes the controller to me.

"Uh, I kinda suck at video games."

Matt groans and hits pause. "I'll just wait for Reggie." He offers the joint to me somewhat begrudgingly, and when I refuse he sets it down on an ashtray in front of him with a heavy eye roll.

I try to think of something to say, fail. I open another beer, realize I'm staring, find myself wishing he would just simmer away. Back to my phone it is, as the awkwardness builds in the living room. Sitting next to Matt. Trying to break the ice, and be friendlier, but for some reason can only think of him as a sauce.

That makes absolutely no sense, Emma responds, from some unseen corner of the party.

Only to the sober mind. Trust me, it's not weird. I don't mean that he's, like, a delicious sauce or anything. Just...you know. He evaporates.

Carlos. Drink some water.

Matt looks like he's about to explode with discomfort, maybe because I keep giggling to myself. Before he does, he looks at me and says, "So, what's that all about, man? Talking to yourself."

I think about bolting, laughing it off, lying. But the booze and my good mood swirl together and turn confessional. After all this time, I'm curious about how someone will respond to the truth. Especially someone I'm not close to, someone who doesn't care about me in the slightest. "My dead brother," I say. "I talk to him."

Matt stares at me, unblinking. He doesn't laugh, doesn't crack a joke. "Are you fucking with me?" he asks, taking a drink from his beer.

I shrug, tell him I wish I were. Tell him how Felix died six months ago but that I still see him. Matt doesn't say anything, just looks down at the controller he's holding. For a second I think he's going to say something nice for a change. That he'll offer a condolence, for Felix or for himself. But then he turns back to his video game, mashing buttons, his gaze focused intently on the screen.

In the kitchen I pour myself a glass of water from the tap, drinking it down quickly. Then I'm back outside, wanting to talk to everyone all at once, not knowing which conversation to choose. Emma's sitting around the fire, and it wouldn't be the most terribly obvious thing in the world to go sit next to her. Except Chef is sitting on the back porch steps with Sue, a full glass of wine in her hands, the fire pit directly in front of her.

So I just look up at the stars, smile stupidly, have another beer.

I make eye contact with Emma and smile goofily at her. I wave and then remember we're trying to be incognito and very conspicuously sit on my hand. Emma grins at me and shakes her head, mouthing the words *you are so drunk* at me.

You are so great, I mouth back. The carelessness feels like love, and maybe that thought is prompted by the booze but maybe not. Emma blushes and turns away. Chef hasn't noticed a thing, thank god.

"That's why," Elias says, nudging me, though he's looking at Memo. "He'd be hanging out with us every day, pero el güey anda clavado."

Memo cranes his neck toward Emma. His eyes are bloodshot, droopy-happy. "I'd noticed."

"Shit, really? I'm trying to be secretive. Chef kinda told me to stay away from her." I get the sense I shouldn't be saying this so openly. But if alcohol is good for anything it's for saying fuck it and confessing.

"Probably a good idea," Elias says. I feel my heart sink a little. This isn't what I want to hear. I take a sip of beer, think about getting up, rejoining Isaiah and Morris, who I hope are still talking about Prime Minister Jackie Chan.

"Not that I'm saying stop seeing her or anything," Elias continues. He is picking at the label on his beer, looking at Emma and then back at me. "Just, you know, appreciate your place in the kitchen. You don't know because you're new to this, but what she's doing for you? It's rare, man." He runs a hand through his hair, rolls a little corner of the beer label into a snowball and throws it on the floor. Memo sits quietly by, listening. "I know from experience that Chef pushes the people she believes in. She gives you opportunities that shouldn't be granted to you because you haven't earned 'em, or, like me, because you've thrown others away.

"But she's hard on people wasting those opportunities. That buddy I opened the restaurant with in Seattle? He was here too, man. But dude fell back into drugs and Chef literally put all his fucking belongings on the ferry back to the mainland the very next day." Elias gives me a hard look. "I'm a romantic. I'm all for forbidden love. Just, you know, be careful."

I look over my shoulder at Chef and then at my phone to see if Emma's responded to my latest text. I wonder if the booze has made me reckless tonight, how many people other than Elias and Memo have noticed me gawking at her. "Yeah, I know," I say. "I am."

"Lo que tú digas," Elias says. Whatever you say. Then he reaches into the cooler next to him and offers me another beer, and since I can't go sit next to Emma, I take it.

I continue to enjoy myself throughout the party, flitting around from group to group, even having a less-than-awful interaction with Matt about the greatness of noodle soups for breakfast. As the alcohol compounds and people leave, I spend more time looking at my phone, wanting to talk to Emma somehow, wanting her to carve a path for us in the woods where we can disappear together. But her phone must have died, and a little while later she waves a silent good-bye.

When my body tells me it's time to call it a night too, I carry myself up to my room, to the mattress on the floor, which I literally plop onto face-first. I entangle myself in the still-unfamiliar sheets, and, while my last few thoughts before falling asleep are about Emma, Elias's words play over them, like foreboding music in a horror film.

CHAPTER 22
GYOZA IN ORANGE-BASIL BROTH

FOR THE FILLING:

1 pound flor de calabaza

2 pounds shrimp, peeled and deveined

½ pound portobello mushrooms, chopped

½ pound shiitake mushrooms, chopped

2 red onions, chopped

6 cloves garlic

2 tablespoons ginger

2 tablespoons sesame oil

FOR THE BROTH:

12 cups veggie stock

4 tablespoons ginger

½ cup packed basil leaves

2 tablespoons sesame oil

2 tablespoons sriracha hot sauce

2 tablespoons rice wine vinegar

METHOD:

The next day, I wake up aware of death.

It's just there, prodding at me, reminding me it exists. It's too early to get out of bed, but I know only activity will drive the thoughts away before they can shake me to my core. I drag myself off the mattress, splash water on my face, go downstairs. I find my phone in the kitchen, battery drained, inches away from a puddle of some unrecognizable liquid.

Before the puddle can shape itself into Felix, I mop it up with a paper towel. I plug my phone in, look around the house to see where I should start cleaning. This happened often those first few weeks. After the funeral, I would wake up with too much awareness of How Things Are. The realization would claw at me that if Felix hadn't been in the way of a bullet, something else would have got him in the end. I'd start thinking about how I too will inevitably die, how everything I know is transient, fleeting, impermanent. Sometimes it's just flashes, in the middle of the day, of how things could go wrong. But when I wake up like this, I know I have to keep busy or else go completely insane.

Though my stomach lurches with movement and my head is pounding, I grab a garbage bag from beneath the kitchen sink and start collecting beer bottles, taking pleasure in the little clinks of the glass, the crumpling of plastic cups and aluminum cans. I open every window and both doors to allow the smell of the party out and the cool morning air in. Memo's still on the couch, Reggie on the floor. They barely stir as I tiptoe around them.

Once my phone is charged and the house is tidy, I text Emma to see if she's free. She might still be sleeping, and so I walk to the grocery store, listening to music. It's a gorgeous day, and it feels like the world is trying to reassure me. I meander through the aisles, waiting for inspiration, hoping that death won't creep into the space I'm carving in my thoughts for food.

On the walk back home, the weight of groceries digs into my shoulder, clouds move swiftly overhead and the leaves flutter as if they're breathing. I set my bags on the counter, turn on the oven, wash the vegetables. The restaurant is closed, Emma asleep; nothing else beckons.

My roommates wake up and turn on the TV. The house comes alive as I cook. Elias goes out for a run. Matt heads to the city to meet up with friends. Before he leaves, he looks around groggily, takes heed of the state of the house. "Thanks for cleaning," he says. The noose around my neck slackens.

When Emma wakes up she comes over, sits on the counter as I concoct dish after dish, things I've never tried to make before, things that might read like a dream on a menu. Every now and then I bring a spoon up to her lips, wait for the steam to dissipate and then tilt it so she can taste. Every now and then I step into the space between her legs, and when a surge of affection threatens to make me say something stupid, I lean in and kiss her.

Some things we eat, some things we only taste and cover with cling wrap. The fridge is full by nightfall, and when Emma lies down next to me, it's hard to think of anything but life.

Tuesday morning, and Chef pushes away another omelet. I try to eat it calmly, hiding the fact that I want to throw it in her face, because at this point all doubts that she's a sadist have disappeared into a puddle of egg yolks. I try to keep Elias's words in mind.

Instead of throwing something at her, I ask if I can start cooking the staff meal early.

Chef looks at the time, raises an eyebrow. "Already?"

"I'd like to be productive, Chef. Don't plan on going home, and there's no dishes for me yet."

She studies her clipboard, leads me to the walk-ins. "Use all this shrimp," she says. She tells me to use any station I want, but that I'll have to clear away as soon as the staff starts to show. "Yes, Chef."

I bring out all the Tupperware I've brought from home. I set them next to the items Chef's instructed me to use up, thinking. Waiting. There's a bunch of basil that's not quite wilting but not pretty enough to use fresh. Good for a sauce, probably, but I feel like doing something else.

I look over at all my potential supplies some more, wash my hands again, place the shrimp in a lowboy fridge. I run over to the pantry, grab some flour and—I don't know what they're called in English— flor de calabaza.

Still not quite sure what I'm going to do, I pick up my gyuto, unsheathe it, watch it catch the light. In the blade, I see my reflection, and a hint of yesterday morning's thoughts come bubbling back, that excessive self-awareness that tells me that one day I too will die. I think of a postcard I got from Felix from Hong Kong a few months before he died, one that stands out because it had these dumplings on the image, and Felix actually described them. All his travels, he almost never wrote about the food.

Two red onions, chopped easily. Some portobello and shiitake mushrooms, the flor, meet the same fate, their resting place a large stainless-steel mixing bowl. Smash a few cloves of garlic with the flat side of my knife; mince them up. I grab a cast-iron pan from its hook in the prep area, squirt some sesame oil into it, slide the garlic from the cutting board into the pan before the fire's lit. This I learned from Rosalba. Fill the kitchen with the scent of garlic before it can burn. Let the heat slowly draw out the garlic's taste. Felix could pick out from the smell alone when the garlic was about to burn.

I toss the entire mass of the basil into the blender and then cut some of the remaining ginger into chunks and throw them in too. A little soy sauce, a little sriracha, a few oranges' worth of fresh-squeezed juice. While the blender transforms the pieces into a wholly greater whole, I turn off the flame on the mushroom/flor concoction. I grab a tasting spoon and take a bite and then run over to the dishwashing station to chuck the spoon into the sink in celebration of the flavors.

The dough has to rest, the broth is at a simmer, the basil mixture tastes like I Belong in the Kitchen. Every piece of equipment I'm no longer using is in the sink waiting to be cleaned, and the surface around my work area is spotless.

Felix is a genius for leading me here, for making sure I stay.

Feeling like I'm in the midst of the kitchen dance, I use a mortar and pestle to crush some Thai chilies along with some garlic. Then I slide them into a deli container with a few tablespoons of olive oil, and fiddle around with a smoke gun I found at the bar, trapping the concoction under plastic wrap. I can't believe this is a profession. That people fiddle around with food, perfect the art of it, and it's a job. That you can provide the joy of a meal to someone else and earn a living. Not the kind of living my parents think is necessary, maybe. But I can't believe I ever considered doing anything else, at Dad's insistence or otherwise.

When there's eight dumplings for every person working the early shift, I finally stop. I look around, only now becoming aware of the fact that the kitchen's almost full. Matt's using a mandolin to slice cucumbers into paper-thin strips, for once not scowling at me. Memo catches my eye and gives me a little head nod. Everyone else is focused on their work, stirring, chopping, tasting. They may have been doing this for much, much longer than I have. They may not have grown up with maids or with two passports. The schools they attended probably weren't surrounded by bodyguards. But right now, I feel closer to them than to anyone I grew up with. I am a part of their world.

I check my texts, getting the feeling that Emma might have passed by without me noticing, but there's only a hi how are you from Mom. Cooking 😊, I respond.

I disappear back behind my partition. It is so much more satisfying to clean pans that I am responsible for dirtying. Even the ones that come in afterward feel easier because of the sheer fact that I have cooked today. Elias shows up around eleven. "What did your crazy ass come up with for us today?" he asks.

"Flor de calabaza, shrimp and mushroom gyoza in an orange-basil broth," I say.

"You are out of your fucking mind," Elias laughs. It's a pretty accurate comment, I realize, which should make me panic that maybe Elias has noticed something, maybe Matt told him about seeing me talking to myself, my ill-advised confession. I have been talking to Felix too loudly, interacting with inanimate objects or nothingness. But this time, for now, it's a compliment, not a diagnosis, and I swell with pride.

Elias doesn't have to tell me to put the music on to let everyone know food's ready. And when I do it this time, I feel no nervousness, no doubt about the food I'm presenting. I don't even wonder if I've gone wrong anywhere. If I have, the struggle will lead to a climb.

I plate a bowl for myself. A mini ladleful of broth, eight dumplings, garnished with the green onions and the smoked chili oil. The dish looks beautiful, worthy of the TV shows Felix and I used to watch.

I might be deluded. I might be good at this or I might be fooling myself—it's hard to tell. In this moment, I don't particularly care which it is. My coworkers serve themselves, slurp at the broth, add more chili oil. Elias is loudest with his compliments. Chef has no discernible human emotions, so she doesn't react. I catch Matt going back for seconds, serving himself quickly and pulling away as if he doesn't want to be seen.

I feel like I've finally arrived. Whatever life was supposed to have been waiting for me after graduation, whatever has been lost since the Night of the Perfect Taco, I know this is where I belong.

CHAPTER 23
THE PERFECT OMELET

3 eggs
Way more butter than you think
A touch of cream
Salt and pepper, added in the pan

METHOD:

On my fourteenth day of training, Chef actually makes it halfway through the omelet before she decides it's not up to her unspecified standards and pushes the plate away. I'm still repeating Elias's words to myself, that she's pushing me hard because she believes in me. But I wish she would just give up on this stupid lesson, let me move on, really teach me things.

That night, Emma and I meet up at two in the morning. Everyone else goes out to The Crown, but it's the first chance we have to sneak away. We're swimming again. I've never loved the act so much. The feel of jumping in, how gravity falls away from my limbs. Everything is light. Emma's a terrific swimmer, so graceful in the water that at times there is barely a radiant ripple in her wake. "I've always had this dream of swimming from here to Seattle," she says as we tread water. "I really think I could do it."

"You should," I say. "Were you on a swim team at school?"

"Nah. Just another by-product of neglectful parents," she says. "Lots of days to escape here, get good at swimming on my own." She dips below the surface, legs barely making a splash. When she resurfaces, she wipes the water from her forehead. "I'm gonna miss this place when I go," she says.

A silence settles in, smoothing even the ripples of the lake so that it's a perfect mirror, despite the fact that we're still kicking to stay afloat. We haven't yet discussed the future, and I'm not ready for it to interrupt this. "How could you not?" I say.

Fireflies dance at the edge of the lake and wispy clouds pass in front of the waxing moon. Emma swims over to me and we kiss. A breeze picks back up, like a breath, like the island itself is sighing in pleasure.

On my seventeenth day of training, Chef eats the entire omelet. Except she doesn't offer a compliment. She pushes the plate away again, holds up a finger and says, "Wait a sec." She comes back about five minutes later with a cup of coffee, and it almost looks like she was on the way to her office, like she'd forgotten I was there at all. "Big fucking whoop, you can cook one omelet at a time. Anyone can do that. Make me five."

Another paycheck disappeared into these morning sessions, but I'm somehow okay with it.

That night, Emma and I go bowling with Brandy and Reggie. It's loud, it's fun, it's normal. It's silly, with stupid trick shots when we get a little bored of the scores. We eat nachos, instead of potato chips covered in hot sauce and lime like we would in Mexico. There's another group of teens a few lanes down, people Emma and the others clearly know from school.

I keep looking around, expecting someone from the restaurant to walk in, discover us. Matt taking pictures on his phone so he can blackmail me. Chef trailing us, suspicious of me from the start, just waiting to catch me in the act.

At one point, when Brandy and Reggie are laughing, changing our names in the scoreboard, Emma tugs on my sleeve. I was looking toward the door again. "Hey. We're all right here," she says. In her eyes I see the sadness of a kid too used to being alone, and I promise to myself to stay present. I remind myself how quickly joy can be undone.

On my twentieth day of training, I finally manage to plate five omelets at the same time. Except they're all different levels of doneness; one's flat-out burnt, one's still kind of runny, the other three are somewhere in between, each somehow a different hue on the yellow scale. It's like Chef is fucking with the laws of thermodynamics or something. On this island, I'm not so sure that natural laws hold steady anyway. It's easy to believe that Chef of all people could manipulate heat.

That night, Chef gets on a ferry to the city, so Emma invites me over. I'm uneasy about it, though, not sure when Chef will come back, so I ask if we can hang out at my place. She shows up an hour late, her words terse and her touches light in a bad way.

"Everything okay?" I ask. Elias was on the couch in the living room, so we're on my bed, a popcorn bowl between us, Emma's laptop set up at our feet.

"Sure," she says, in a tone of voice that makes me tense.

Usually, we make out before movies. Now she leans over and clicks a few times until the credits start to roll. She's quiet, withdrawn, and I tell myself she's just tired. Maybe her dad pissed her off again. We watch the movie quietly, wonderful weight of our bodies pressed against each other. I try not to ask myself if we're as close to each other as usual. I try not to think of August.

July's nearing its end, and I'm nearing a month into my training with Chef Elise. Felix is in the kitchen with me, hovering over the five pans I've got going, little fairy wings on his back. "Looking good," he says, but Chef is hovering nearby too, scrutinizing my every move.

I turn off the burners and start to plate the omelets, starting with the one that I know has been cooking the longest, even if just for a few seconds. Five golden omelets at a time, each identical. I stack the pans I used on top of each other, look around to make sure nothing's out of order.

Chef leans in, takes her fork to the corner of each omelet. I swat at Felix, who's buzzing irritatingly by my ear. "You're not a cook," she says. "You're a kid playing pretend. You're just fucking around, wasting my time, wasting yours, wasting food." She slides them into the trash. Five omelets, three eggs each. I'll need to buy another dozen for tomorrow's session.

Felix climbs out of the trash can, all five omelets on a plate. "The food waste feels particularly sad in this situation," he says. "You'd think someone in her line of work would revere food a little too much to chuck it in order to make a point." I haven't seen much of him lately, and it's just now that I realize that.

Later that day, when our breaks line up, Emma and I don't sneak away for a rendezvous. We don't steal kisses in the walk-ins the way some of the servers who are hooking up do, muffled moans emanating from within that everyone either ignores or draws attention to for kicks. We don't text each other across the room, because I feel eyes on us all the time, and I'm terrified they're Chef's. Emma looks annoyed, and she leads us to the back.

"This shit is getting old," she says. She pulls a berry from the meadow from her pocket, digging a nail into the rind and pulling it free from its fruit. "I'm all for sneaking around. But I barely see you. When I do, you're constantly nervous, your mind on other things."

I fall quiet. That perfect view of the island and the ocean grows a shade darker, and I look overhead for the cloud that caused it, but the sky is clear.

"It makes me feel lonely." She takes a bite. A trail of juice leaks down her chin, and she uses the back of her hand to wipe it away. "I want to spend time with you, Carlos. You get that, right? If I didn't..." She trails off, finishing the berry with another bite. "Which, you know, whatever. I'm not someone who needs to spend every moment together. I know the kitchen means a lot to you, but the summer's gonna end eventually and then..."

"You're right," I say, before she can finish the thought. I don't want her to go down that rabbit hole. "I'm sorry. Let's go on a date. Let's go to the city, spend a whole day together."

Emma smiles halfheartedly, puts a hand on my cheek and quickly pulls it away. She walks over to the Dumpster and tosses the rind inside. "Okay," she sighs when she comes back. "Just...you know, I heard empty promises from my parents a lot. I know what it's like to lose battles of importance to a restaurant." I try to cut in again to argue, but she interrupts me. "I'm not saying you're doing that. I'm just saying that my parents made promises too."

I nod eagerly. "I won't do that. I couldn't live with myself."

"You could," Emma says. We stand side by side with our backs against the restaurant wall for a bit, looking out at the water, legs touching, beauty surrounding us. Tightness clutches at my chest.

CHAPTER 24
OMAKASE

A ton of sushi

METHOD:

I'm at the dock, waiting for Emma to arrive. I almost want her to be late, so that we'll miss the ferry and not leave the island, have our date within its magnificent borders. But I want things between us back where they belong, moments shimmering with lake water and joy.

I still went in for my training today, served Chef five omelets with sundried tomatoes, goat cheese and basil. She devoured one in minutes and then offered a couple of the others to Sue and the guys delivering produce. It's the best I've felt hanging up my apron at the end of our sessions, and it almost made me wish that Emma and I could move the date to another day.

But that feeling falls away when I see Emma. She's in a sundress, her bag's strap across her chest. I can see a cardigan tucked inside the bag and the corner of a book sticking out. The smile is automatic, and, by now, if we're not near the kitchen or our coworkers, so is the kiss hello. It is an incredible thing to have every day, this kiss hello.

"Fancy date time in Seattle!" I say, doing a weird little jig.

"That was interesting," she says, eyebrows angled in amusement.

"Yeah, I don't know where that came from. Let's pretend it never happened."

"Okay, but I accidentally took a video and uploaded it to the internet. Sorry."

We take a seat on a bench at the dock, hiding from the afternoon sun. There are a couple of cars waiting in line to drive onto the ferry, which is just now in view. Inside, families of four and five sit looking bored. One kid is crying, while his mom tries to calm him and his siblings try to sleep.

"How's your day been?" I ask.

"Pretty good. Slept in. Went to my meadow to do a little yoga. Now I'm here with you," Emma says, folding her hands in her lap.

"Well, I guess it was good for a while, then. Sorry to ruin things."

She nudges me with her shoulder and smiles. "How's your day been?"

"Not bad. I think I'm the best omelet maker in the world right now. Your mom asked for some tips today. I think I'm going to start charging her for the lessons or maybe go start my own restaurant."

She gives a little tight-lipped smile and cleans her glasses on the hem of her dress. She gets a little quiet. I should know better by now than to bring up the kitchen all the time. A sea breeze passes by, cooling the sun on my face. I close my eyes to it for a moment, try to let everything else float away. I'm young. I'm alive. I'm here. "Thanks for coming with me," I say and give her hand a squeeze.

It brings her back to me, removes her mind from whatever worries her when she quiets down. She scoots closer to me, lays her head on my shoulder and we look out at the steel blue of the Pacific extending beyond us. *No worries today,* I tell myself. *Just Emma.*

The ferry arrives from Seattle with a couple of horn blasts and unloads a fresh smattering of tourists. "If you could start your own restaurant," Emma asks, "what kind would it be?"

"I don't know. I haven't really thought about it," I say. We rise to our feet as people start to shuffle onboard. "I've been so focused on just learning little things. I'd have no idea where to begin. It feels impossibly far away."

"Throw something out there."

I think for a while, and the only thing that comes to mind is crazy concoctions, things that I would have no idea how to pull off technically, things that might not even be able to exist. "I don't know. Something unreal."

Emma laughs, leads us to the stairs to go up to the second level of the ferry. We stand at the front of the boat, leaning against the rails. "Unreal? Like...those every-flavor Harry Potter jelly beans? A whole restaurant of that?"

"I mean, not exactly, but that's not far off. It'd be like...fusion. But not between different cuisines. More like between something real and something magical. Have you ever read *Como Agua Para Chocolate? Like Water for Chocolate?*"

Emma shakes her head.

"It's this crazy love story where the food being cooked in the chapter has an emotional effect on the characters. Like, the main character cooks with rose petals given to her by this guy she's in love with, and it causes her sister to go into this lustful state and run off with a revolutionary soldier."

Emma takes her phone out to write down the title. "So, you want to cook so well it makes people horny."

"Exactly," I say, laughing. The ferry blasts a few deafening horns again and then pushes away from the dock, creating a slight breeze. "If I ever owned a restaurant like your mom does, I'd want the menu to read like that book. Dreamy ingredient combinations, entrées that sound like poetry." I think for a second, look at Emma, who's looking out at the water. "I guess what I'm saying is I'd want a superpretentious restaurant."

"With really long menus," Emma says with a smirk. She leans over the rails, looking down at the hull splitting the water. "I guess you have time to figure that out."

"I'm in no hurry," I respond. We both fall quiet, looking out at the San Juan Islands passing us by. What a crazy notion, I think, that there's a wealth of time out there for all of us.

After about thirty minutes, the Seattle skyline appears in the distance, and Mount Rainier, snowcapped and unobstructed by clouds. It looks superimposed onto the scenery, like skilled but still-obvious Photoshop. The city gets closer; the waves are a little rougher, sending a fine mist up to their deck, the tiny droplets sticking to Emma's glasses and her hair. I wipe at her cheek and wonder how it is that I still get goose bumps at her touch.

When we reach Seattle, Emma and I follow the small crowd downstairs, toward the exit. "We've got a couple of hours before our reservation," I say. "I figured we could just explore for a bit? If you know any cool spots you can lead the way, but no pressure. I like wandering."

"Sure," Emma says. "Do you want to see the touristy spots?"

I shrug. "If they're on the way. I just want to walk with you. Then shove food in your face."

"So romantic," Emma says. "You pick."

I look left, look right, pick the direction that seems more interesting (crowds, trees, restaurants). "You never told me what really made you decide to leave Mexico," Emma says. "I know you said your brother had something to do with it and that you ran away against your parents' wishes, but what was the thing that made you actually bolt? Was it a train of thought, an epiphany?"

I sigh, try to guess what her reaction would be if I said, *A pigeon told me in my brother's voice.* She'd think I was joking.

"A little birdie told me," I say, following it up quickly with a shrug. "It had been building up for a while, I guess. I'd always looked up to my brother, and I had never really thought of doing what he did when he said no to college and just went traveling. I admired the fact that he could find random jobs as a construction worker in countries where he didn't speak the language, that he'd seen so much of the world because that's what he wanted to do. But I never wanted it for myself.

"After he died, though, I started thinking about it more and more. Not exactly doing what he did, but, just, reconsidering doing what my parents expected. The life path I was on being the only one I could choose. It was like he was telling me that the world had more to offer. Every day it got a little louder. I'd find myself hearing—" I pause, think better of the phrasing "—or thinking more and more: leave. Find a change of scenery. Get out. Then at my graduation party, my dad made a stupid speech basically saying we should all forget my brother."

"Jesus."

"Yeah," I say. "He just put on this whole act like he was heartbroken, but when he wasn't in front of a crowd…" I trail off, not wanting to rekindle these thoughts about Dad. "It was just the tipping point for me. I had to finally heed the voice and leave."

We cross the street beneath the overpass, head away from the water up a street that slopes upward at a ridiculous angle, one that I would imagine in San Francisco, not Seattle. The sun's at our backs as we climb the hill. It glints off the myriad windows on the surrounding buildings and stretches our shadows out along the sidewalk.

The hours pass quickly with Emma. The nervous thought *this is a date* doesn't even enter my mind. Usually, even with Isa, months into our thing, I never really felt completely at ease. I'd have to think of ways to be funny, talk nonstop to fill in the spaces between conversations. I was constantly aware of my hands, the not-white shade of my teeth, constantly wondering how our night together would end, whether we'd have sex. None of that happens with Emma.

We comment on the things we see (a guy speed walking past us in tiny shorts, a woman having a heated conversation with a customer service rep on the phone, two dogs walking side by side with no owners nearby), or the perfect evening weather, or the strange thoughts we've had that we've never voiced before. How Emma did mushrooms once and had a bad trip but was saved from freaking out because she was certain that her friend's dog knew what was going on and stayed nearby to comfort her. I come close to admitting that I see Felix everywhere, but I end up sugarcoating it to keep myself from sounding insane. "It's like he can still speak to me," I say. "Like he never went away at all."

Emma is quiet for a second. "This is going to sound awful, but, since we're on confessionals, I want to say this. I've never allowed myself the full thought, because it's awful. So if you think I'm awful, just stop me and I'll shut up and we'll only talk nice things from now on."

"No," I say. "Go ahead.'"

Emma moves her glasses from her head down to the bridge of her nose. The sun's not quite setting but beginning its orange crawl toward the horizon. We're walking back downtown, toward the restaurant. "Okay, so what I was going to say is that, well, I've never really experienced death. Not like you have. A couple of grandparents I wasn't all that close to, some kid I kinda knew from elementary school. And I keep having this awful thought that I want to experience it. That I want it to happen to someone close to me, I want to feel that loss."

I don't tell her that no, no, she doesn't. I nod, let her go on.

"Obviously I don't *want* anyone to die. But I know I'm going to experience it sooner or later in my life. Of course I am. And part of me just thinks: let's get it over with. And another part of me is just…" She hesitates, either trying to find the right word or making sure I'm not going to run off. The golden cinematic light of the sun catches on some fine hairs on her cheek, and I want to cup her face in my hand. "Curious. Morbidly curious at what it's going to be like when it happens. How will I react? Will I be destroyed, or will I know how to celebrate their life? Will I get stuck in one of the steps of grieving you always hear about? Denial, sadness? I hate that I even think about it like this, that I devote any time at all to it. I shouldn't worry, shouldn't dwell. I shouldn't want it to happen ever. I shouldn't think about it. But I can't help it." She folds her arms over her chest, looks over at me. "Was that the most insensitive rant you've ever heard? Am I awful?"

"You're not awful," I say. "I kind of wish I'd thought about it more before Felix died. I don't think it can really prepare you for how it feels, how much you miss them. But maybe it would have."

"You seem to be doing okay, though. Did it, like, pass with time?"

I wish the answer was a straight-up yes, but it says something that my instinct is to look around to make sure that Felix isn't around. "I still have my moments."

Emma reaches out to me, hooks her arm around my elbow. I turn my neck and kiss the top of her head, and we walk the rest of the way in silence, death hovering around us.

The restaurant, when we finally reach it, is an unassuming place, laid out like most sushi restaurants. There's a bar that seats maybe eight people, behind which three Japanese sushi chefs lean over their counters, blades in hand. There are a handful of tables, mostly business types or couples. I check in with the hostess, and she leads us to two seats at the bar.

The chef bows down and greets us in Japanese. "Can I start you with anything?" he asks, accented to the exact same level as Felix, the English fractured, not broken, though in a different way. As if each language has its little faults with which it cracks another.

I tell him we'll be doing omakase, which is where the chef decides what to serve you depending on the freshest fish of the day along with the restaurant's specialty. Emma says that he doesn't have to bother serving on plates; he can just place the food directly in our mouths. The chef laughs and then reaches across the bar and sets a plate down in front of each of us. It's a simple piece of nigiri, just the rice and a sizeable, expertly cut slice of fish on top. "Red snapper," he says.

Emma raises her piece without any trouble holding her chopsticks and moves it toward me, as if she's going to feed me. Then she stops halfway through, looking at me expectantly. I give her a puzzled look. "Cheers with me," she says, smiling.

I raise my piece too, and we touch them together and then dip them slightly in the soy sauce and chew slowly. I usually love big, extravagant flavors, unapologetic spice and heat. But I respect the subtlety of this, how unencumbered the taste of one piece of fish can be.

"One of my goals in life is to always have a toast ready, for any occasion," Emma says, when she's done chewing. "I think Ireland is high on my list of places to travel to, 'cause I picture them just toasting everything, every moment of the day. It's sunny! We have a toast for that. This coffee is particularly good! We have a toast for that."

The plates get whisked away in an instant, and the chef is looking at the galore of fish in front of him, trying to decide what comes next.

"Do you know any?"

"Toasts?" She takes a sip of water, thinks about it. "Of course I can't remember any on the spot, but I've definitely Googled the shit out of this." Someone in the restaurant erupts in laughter, and I turn around to see who. Dudes in suits raise sake glasses, laugh with their mouths full. Two women watch as their friend tries what looks like sea urchin, eyebrows high, waiting for a reaction. Life between the cracks of everything. "Oh, I know!" Emma reaches into her purse and pulls out a flask.

"You carry around a flask with you?"

"Yeah, for exactly this sort of occasion." She raises it up but not too high so as not to arouse suspicion. Then she continues in a pretty solid Irish accent. "'There are several good reasons for drinking, and one has just entered my head. If a man can't drink when he's living, then how the hell can he drink when he's dead?'" She takes a pull from the flask and then passes it on to me. "I figured it'd be appropriate, in a way. For your brother."

She smiles, and I try to ignore the fact that the wasabi has just shaped itself into Felix and is trying to high-five me. "I like this girl," the wasabi squeaks and then goes back to being a little green blob. I've been seeing so much less of him lately.

About seventeen dishes later, Emma and I have pushed our stools away from the bar, as if we're begging for mercy and distance is the only way they can express it. We try to finish the green tea ice cream in front of us but have to moan each bite down.

When we leave the restaurant, Emma reaches out to squeeze my hand, and I feel like I've been fully forgiven, like the night has done what I wanted it to. "I wish more places were like this," she says a moment later. "Like, forget what *I* want. You're the expert. Shove a bunch of food in my face and then I'll tell you what I liked best."

I laugh, pull her closer to me. We're not in a particularly pretty part of downtown Seattle, but the night feels perfect. It's moments like these when people say stupid, rushed things to each other. Instead I bring our clasped hands up to my mouth and kiss each of her knuckles.

"So, my dad's coming into town next weekend," Emma says on the labored walk back to the harbor. "Some special event thing that he wants me to come to. He's receiving an award, I think. Or maybe cooking for someone important. He's the worst phone-mumbler, so I don't actually have any idea what it's for."

I laugh. "That's cool that he wants you to come, though. Do you get to see him much?"

"No, so it's cool that he invited me. Except..." She sighs. "I know he's just trying to apologize for last time, and he's gonna be running around schmoozing. I'm gonna be left alone with a bunch of adults feeling uncomfortable and abandoned for three hours."

"That doesn't sound fun."

"No," she says. "It's like my childhood all over again." She's looking down at her feet as she walks, kicking pebbles, running her thumb over mine while we hold hands. "Could you come with me?"

"To your dad's thing?"

"Yeah. He'll be thrilled for the excuse to not actually spend time with me. I'll be thrilled because I'll actually enjoy myself with you there."

I stop walking, step in front of her while hanging on to her hand. I may not have been Dad's biggest fan since I left, but I can't imagine what a whole lifetime of disappointment would feel. "Hell yes," I say.

We kiss, and again I'm completely aware of being exactly where I am: alive, with her.

That night, in my bed, Emma takes my shirt off. It's an incredible feeling, nervousness in this situation. I thought I'd left that in the past. Nervousness was for someone who had not yet lived out fantasies, someone who hadn't seen tragedy, or magic. I'm eager, of course, but anxious. Not just about the ways my body might betray me, but in how I might disappoint Emma, in ways I can't even predict.

We don't have too many more nights like this left. Emma won't be here for long. But I don't feel like rushing myself, and I don't want to rush Emma at all. I let her advance things as she likes and am thankful that she seems to savor the steps in between one thing and the next. I'm thankful for time, however much of it she and I will have. The feel of flesh on flesh, every new part of it. The exquisite sensation of previously unexposed skin, seen for the first time, felt, kissed, held. Nakedness for the first time. Love, if that's what this is.

There's something here that's unlike every other time. Something in her lips and how they fit into mine. The joy of someone who moves when you do. Who knows when to touch, and where, and how, even if there's a lot of fumbling about.

A part of me is aware of my phone ringing somewhere nearby. But *somewhere nearby* probably means not on this mattress, which means it's in a different world, a much less important and far-off one. I press myself harder against Emma, and she gives out a soft moan, beckoning me even closer.

CHAPTER 25

PAN DE MUERTO

4 cups flour

1 tablespoon active dry yeast

½ cup water

3 eggs

3 tablespoons orange zest

½ cup sugar

½ teaspoon salt

¼ cup orange blossom water

¼ cup butter

METHOD:

I wake up, disentangling myself from the bedsheets and my dreams. I get dressed and leave the house even earlier than I have to.

The island feels like it's just for me. The fog, the dawn-hued water, the leaves stirring gently. I cut through the woods, across Emma's meadow. There are considerably fewer fireflies, either because of the time of day or the fading summer. I run my fingers over the tall grass, the dandelions grown wild. Mom still calls every couple days, worried, but she wouldn't if she saw this, if she felt how peaceful and beautiful this place is. I try to take a picture on my phone, but something gets lost in the process. On the screen, it just looks like an empty field. I don't even expect Felix to show, and he doesn't.

Popping back out on the road that leads downtown, I check the time, put my hands in my pockets and slow my pace. At the bakery, Anne the nose-ringed barista throws in a cardamom roll free with my coffee. ("Just came out!" she says.) A jogger smiles at me as I go down the block; a line cook from the diner recognizes me from The Crown and waves. I feel like I'm starting to forget what life in Mexico City was like, what it was like to be me, lost and confused, haunted, missing.

I knock on the side door, sip my coffee while I wait for Chef, look beyond the patio at the majestic view. Once inside, I head for the usual station we've been using for our sessions, but Chef tells me to follow her instead. We go into her office, where she's got music playing softly. A huge coffee mug sits steaming next to the computer. She takes a seat and looks at me over the rim of the mug as she takes a sip. As always, she looks slightly villainous, but today there's something not quite as intimidating about her. Softer, like she can see the same things about the island.

"How familiar are you with our menu?" Chef asks.

I hesitate. "I've looked at it a lot," I say. "And I ate here once before getting hired. I've got the descriptions pretty well memorized."

She leans over, grabs a clipboard and hands it over to me. "Take this, and go sit with a menu for a while. We're gonna run a line check in a bit, so I want you to know what goes in each dish."

"Yes, Chef," I say, probably too enthusiastically. I take a seat on the counter of my dishwashing station, the way Emma does sometimes, poring over the itemized list and then comparing it to the menu. It feels like a backstage pass to meet my favorite musicians, like Chef just handed me a recipe.

I read for who knows how long, like I'm studying for an exam. Then Chef comes by and says, "Don't sit on my counters, asshole. You ready?"

I hop off and follow her to the line. She holds in her hand a box of tiny plastic spoons. "We're going to taste everything," she says. "One spoon per taste and then you throw it out. Every sauce, every oil, every little bit of mise doesn't see a plate until we taste it. A dish can get screwed up way before it hits the pan, and a line check is to make sure that doesn't happen."

Barely containing how much I'm geeking out at this, I nod, try to look serious. Chef grabs a spoon, motions for me to do the same. We start at the garde manger station, where it's mostly veggies, salad dressings, different infused oils.

The cilantro oil is great, the champagne vinaigrette incredible. There's some pickled veggies that maybe have another day or two in them, so Chef tells me to make a note. We go down the line like that, tasting every little thing, double-checking amounts and dates and flavors. Almost all of it tastes unbelievable to me, but Chef yells at me when I think the red wine aioli is good. "Jesus, kid, grow a palate," she says, tossing the deli container in the sink, where I will have to clean it soon. Aside from a few of her outbursts, she's actually really good at explaining what everything should taste like, and why, and how it'll balance with the other components of the dish it belongs in. For once, I do not have to guess at how a dish is made, don't have to guess at how

I might be able to recreate it. I don't even think about what changes I would make, because that feels like blasphemy.

A little while later people start showing up for shift. Elias sees right away what's going on and gives me one of those Felixesque beaming grins. Memo, Lourdes, Isaiah, Vee, Morris—they barely bat an eye. Matt comes in, and I find myself hopeful that the tide has turned, that he's done being a dick.

But the first thing he says is "What the hell, Chef? You're taking the dishwasher on line checks? What's with the special treatment?"

Everyone goes quiet, shares looks like they know shit's about to go down again. Chef, though, doesn't even look up. She chuckles. "When you have your own kitchen, you can decide how to run it, Matt. Until then, just do your job and don't worry about my choices."

"No offense, Chef, but the kid's been here for, like, a month. I've been here for over a year."

"And that entitles you to what, Matt?" Chef says, tossing another tasting spoon into a nearby trash bin.

Matt seems taken aback. He stammers, looks around at the kitchen as if asking for support, but everyone's minding their own business. "I'm just saying, Chef…" He trails off.

"No, Matt, you're just whining." She turns to me and says, "We need another ten pounds of bacon—write it down," effectively ending the conversation. When I finish writing the note, she grabs the clipboard from me and then walks away.

Matt's already turned his back, but I can tell he's fuming. Every move he makes is angry, even tying on his apron and washing his hands at the sink. It feels like I've got a noose around my neck again. I'm terrified that this is all he needs to give it a nice solid yank, watch me choke.

I keep going out during my shift to the floor, making excuses so I can see if he's still pissed, if I'm in danger of getting told on. At one point I see him walk out the side door with a cigarette in his hand, so I run over to Roberto and tell him I'm going to take a break. When I push open the door, Matt's smoking with his back against the wall. He sees me and exhales with a groan, a puff of smoke escaping in my direction. "What do you want?"

I hesitate, not knowing exactly why I came here chasing after him. Then I think of Felix, his unabashed honesty.

"Look, Matt, I don't know why you hate me. I don't know what I did to you. If what you wanted was to see me suffering, trust me, I've had my share." I take a deep breath. Everything that I've escaped is coming back with these words, the mere acknowledgment of suffering bringing it back. I close my eyes, trying to find the rest of what I wanted to say. "I don't know what you've been through, so I won't pretend to know that I've lost more. If you want to keep giving me shit about being a Fake-xican or whatever, I won't complain. But please don't tell Chef about me and Emma. Don't take this away from me."

He takes a slow drag from his cigarette. I can't tell if he's smiling or not. He holds his breath for so long that I feel like whole meals were cooked during the span. A whole new set of customers were seated during his breath.

Finally, he exhales, no Felix in the smoke. "I don't hate anybody, man." He tucks one of his tattooed arms beneath the other, ashes the cigarette onto the ground. Little gray specks of ash saunter away in the breeze before they even hit the ground, as if the island is carrying them away. "You're a weird dude," he says, shaking his head. Then he stubs his cigarette out and walks back inside.

CHAPTER 26
MOM'S SPAGHETTI BOLOGNESE

6 stewed tomatoes

1 onion, diced

4 cloves garlic, minced

1 bunch basil leaves

1 pound ground beef

½ cup red wine

¼ cup parmesan cheese

2 tablespoons red pepper flakes

1 tablespoon oregano

2 bay leaves

3 tablespoons olive oil

Splash of balsamic vinegar

METHOD:

It's late afternoon, in between lunch and dinner service. I'm facing a mountainous heap of dirty dishes, and over the sound of my spray hose I can hear the kitchen clamoring. Out of the corner of my eye I notice someone poking their head in.

It's Emma's lovely face. She's somewhat stoic, as she tries to be when we're in the restaurant and her mom might be lurking. I can always spot a little glimmer in her eyes, though, meant only for me. It makes me want to rip my apron off and take her to the lake, watch her swim, read, watch the world become secondary to her, its beauty just a backdrop. "Um, Carlos, someone's here to see you."

The first thing that crosses my mind is that Emma's making up some cover to sneak me away for a few minutes. I peel my gloves off and hang up my apron, and then I follow her out of the kitchen and into the empty dining room, where bussers and servers are seated at a table, folding napkins. Out of habit, I look beyond them to the patio, the golden light of the sun drawing out the shadows of the chairs outside. What a world.

When I turn my head, Emma is holding the front door open, and I still think for a moment that she wants to take me somewhere, until I see Mom standing outside. I freeze, my brain trying to wrap itself around the fact of her presence.

Emma gives me a little smile, while Mom looks like she's about to cry. She's wringing her hands nervously, and a few tourists are walking past, looking into the restaurant curiously. Emma tells them that we're still closed and then puts a hand on my shoulder before closing the door behind me.

It's so bright outside compared to the fluorescent lighting of the kitchen that it takes a moment for my eyes to adjust. "Mom, what are you doing here?"

She wraps me in a tight hug, and I'm pretty sure I feel tears on my neck. "If you ever greet me like that again, I don't care how old you are, I'm giving you a spanking."

I laugh. "You've never spanked me."

"Oh, trust me, I feel like doing it now." She pulls back and wipes at the tears on her cheeks. Then she breaks out into a smile.

I can't believe how long it's been since I saw her. It's the longest I've been apart from my parents my entire life. Still, I can't resist looking over my shoulder into the restaurant to see who might be watching. It's so strange to see her here.

"Can we go somewhere to talk?"

I hesitate. "I'm working."

She looks like she's about to cry again. Rummaging through her purse, she pulls out one of those miniature packs of tissues and blows her nose a couple of times, and then she crumples the tissue in her hand. Spotting the bench, she walks over and takes a seat. I follow her.

We sit quietly for a while, Mom looking around as she occasionally dabs at her eyes. "Pretty town." Then her eyes flick forward to the Provecho sign. "I've been hating this place ever since I found out you were here," she says. "I even left it some bad reviews online."

I chuckle. "Why?"

She turns and gives me a heavy look. "Oh, please. You know." When I don't say anything, she looks away. "It took my baby away from me." A family walks by, comically eating ice cream, happy, careless. I watch them uncomfortably, aware of the time that I've spent away from the sink, the work piling up. Aware, too, of Mom thinking about what to say. I can practically hear her mind whirring. Mine's still wrapping itself around her presence. It's so unexpected, as if I haven't told her where I am, as if I've been hiding out from a whole other world.

Felix's absence weighs heavy in our silence.

"You know, I've caught your dad a few times looking at the satellite images of this very street. He tries to hide it, clicks out of it as if I've caught him looking at…" Thankfully, she doesn't finish the thought. "I can see how the stress of you leaving has affected him. He can't sleep." She turns to look at me, puts a hand on my forearm. "Please just come home. We can talk about everything else once we get back. But we want you to come back."

Of course. I should have guessed this was coming as soon as I saw her. They don't want another Felix on their hands. They don't care about how well I'm doing, how happy I am here. My first reaction is to just stand up and leave, go back to the kitchen where I belong.

But it's Mom here. She flew all the way to Needle Eye to talk to me, and I've missed the hell out of her. The least I can do is stick around and listen.

"Please, Carlos. We miss you. You don't know how much this is affecting your dad."

"You're right, I don't," I say, rage bubbling up. It's been easy to forget how I felt when I left, but their attempt to guilt me brings it all back to mind. "He doesn't ever bother to call, does he? Not that I'm surprised, after the things he said about Felix in his stupid little speech, and before I left."

She reaches into her purse again and grabs another tissue. "You don't understand. Your father doesn't show his emotions well."

"Oh, I'd say he does a damn fine job of showing how he feels." I stand up, ready to end the conversation. "I'm sorry, Mom. I miss you, and I wish it didn't have to be like this. But I can't leave. Did you guys not notice how badly I was doing back home? Could you not see me disappearing right under your fucking noses?" I hold up my hands, knowing I'm making zero sense, but I'm not able to stop. "Look at how much better I'm doing here! I can feel every moment I'm a part of now. I'm not thinking of the future or the lack of one. I'm happy!" I'm shouting. I take a breath to calm down. "You want to take this away from me?" I say, much softer.

Mom lowers her head, and it hurts me to see that this fresh new batch of tears is without a doubt my fault. But I'm not going to unravel everything I've built for myself here because Mom's sad or because Dad's Googling stuff out of guilt. I take a breath or two, lower my voice.

"I hope Dad feels better. I really do. And if he wants to call and talk or if he decides to come visit, that's great." I sigh, realizing how many people passing by are doing little double takes, interested in the sidewalk drama. It's been too long, I should go back inside. "This is my life now. This is what I want for myself. And I'm not just going to step away from all of it because Dad's guilt is chewing him up."

I walk back to the restaurant, open the door, turn back to look at Mom, who's trying to contain her mascara from running. "It's nice to see you again. I'm sorry you wasted your time coming here." Then I step back inside, letting the door slam behind me.

CHAPTER 27
TUNA THREE WAYS

1:

3 ounces sashimi-grade ahi tuna

4 tablespoons toasted sesame seeds

½ small cucumber, spiraled

1 roasted Scotch bonnet pepper

1 clove garlic

3 tablespoons ponzu sauce

3 tablespoons basil leaves

2:

3 ounces sashimi-grade ahi tuna

2 tablespoons Cajun seasoning (thyme, cayenne, paprika, garlic, onion)

½ cup cauliflower florets

1 cup veggie stock

1 sprig fresh thyme

1 clove garlic

1 teaspoon lemon oil

3:

3 ounces sashimi-grade ahi tuna

2 tablespoons chili ancho aioli

2 teaspoons Mexican chimichurri

1 flour tortilla

berry

METHOD:

It's been a week.

I met up with Mom for dinner once before she left, but she kept looking at me with tears in her eyes, like I'd told her I was never going to see her again. We ate quietly at a place down the street from Provecho, avoiding all sorts of elephants in the room.

If guilt comes knocking (it does), I have plenty with which to keep it at bay: the kitchen, Emma, the knowledge that Dad's at fault. The electric lake, fireflies, impossible full moons. It was hard to see Mom take things so hard, but she should have known that I wasn't just going to come running back home. Hasn't she noticed how how much more present I am, how the island has given me back my full self? Felix makes a few appearances over the week, playing in the clouds, swimming in a sauce, but he doesn't say much.

I wake up on another day off, as early as any other day. Elias is downstairs making coffee. "Hey, man. I thought you had the day off today."

"Still have a training session with Chef," I say.

"Always at it," Elias responds, opening the fridge and grabbing some eggs. "You doing anything with the day off? Sleeping?"

"Going into the city with Emma. Her dad's in town for some event thing. She wanted me to go with."

"That's cool," Elias says. "Getting pretty serious, huh?"

I shrug, play it cool, though the fact that Elias is even asking makes my stomach flop around with giddiness and nerves that he isn't the only one who's noticed.

I leave the house with a good-bye, my knife tucked under my arm. Sunrise, the fog reaching out for its usual morning embrace with the island. The forest is a dream to walk around in at this hour, and I'm still good on time, so I veer off the road. The paths that once seemed only visible to Emma are now familiar to me. I can spot where the grass has been matted by our footsteps; I recognize minute differences in the trees pointing the right way, like a map in invisible ink.

In the meadow, I pick out a handful of the orange berries, peeling them carefully and popping them in my mouth throughout my walk. I can't help thinking of how I would cook with them, and though I vaguely remember Emma saying something about wanting to keep them a secret, I think maybe she'd be okay if I was the one who cooked with them. I keep a few in my pocket, just on a whim.

My lessons with Chef have varied lately. One day, she will put me back on omelets; the next she'll tell me to roast a whole chicken, peel potatoes, sharpen every knife in the kitchen. Whatever the lesson is, I carry it with me the rest of the day, repeating the motions in my head so that the next time I'll be better at it, faster, more precise.

I arrive at the restaurant, the tang of the berry still on my lips. Chef opens up, leads me in. Today, she heads straight for the walk-ins. The excitement of stepping inside has not dissipated. The instant chill, the sensory overload of all those colors, all those flavors waiting to be drawn out. Making sure I appreciate that first step into the walk-in is my nod to Felix, how he would want me to treat this place with reverence.

I look around for him, some acknowledgment that this is true. But it's just me and Chef. She chews her lip, looks at me like she doesn't have a plan or is second-guessing the one she already had. There's a brief moment where I can see Emma in her face, and it freaks me out a little. It passes quickly, because she tosses the clipboard at me and I have to catch it before it hits me in the nose.

Save for the far-off whirr of whatever engine keeps the room we're in cold, it's dead quiet. I'm not quite sure what's going on yet and am still a little scared to say anything to Chef unprompted. After way too long, my skin pinpricked because of the cold, Chef finally speaks up. "A prep garde manger position is opening up. I thought a little test for you would be fun. You've been working hard, both with me in the mornings and doing what you're paid to do. Your staff meals are good, but those don't really mean shit. It's a little soon, but let's see what else you can do."

My heart quickens.

"I need specials for the day." She crosses her arms in front of her chest and nods to the clipboard. "You get to come up with one of them. If I like it enough, maybe I'll put it on the menu." I want to run and hug her. All those early mornings, those double shifts made harder by the extra work—this is what they were for. Elias was right. "And," Chef adds, "I'll promote you to the line."

I can't help but smile at the clipboard in my hands. My mind's already going to what I could make, using the flashes of ingredients that I can see on the menu. Braised short ribs with mole colorado and a corn puree. Lamb vindaloo pizza on naan crust, topped with cilantro chutney. I'm not throwing this opportunity away.

"I want to see a detailed recipe with exact quantities of every ingredient you'll use per portion. Make sure we've got enough for at least the day. I don't want to eighty-six it before we're even setting up for dinner."

"Yes, Chef. Thank you, Chef."

She nods and heads toward the door.

"Um, Chef?" I ask, remembering all of Chef's outbursts, thinking there's gotta be some sort of catch to this. "What if you don't like it?"

"Then I don't make it and you don't get the job, genius," she says, not slowing down. "And I don't let you cook again for a year. You have until the prep cooks show up."

Having imagined this scenario plenty of times before, I expect to feel like I'm in one of those cooking shows I've watched over the last few years. I wait for the surge of adrenaline, the scamper to the pantry. I expect a giant timer to show up over my head.

Instead, what I do is stand there in the middle of the walk-in, looking at the produce, studying the clipboard, suddenly impervious to the cold. I check the time. I wasn't expecting to be here long today, but there are hours to go before I have to meet up with Emma and take the ferry into Seattle. Plenty of time to just think up a dish and explain it to Chef, maybe even cook up an example the way I'm envisioning. Emma's probably still sleeping. I put my phone on a nearby shelf to see what's hiding in the back.

I find a scrap of paper, write a bunch of notes to myself about the ingredients, leave the walk-in. I spend about an hour on the patio, tapping a pen against the table, urging brilliance from myself.

I'm surprised but relieved to look up and see Felix at the table, eating a plateful of chilaquiles, tendrils of steam rising from the dish as he scoops forkfuls into his mouth. I was starting to worry that we weren't going to get a chance to say good-bye. "How about some of these?" he says.

I give him a look. "Please."

"Okay, chilaquiles with, like, foie gras and a mango demi-glace and truffle shavings?"

"You're just throwing as many Food Network words out there as you can."

He chuckles to himself and takes another bite, following it up by running a piece of bread through the sauce on the plate. "What about some tacos? We never found the perfect al pastor. You could make that."

The suggestion stirs a thought. I hold up a finger, though asking for quiet has never worked with Felix, dead or alive.

There's a big hunk of prime ahi tuna that has barely been touched and needs to go. It might have been a provider's mistake, or maybe people just aren't ordering the tuna this week. An image pops into my head, the fish done three different ways, kind of like the salmon at the sushi place the other night but not quite. I lean over my sheet of paper, separate it into three columns.

I look up, trying to decide what else the dish would need. Felix is still eating. He's got his mouth full, and he tries to offer a suggestion but ends up choking on his words and spitting out little droplets of sauce all over me.

"Gross."

Behind me, I hear the door from the restaurant open up. Elias comes out, and when I turn back Felix is gone. "Hey, man. What are you still doing here? I thought you were peacing out today."

I tell him about Chef's challenge for the day. "Is that it?" Elias asks, motioning to the paper that I have been scribbling on all morning.

I hand it over, mostly confidently. Elias nods as he reads, like it's a song he can hear in his head. "Butter in the puree?"

"Yeah, right?"

Elias nods. Felix reappears, chewing on his nails, scrunching up his nose. "This guy to the rescue again?"

I roll my eyes while Elias is still focused on the page.

"Sounds pretty good, man. The taco needs something else. Some acid, maybe. The chimichurri's good, but you need something that'll make it pop."

"Yeah, I was thinking that," I say. Just then I feel the weight in my pocket; the berries only Emma and I know about. That tang of theirs would be perfect. I wouldn't have to do a thing to them, a couple of thin slices on top, or maybe chopped in with the tuna itself, along with the aioli, so that they're in every bite.

"Anything else you can think of?"

Elias rubs his hand around his mouth, along his goatee. "Hope you're not thinking of using packaged tortillas. We don't even have them."

"Yeah, I know. I was gonna ask Lourdes if she could make them."

"Good call." Elias reads through a couple more times and then hands back the sheet of paper. "Not bad at all, man."

At that moment, Chef steps outside. "Carlos. Were you gonna take the rest of the fucking day?"

I stand up, scribble one last addition to the recipe. "Sorry. I'm ready." I walk over to her, list held out. She stays there in the doorway, reading. I'm standing in the sun, she in the shade. Behind us, Elias types a message on his phone.

Chef looks up from reading. "What's this?" She's pointing at where I just scribbled the word *berry*.

I pull one out of my pocket, show her. She grabs it, examines it for a second. "What is it?"

"I'm not sure. It grows here. In the woods."

She digs her fingernail into the skin, peels it open, smells it, peels farther so she can get a taste. Chewing, she gives me a weird look. I wonder if I should feel guilty, but before I can linger on the thought, Chef says, "Follow me." I look over my shoulder before following her inside, see Elias raise his eyebrows at me.

Inside, people are setting up. They're looking over their lists, checking their supplies. Lourdes has atole going. I can smell it as soon as I step in. They're sharpening knives, arguing over what music to play, talking about last night's bar outing. Ah, to be in the midst of all of this.

We enter the prep kitchen, where Lourdes is indeed ladling out atole into Styrofoam cups. Memo and Isaiah are sleepy-eyed, both leaning over to look at their mise. "How you doing on onions?" Isaiah says. Memo slides a deli container his way without answering. Matt's in there too, leaning back against the wall, looking at his phone.

"Alright," Chef says, quietly to me. "This looks good. We just have to figure out where you can actually cook without pissing everyone off and fucking up the whole day."

I see Matt look up from his phone and can swear he's tuning in, that he's heard every word. I hope Chef tells him to fuck off again, to mind his own business. If he finds out she's letting me cook a special, I can't imagine he'll keep my secret about Emma any longer. He'll sabotage everything.

To my dismay, Chef just calls out: "Carlos has a dish for us. Might go on today's menu. Don't let him get in the way, but I need you to give him a hand. He'll tell you what he needs from you."

Everyone exchanges a glance. Isaiah leans in to take a closer look at his prep list, mutters a curse under his breath.

I can taste the disappointment. If everyone's busy, I'll be screwed. The ingredients available will be different tomorrow. What if I can't come up with something else that she likes? I'm so close now, and I don't want it ruined by the off chance that someone has too much shit to do.

"Just let him cook, Chef. He can use my station if he needs it."

I look up. I think I know who said that, but it can't be right. It sounded like Matt.

"You sure? You're set for service?"

"I'm set, Chef. Don't need a burner at all. Just a counter for a board and a knife." He stands up straight, sticking his hands in his pockets, his tattooed sleeves showing. "I'm all for testing the kid."

"Great," Chef says, always happy when things run smoothly. She turns to me. "Just one portion right now. Don't waste any of my food until I decide it's good enough. Let me know when you're done, and don't take your sweet time." She walks out the door while I'm still making eye contact with Matt, not sure what's going on.

Everyone looks away, the flurry of prep hour returns, flames sizzling and knives coming down on cutting boards.

"Thanks, man," I tell Matt, approaching his station. "You didn't have to do that."

He keeps his eyes on his phone, as if I'm still not worth his full attention. "You give me the creeps, man. But I see you working." He gives the slightest of nods. "Do your thing."

The next hour is a blur. Lourdes helps out with the tortilla and gets a small saucepan full of veggie stock going for the cauliflower waiting to be pureed. Matt roasts a single red Scotch bonnet pepper for the basil tuna's topper sauce, which I throw into a food processor with lemongrass and garlic. I scoop that into a ramekin and then push it aside until I'm ready to plate.

The steps, of course, are enjoyable. Seasoning the tuna and then searing the pieces, watching the flesh change colors like a magic trick. Cutting into the fish and seeing that beautiful almost-maroon in the center. Dipping a tasting spoon into the cauliflower puree and, even though I try to set the bar of expectations high for myself, being blown away by the flavor. Taking a single berry out of my pocket, rinsing it clean, using my gyuto to chop it into tiny cubes, its tangy aroma releasing into the kitchen.

There's something special about plating a dish for the first time. Making something in real life match what was in your mind's eye. I use one of those long, rectangular platters with three separate compartments. The colors are almost exactly what I was envisioning. The darkness of the sesame crust and the ponzu in the first one, contrasted with the bright green cucumber beneath and the bright red sauce on top. The cauliflower-thyme puree in the middle dish, perfectly off-white and flecked with green, the orange Cajun exterior, the drizzle of lemon oil over all of it. And the taco. The perfect spice of the aioli, the cilantro smelling like home.

It transports me to the Night of the Perfect Taco. Felix leaning in to take a bite, chewing thoughtfully. It was late, maybe the second-to-last stop. I felt drunk off the night, exhausted. Felix picked up a chunk of salsa-covered pineapple that had spilled and popped it into his mouth. "So, how's this one rate?" I asked. "Perfect?"

He didn't answer right away, just looked around. Who knows where we were. Some hole in the wall, two tables and a counter, paint peeling mid-meal. Across the street there was a cantina, and we could hear a group of drunk dudes singing. "Not much is," he'd said. Another smirk, one of the last I saw the real him make.

I focus back on what I'm doing. I arrange the pieces of tuna exactly how I had pictured them and place a basil leaf, a sprig of thyme and a cilantro leaf respectively atop each piece of tuna. It looks perfect. Everything tastes perfect on its own when I try it, and I feel this surge of excitement when I think of how good it will be all together.

There's a small crowd gathered when I tell Chef I'm ready. They pretend they're doing their own thing, but everyone focuses at least one sense on us. Isaiah is looking over his shoulder while he stirs something. Memo's actually leaning toward us to try to hear better. I wish Emma were around to see this, and I quickly check the time on the wall clock to make sure I'm still fine to catch the ferry.

Usually, no comment from Chef is a good thing. She can think of criticisms fairly easily. Compliments, not so much. She takes a bite of the basil tuna, making sure to get some of the sauce and the cucumber in the bite, dragging it across the ponzu reduction. She chews, nods, says nothing. A wipe of the mouth, a sip of water. Then she uses her fork to cut into the Cajun tuna, scooping the puree up this time and again dragging it through the lemon oil. Chew, nod, nothing. A wipe of the mouth, a sip of water. She looks closely at the taco and then grabs the tortilla and folds it. The lean-in is so familiar to me, I can't help but think of Felix, replay every lean-in he made that night before it came to an end. I shake the memory from my head, bring myself back to the present.

On the first bite of the taco, Chef closes her eyes. She chews, maybe slower than usual. Was that a sigh? Was that a fucking sigh?

I hold my breath. Oxygen is actively leaving my lungs without my permission. Chef chews. Swallows. Sets the taco down on the plate. She looks like she's going to speak, but she reaches for her water and her napkin. Oxygen doesn't exist anymore in my world.

"We've got a special," Chef says without much fanfare. "Good job." She reaches for the taco again, takes another bite. "You better have written down exactly how to fucking do this one, or I'll never forgive you."

I smile. "Yes, Chef."

"Good." She feels some aioli on the side of her mouth and uses her finger to lick it up. "Teach these guys how to make what I ate. A little more butter in the puree. Don't overdo the spicy shit for the first guy." She takes her last bite of taco and then shakes her head, and I swear I hear her go "mmm" as she walks away.

Still plenty good on time, I spend the next hour before doors open teaching the guys on the line how to make the components. Not that I really have to teach them much. They all know how to read my recipe and execute each element better than I can, but these guys treat the creator of a dish with a certain reverence, taking no artistic liberties, though they're fully qualified to make adjustments and infinitely more experienced than I am.

It's not a bad feeling.

Then doors open, and the waitstaff is starting to offer my dish as one of the day's specials. I'm not technically on the clock and don't need to wash dishes, but I hang around with my apron on, helping out in any little way I can. I don't want to step away, don't want to miss any of this.

I find the exact spot where I can stand out of the way but still in plain view of the line, watching my dish come together over and over again. I watch Chef call out from the pass, "Order fire, two tuna specials, table seven."

Lunch service stretches into dinner. I'm glued to my spot in between the sink and the wall. Elias comes around laughing, saying, "You're still here?" And I check the time and see I'm still fine. Since I'm not in a rush, I offer to peel the berries. I watch the stash I brought with me—stroke of luck—dwindle.

I watch Vee butcher the tuna down to nothing. I set the garnish, drizzle the sauce. I know time is running late, but I also see the portions disappear, and in their wake my future at Provecho sets its roots. I've never been prouder of anything in my life, and I want to see this through. I know I'm cutting it close, but at seven o'clock the dish gets eighty-sixed. Elias and Memo give me fist bumps as I hang up my apron. I think Chef almost smiles.

I run into the walk-in, where I now realize I left my cell phone at the start of the day. Emma called exactly once, twenty minutes ago. It dawns on me that our ferry leaves in ten minutes. I say a quick good-bye to anyone who can hear me shout it out, and I bolt out the back door. It's beautiful out. The sky is golden. Not just tinted by a golden sunset, but entirely golden, as if that's a normal color for the sky. Not much is perfect in this world, but this isn't far off.

I sprint, thankful I brought a button-up shirt with me, trying to keep it free from wrinkles in my clutched hand. Things don't go wrong here, so I have faith in the island's ability to do whatever it wants to time in order to help me out.

I've apparently forgotten that happiness is a knot easily untied. I arrive at the dock eleven minutes late, slipping into the shirt even though I'm about to sweat through it. I can see that there's no one here anymore, and still I'm hanging onto some idiotic notion that this place does not adhere to the laws of nature. The ferry is fading into the horizon, steam billowing up and joining the golden sky. Stupidly, I look around the docks for her, phone pressed against my ear, saying "Fuck" every time it rings. It's like burning a piece of food, this feeling. Like I know no matter what I do, the mistake is done; there's no going back.

I know without the shadow of a doubt that things are useless, calling Emma again is pointless, except maybe to say how much of an idiot I am. No answer. Maybe she's already out of service range. Maybe she's pissed at me right now. Maybe she always will be. I check the upcoming ferry schedule and realize with a sinking feeling in my stupid gut that there aren't any more tonight.

Night falls much faster than it has any right to. It gets dark in between phone calls, from one dial tone to the next. The stars are barely out. There are no clouds out to cover them up, but they're hardly twinkling, as if they're only showing up for a job they hate.

I stand there a reasonably long time, calling her, texting her apologies. I consider swimming to catch up with the ferry. I consider swimming all the way to Seattle, faster than the boat, so that when Emma steps off she sees me and I can pretend I left too early. I call again. The night gets darker. I stare at the horizon, unable to do a damn thing about it.

CHAPTER 28
NOTHING

METHOD:

The worst night of my life was all sobs and sirens. This one is much quieter.

It's a slow dark walk through town back home, though halfway through I veer off into the woods. There's nothing but the squish of my shoes on damp leaves, branches brushing against my clothes. My mind is desperate to find some explanation that doesn't make me an asshole, coupled with the horrible feeling in my stomach (right above my stomach, actually, where shittiness is felt). I get too distracted and lose myself. I'm far off from any path that Emma might have showed me, pushing aside branches blindly. The moon should still be bright enough to see where I'm going, but it's nowhere to be found. Even the fireflies are nowhere to be seen, perhaps prompted by my behavior to announce summer's end.

Nothing looks familiar. I can't find the meadow or the hill with the view. I can't even find the lake. The thrill of the day in the kitchen is buried deep beneath shame and regret and a general mix of emotional awfulness. I'm not sure what time it is when I get back home, since I call Emma so many times that my phone dies along the way.

I flop onto my bed, knowing sleep won't come easy. The sun rises almost instantly, the world decreeing that I do not deserve to rest. Emma hasn't responded, except for in the millions of imagined conversations I've had while lying down. My alarm rings, pulling me out of bed. I feel half-dead, like I'm disappearing again.

All throughout the twenty-minute walk to the restaurant, my brain continues to point out how much I've screwed up. How Emma might be a forgiving person but definitely not when it comes to playing second fiddle to the kitchen. The betrayal, my mind tells me, started with the berry. As soon as I picked it up, I was telling the universe I care more about food than about her. And I want to argue but a) my brain is right, and b) my brain is one of those assholes who won't even listen to arguments.

Felix doesn't show his face either (any version of it), which is a damn shame because I could use some of his platitudes right about now. Something about second chances or losing track of time, the distractions of a dream coming true.

Even as I'm thinking this, I know what Felix would say, the real version of him. He'd say that I didn't need to stick around in the kitchen the entire shift in order to stroke my own ego. I could have had my little moment and then left on time. Felix would have said all this calmly, softly, the way difficult-to-hear-but-wise things are always said.

I want to yell at my brain to shut up. On Main Street, everyone is having another summer day, taking their little jogging trips, getting breakfast before another day at the beach. They look like they're basking in the sun already, even though the sun has barely risen and fog is smothering the light before it can really reach the people on Needle Eye Island. I grab my phone, desperately hoping all of this will be resolved with a miracle. I was confused about the day or something. Emma will text and say, Oops, phone died. Still on for our date tomorrow? Or maybe: No big deal. Had a pretty good time with my dad anyway. How was your day?

But there's nothing there, no relief, which means I'll be thinking about all of this on a loop all morning. Emma's working today, I know, and I should at least be able to sneak away long enough to apologize in person.

I knock on the back entrance to Provecho. Sue opens the door and tells me that she and Chef are taking inventory and to go wait in the office. I take a seat and my stomach shoots out of my gut and starts pacing around the room, muttering to itself. God, what an awful feeling to have fucked up this badly.

Chef has me wallowing in it for what feels like an hour, just sitting there with no distractions except for the wall calendar sprawled with notes that I can't read from where I am. If only I'd left an hour earlier yesterday. Hell, twenty minutes earlier. If only I'd been a decent person, appreciated the luck granted to me.

The wall clock ticks as loudly as humanly possible, just rubbing every passing second in my face, both the ones I wasted last night and the ones I'm forced to sit through right now. Why the hell can't time be reversed, mistakes unmade?

Finally, Chef comes in, heading straight for her chair behind the desk. It's (undeserved) relief to no longer be alone with my thoughts, to merely have another person's presence in the room.

Chef sits down, not wearing her whites. She's got a stray streak of black ink on the back of her hand, the pen it probably came from tucked behind her ear. She sits quietly for a while, looking at me longer and more inquisitively than she usually does. There's something in that look that feels off. Almost like sadness or pity, instead of the usual disappointment-tinted impatience. Am I that transparent?

She sighs, and I'm momentarily thankful that I've got something other than Emma to think about. Then she says, "First things first, that dish last night was great. Incredible, actually." She pauses to pull the pen from behind her ear and twirl it between her fingers like a drumstick. "For someone with no experience, especially. There wasn't anything crazy hard to make, technique-wise, but the creativity is… well, frankly, enviable. Lots of people would give up their technique for your ability to think up dishes. The techniques you'll pick up with experience. I have no doubt you will, 'cause you work hard. You've proven that much." The clock's ticking seems to have been turned down a few notches, volume-wise.

Chef twirls the pen a little longer, taps it twice on the palm of her hand and then tosses it on to the desk. "You've got a rare thing going for you, that combination of hard work and talent. It'll make you a great cook one day."

I want to smile, but Chef's tone is confusing me. She looks tenser than usual; her body language doesn't match anything she's saying. "I have no doubt about that," she continues. "I see that potential in you, and I get pleasure in seeing potential realized. Give it some time and you'll be able to do whatever you want in a kitchen. It just won't be in mine."

For a long moment, I'm sure I've misheard that last part.

"I told you to stay away from Emma not because I'm overprotective or territorial but because I know what happens when people like us love the kitchen." She sighs again, slumps in her chair a little with her head leaned back so she's looking straight up. "I don't even care that you went against my wishes. I was willing to overlook your sneaking around because I wanted to see you do great things and because Emma seemed happy. But what you did last night was unforgivable."

I start to stammer an excuse, or an apology, anything that'll undo all of this. Chef promptly interrupts.

"You broke her heart, Carlos." She says it loudly, like she wants it to sink in. She reaches for her pen again, starts tapping it against the palm of her hand. I swear I can see the words leave her mouth, and I have to fight not to pluck them out of the air and shove them back in, make them unspoken again. "I'll be sad to see you go, because I really do believe you'll do great things. But I care about my daughter more."

A pause. And then:

"You're fired."

She sighs one last time, sits up straight, pushes away from the desk. Just like that, she's done with me. Way before I'm ready to be done with her, with Emma, with this restaurant. I want to cling to this chair, to this island, to yesterday. Then Chef stands up, shakes my hand and, in that motion, pries my fingers away from all of it.

CHAPTER 29
ISLA FLOTANTE

4 eggs
2 tablespoons cornstarch
6 cups whole milk
1 ⅔ cup sugar
2 tablespoons rum
1 cinnamon stick
1 teaspoon vanilla extract
½ teaspoon salt
1 tablespoon lime juice

METHOD:

Another lonely walk across the island.

I think of the curious English term, *silver lining*. What shitty thing, exactly, was supposed to have been lined in silver? Again, I look for Felix to appear and enlighten me, since finding silver linings was pretty much his life philosophy. But he's nowhere to be found.

Okay, possible silver lining: I am now free to date Emma. Out in the open, hand-in-hand kind of stuff. I could just work at another restaurant. Give it time, like Chef said. Keep practicing fancy shit at home, learn all of Emma's favorites and cook them for her.

I pass by all the tourists. I walk through the familiar forest paths, hoping that if they regain some sort of glimmer it'll mean there's a chance for forgiveness. When I see no evidence of that, I look for my brother. In the trees, the wind, blades of grass, pebbles, insects, in the sunbeams that are cutting through the leaves.

It's just me and the island, though. Crickets and cicadas, the occasional sound of wheels grinding against the pavement, on the way to the ferry or emerging from it. Horn blasts and the ocean gently lapping at the shore, locals at the lake.

I drag my feet across the road. Only now do I realize that I've felt like this before. In the months after Felix's death, when I was marching my way toward a future Dad imagined for me. It was dread. I felt it then, and I feel it now as I shuffle across the road toward Emma's house.

I sigh and step up to the door. I ring the doorbell. Why do these things always sound so normal when nothing else feels that way? *The inanimate things in our lives should reflect our joys and sorrows,* I think. *They should act accordingly.* I remember thinking this the day of Felix's funeral too. In the elevator on the way back home. How normally it functioned, whirring and groaning and lighting up the way it always did, as if the world was no different.

The chime happily echoes throughout the house. My stomach turns to stone and settles in my gut. The rest of my insides take the hint and decide to calcify too. Nothing happens. No one answers. I call her again, but, useless fucking thing, it doesn't get me anywhere closer to her.

So I sit. I wait. I wallow in the awful feeling I've brought upon myself. I think of nothing but what I can say to her. I go hungry, because I deserve it.

At midnight, I hear voices approaching. I've got my forehead resting on my knees; my lower back is so stiff it's as if I've spent a couple of shifts at the sink. I look up, see shadows stretched out on the asphalt. They turn the corner, ten or so of them. When they get close, I spot Emma at the front. Some tourist-looking dude in khaki shorts and a striped polo has his arm around her shoulder. The whole group smells of booze and joy.

When our eyes meet, she doesn't burst into tears or demand an explanation. She almost looks bored, like she's been expecting me, and knows exactly what I'm going to say already. Brandy is with her, and she makes quick eye contact with me before leading the group inside.

Emma gives the tourist guy a hand squeeze, says something about seeing him in a bit. I wait until it's just me and her on the porch.

I've familiarized myself with her mannerisms in the last couple months. The slight ways in which she moves her body, the way her facial features contort depending on what she's feeling, the variations in her voice. But it's still only been a couple months. I don't know her well enough to know what she's thinking. This is still so new.

Emma leans her arm against the door frame and her head against her arm and she raises her eyebrows, "Just fucking say it so we can move on with our lives," she says.

"Never again," I say. I wait for more to come bubbling out, but that seems like that's it. I open my mouth, begging for more of an explanation to present itself. Nothing. It feels like I'm reaching to undo time. Emma, understandably, does not look impressed.

"'Never again' what?" Her voice doesn't break at all. She's solid, the exact opposite of me.

"I don't know. I never want to feel this way again."

"Great, a selfish sentiment to explain a selfish act." She sighs, almost exactly like her mom did, wipes at her eyes. "Are we done here? Is that it?"

"No," I say quickly. I feel like throwing up. I feel like entropy, like the toothpaste has been squeezed out of the tube and I'm trying to get it back in. "I mean, I never want to make you feel the way you probably felt last night. The way you must be feeling now. I never again want to…" I trail off lamely when I should be rattling off a list of my grievances. The whole silver-lining thing is not looking good.

"Look, Carlos, I appreciate you coming over here to try to ease your conscience, but you made your choice last night. You chose the kitchen." She stands up a little straighter, looking over my shoulder. Inside the house, I can hear cupboards clattering, glass bottles rattling on granite countertops, people whooping.

"I just lost track of time," I say, in a whimper.

Emma either doesn't hear me or the comment means nothing to her. "My mom chose the kitchen instead of me. My dad chose the kitchen instead of me. You're asking me to let someone else do that to me." Now, finally, she does cross her arms. She definitely seems like she rehearsed some of this, like she gave this speech thought instead of hoping for silver linings, magically unearned happy endings. Her cheeks are flushed with booze and anger, but she knows what she wants to say. I've been sitting here for hours and am still struggling to figure out what my lines should be.

How I wish Felix were around to whisper advice in my ear. "I'm not asking you to," I say. "I know how that sounds. And I'm sorry. I'm so sorry. But last night was not a choice for me. It was just—" I gesture lamely "—a mistake. It's been a crazy couple of months and I'm trying to juggle certain things and maybe my head isn't taking everything well. But I'm trying to figure this new life out, trying to get over Felix, and I made a mistake."

"Don't do that," she says. "Don't blame this on your grief. It's not fair to your brother. You being on Needle Eye? Sure. You spending time with me and the kitchen because it helped you feel better? Yeah, I get that. But last night was not that."

"Okay," I say, my voice breaking, tears gathering at the corners of my eyes. "You're right. But it was still a mistake. A stupid mistake I won't ever make again. You are not less than the kitchen for me."

Emma keeps her arms crossed. If she were wearing glasses I think she might push them up to her head, but she's not wearing them at all. I can picture them folded on her nightstand, in between her glass of water and the lamp she uses to read before going to bed. The tears that have been gathering in my eyes spill now, and I'm not sure if it's out of hope or resignation.

Emma opens her mouth to say something and then changes her mind and looks down at her feet. She combs a loose tress of hair back behind her ear, though the motion doesn't accomplish much. Her arms uncross, fall limp at her sides. "Whatever the reason, Carlos, you chose the kitchen. And that's fine. That's fucking great, actually. You're dedicated. You're passionate. All great things for a chef. And I hope the kitchen helps you with your grief.

"But you made me feel so fucking lonely." She wipes at her eyes again, tears that I'm responsible for. A quiet moment passes, and I know there's still sounds coming from inside the house, but I can barely hear them. It's just me and her. "In the end it doesn't matter," Emma says. "You want to stay here, and I'm leaving for school soon. This wasn't going to last anyway."

I want to argue, want to prove how much she means to me. This is a mistake we can overcome. But all I can do is stand here feeling so empty I'm surprised I'm not just floating away in the breeze. I should tell her I was fired, tell her we don't have to sneak around anymore. I should tell her it was Felix who convinced me the kitchen was more important, tell her exactly what I've been dealing with.

Or I could stand at her door looking at her midsection because I can't handle eye contact, because I know all of those things don't matter and what she said does.

Behind Emma, fireflies light up, the moon shines in full, Felix says nothing.

"You're not second fiddle to the kitchen for me," I say finally, and the way the words leave my mouth it's like they're giving up on my behalf, like they don't even believe in themselves. "You have no idea how much you mean to me." Emma crosses her arms in front of her chest, kicks at a pebble at her feet. There's not another single sound on the entire island. No magic, no ghosts, nothing at all.

Finally, Emma opens her mouth, and it take a long time for the sound to come out. "Take care, Carlos," she says. Then she walks past me, shutting the door behind her.

CHAPTER 30

BOMBA

1 bolillo

1 generous scoop red or green chilaquiles

4 ounces cochinita pibil

1 breaded chicken breast (milanesa)

1 habanero, seeded and sliced

1 tablespoon Cotija cheese

1 tablespoon Mexican crema

METHOD:

This time, I stick to the roads. I can't handle seeing any more magic drained out of this place. I'd kick at pebbles, but it would remind me too much of Emma, and so I just stare at them as I amble by.

What now? There's nothing here for me anymore. There is no cake left, nothing to have or to eat. I could hang around the island and hope for Emma's forgiveness; I could show the persistence that led Chef to hire me. Except Emma didn't seem angry or even disappointed. She seemed like she'd simply moved on. She seemed like she was hurt, but it was as if she'd only nicked herself while chopping vegetables. It was a bit of pain that would pass. She seemed ready to leave the island and forget about me.

Even if I wanted to, I can't return to the life Dad had planned out for me a) because I withdrew my name from the University of Chicago, and going back to Mexico will not undo that, will not just reinstate Dad's plan, and b) how the hell could I, having tasted this life?

So, what now?

I can't even think of where to go right this instant. All the spots I love on the island would just be painful reminders of what I've so quickly lost. It'd be like holding my hand over a fire. I loop around the island a couple of times, from the dock to the boardwalk to downtown, turning around right before I reach Provecho on one end, Emma's street on the other.

An hour or so into this tired circuit, a stray dog starts following me. It's got dark brown fur and is wearing one of those dog-sweaters, which is off-white and threadbare.

"Rough," the dog says, dog-like but not.

"Dude."

"Sorry. Didn't know if you wanted me to try to make you laugh or if you're in a wallowing kind of mood."

"Definitely wallowing," I say, shoving my heads in my pockets.

"You should call Mom. She's good at cheering up people in these situations. She was the reason I didn't try to run away to the woods for a month to record a mopey folk record after my first breakup."

I can tell Felix is still trying to make me laugh, even if I can't find it in me to. At least it does help quiet my thoughts for a moment.

"Well, look at this way, at least you've had the experience of getting fired and getting dumped on the same day," Felix barks.

"Why the hell did you make it sound like a good thing?"

Felix seems to be thinking for a second. "It's like what Emma was saying. How when you experience it at least you know what it feels like. Silver linings."

I don't respond to this. I can't imagine going through the rest of my life (or even the next few days/weeks/whatever) feeling rattled in my gut at the sound of her name. Just like that I'm back in the thought circuit, feeling like an asshole, feeling lost, feeling aimless, feeling the irreversibility of time, how it stupidly just marches onward in one direction.

We reach the Provecho end of Main Street and turn back around. There's a crowd outside the door, hoping for early lunch availability.

"How did everything go to shit so quickly?" Maybe the tourists can hear me talking to the dog, or maybe there is no dog at all. I don't really care either way.

"What can I say? Life's a bitch."

"Felix, shut up with the puns already."

We pass by the bookstore, but I don't want to look at it because it reminds me of Emma. We pass that upper-middle-class-white-people store where I bought my knife; we pass the diner, the bakery, The Crown.

How the hell do people in small towns ever get away from the places that remind them of their sadness? In Mexico City, at least I could easily avoid the fourteen taco stands from the Night of the Perfect Taco. Here, every corner I turn there's something new to remind me of either Emma or the kitchen. We keep walking in loops. A few times Felix goes into a trot or disappears to chase after nearby birds. But he keeps coming back, each time with that near-grin dogs often have and Felix always had.

"Listen," he says one of those times, "I hate to sound like Dad, but

I've got an unsolicited speech to deliver. Is that okay? While we're still moping?"

I grunt. I don't really want hear whatever Felix is about to say, but it'd be more difficult to get into an argument, so I just keep walking.

"This isn't going to help right away. I know that. But sometimes the things we hear when we're not exactly open to hearing them sink in more than the advice we seek ever does." He stares up meaningfully at me, which is a strange look for a chocolate Labrador. "Carlos, you are not dead yet. I know how your brain works. I know how you've been fighting to keep thoughts of death away. This time, it might help to keep it in mind."

Strangely, that queasy existential feeling doesn't sink in now. It's still just gut-wrenching guilt and regret. The road turns darker as a cloud moves in front of the sun.

"This is part of life, brother. Not the best part, granted. But it's part of it. The great thing is that it keeps going. Usually." He offers another stupid Labrador grin, but I don't bite. "Look, this is not the last good thing you will find and enjoy. I know you think I speak in clichés, so here's a good one for you: there are other fish in the sea. There are more girls, more kitchens, more magical places in the world. There is more in store for you, as long as you're alive."

I'm exhausted, not from the walking but from thinking the same thoughts over and over again. I'm tired of the same fear and worry and regret and longing that are gripping my organs and shaking them.

"Remember what I said before you left Mexico? The world is a much bigger place than you realize. You've uncovered another beautiful corner of it. But there's still more. You could go find it."

"Fuck, man, is that your answer to everything?" I'm suddenly shouting. "Just run away?"

"I didn't say 'run away.' I said move on to the next thing."

"You know what, Felix, I think I get it now, why Dad was so pissed at you." I stop walking. We're at the edge of town, where few cars ever pass by. If it looks weird that I'm yelling at a dog, so be it. "You feel a little discomfort, and so you run. That's your resolution, isn't it? That's why you kept moving from place to place? Just leave everything behind, wash your hands of it, move on to the next thing. There's more joy out there, so if sadness comes along, why stick around? Didn't you ever fight for anything?"

Felix sits down on the side of the road, panting. He doesn't say anything, so I keep going.

"That was your entire life philosophy. Take things easy. Escape. Seek out the next adventure. Did you not care about anyone that you met on your travels? Was it really that easy to just leave Mom and Dad and me behind?" Tears build up in my throat, and I pause to catch my breath, wipe away spittle on my lips. "To leave home? How many other people did you leave in the same way, without another thought? If this is what you're here to teach me, I get it now, thanks. You can move on."

A cyclist is approaching, so I pause, waiting for her to speed down the hill out of earshot. When she turns the corner, I feel like I've run out of steam. I'm too tired to yell anymore. "It's not that easy for me,

Felix. I can't just…forget. I can't fathom the idea of leaving this place behind, and even less the idea that I could leave her behind."

Felix keeps panting, looking up at me serenely. "It felt like I was so close," I say. We look at each other, and for a second I'm sure it's really been him this whole time. Not me, not my head. "Why am I still seeing you, man? Why do I have to go through this?"

No longer a dog, just himself now, Felix looks at me, leans back against the air like it's a wall. He thinks for a long while, but it's just us in the dark woods, nothing to track the passing of time. Finally, he holds his hands out in front of him, palms parallel with the floor, one hand above the other. "This is happiness," he says, signaling the lower, left hand. "It's good. But vulnerable, breakable." Then he moves his right hand a little higher. "This is happy enough to survive all the things life will send your way."

Then my phone rings out. I scramble for it, hoping it's Emma. I answer before really looking at the screen. "Hello," I say, eyes back up. It's just me on the road.

"Carlos." It's Mom. She doesn't sound okay.

"Mom? What's wrong?"

"It's your dad," she says. Then she starts sobbing.

For the second time in as many months, I'm packing a bag up, ready to leave. This time, it's both easier and more difficult.

There's no fear of getting caught before I flee, no one chasing after me. No choices to make about where to go or what to bring. Once Mom told me that Dad was in the hospital after a heart attack, I knew my time on Needle Eye was over.

Now I try to shove the comfortable shoes I bought into the suitcase. I sheathe my gyuto, wrap it in the rain jacket I never had to use. I have to put a knee on top of my luggage to get it to shut, and I try not to think of the finality of the zipper reaching the end. My whole life here is locked away inside one suitcase. Dad's on a hospital bed and we haven't said a word directly to each other in two months.

I check my phone to see if Emma's changed her mind in the slightest, see only that Mom's emailed me some flight information. I've got six hours to make it to the airport. It's not enough time, it's too much time. I keep picturing the heart monitor flatlining, keep remembering how much blood there was with Felix. I keep thinking there's a chance I never see my dad alive again.

After I prop my suitcase up in a corner of the room, I go down the hall to see Elias. I knock a couple of times on the wooden door frame and then step inside. He's in bed, sitting up with his back against the wall, a computer on his lap.

"What's up, man?"

With no warning, I find myself unloading. Close to tears, I tell him how literally everything in my life has been flipped upside down in the last twenty-four hours. How I fucked up, and there's no undoing the mistake.

"Shit," Elias says, shutting his computer.

"Basically. I'm sorry I have to go on such short notice." I suddenly realize that I might never see Elias again, that this is a good-bye. "I'm sorry I have to go at all."

"Shit," Elias says again, folding his hands in his lap. "That's a shame, man. I'm gonna miss your cooking."

I smile, feel myself come close to tears again. "I can't thank you enough for all you did for me."

"Don't mention it." He stands up from his bed and goes to put a shirt on. "When do you leave?"

"Now, I guess. My flight's in a few hours."

"Goddamn." We stand there quietly for a moment, Elias with his hands on his hips. "At least you get to go back to some good Mexican food."

"True." I smile but find little solace in this silver lining. I look out the window, see the faintest glimmer of ocean beyond the trees. "I know you said, 'Don't mention it,' but I have to. I don't know what I would have done if you hadn't helped me out in the kitchen, if you hadn't talked to Chef and stood up for me all those times. If I have any future in restaurants, it's thanks to you."

"Shut up. You're making me tear up," Elias says.

"I mean it," I say. "I know we haven't known each other long or anything, but you felt like a big brother to me. So thanks."

Elias looks down at the floor, maybe trying to cover up the fact that he really is getting teared up. "It was my pleasure, every step of the way." He surreptitiously wipes at his eyes and then looks up and steps over to hug me. "And, trust me, you most definitely have a future in restaurants."

We embrace, and I feel myself about to crumble. I can't believe I have to leave. This beautiful corner of the world, my place in it. It wasn't perfect, but not much is.

Within an hour I'm on the ferry toward Seattle. I try calling Emma a few times, texting her what's happened, tell her I have to go. I want to see her again, say good-bye in person, but without a response from her I have no choice but to board the boat and hope that, somehow, I'll see her again. Even with the meal yesterday, the fact that I've cooked a dish that was served at a restaurant, Emma was the best thing that happened to me here. Shitty to know that for sure now that I've thrown it away.

When I roll my suitcase off the ferry and hail a cab, I can't help but think that I'm leaving a part of myself on the island. I was whole again for a second there. Now it's all unraveling.

The driver steps out to open the trunk, granting me time for one last look in the direction of Needle Eye. Except I can't see a thing, no far-off silhouette, no sign of the green island in the distance and all it holds. The cabbie is in the way of traffic, and he tells me we have to move. So I climb into the car with a good-bye that feels as rushed as my arrival.

CHAPTER 31
HOSPITAL COFFEE

2 scoops instant coffee
2 packets sugar
1 packet gross non-diary powdered creamer
1 cup tepid water

METHOD:

Mexico City is a creature too big to see.

It's strange how quickly I have forgotten what it feels like to fly in. How small you become when faced with so many lights. The city just keeps stretching out, like colored handkerchiefs being pulled from some magician's sleeve. When we finally touch down on a recently rained-on runway, my neck hurts from craning to see the sights of my hometown, so much humanity sprawled out across a single valley. The whole time, I was trying to picture what Needle Eye would look like from above, how quickly it would pass by below, how hard it would be at night to spot its handful of lights. The lake would just be a stretch of darkness like everything else around it.

I replace the American SIM card in my phone with my old Mexican one, let Mom know that I've landed. She sounds thankful but exhausted and not just because it's nearly one in the morning. I pass through immigration, pick up my suitcase from baggage claim and then get a taxi, feeling weird that everyone around is speaking Spanish again.

I go straight to the hospital. The nurses give me funny looks because of my luggage. It makes me think of showing up to the restaurant this same way, disheveled and lost, dragging a hastily packed life behind me. It's not the same hospital that Felix was taken to on the Night of the Perfect Taco, though who the hell can differentiate between hospital hallways. I roll my suitcase down the linoleum, following the signs to try to find Dad's room.

After a few wrong turns, I see Mom walk out a door, and I half call out, half whisper to her. She's clearly been crying. And when she sees me there's a fresh stream pouring out even as she runs to me. She holds me for a long time, tighter than she's held me since I was a kid. She tells me that Dad underwent bypass surgery, and he's stable, but they're going to keep him for a few days.

She tells me she was about to get some coffee, that she's afraid to fall asleep. She tells me not to go anywhere and then leaves me alone for a moment.

Inside the room, Dad is sleeping. He doesn't look frail, because he's always been kind of big, with a hefty belly and thick fingers that I now think would be good for a butcher, because they look like Vee's. There are breathing tubes in his nose, saline solution dripping into his arm, those little electrode things hooked up to his chest. The TV on the wall is on but muted, and there's a blanket crumpled on the chair where Mom was fighting off sleep. It's a difficult sight, mostly because he doesn't look peaceful. It's hard to see someone sleeping and not be at rest.

Not wanting to wake him, I roll my suitcase to the corner and then take a seat. There's no real beeping going on, just the calm sounds of breathing, the quiet hum of fluorescent lighting in the hallway. The more I look at Dad the more I start to see a gauntness there, hollowed cheeks. I wonder if he's really deteriorated over the last couple of months like Mom said or if it's just the hospital lighting.

I have no idea what I'll say when Dad wakes up. I look at my phone; even now, every other thought is still focused on Emma. Death or Emma. Everything just ends up floating away.

Mom comes back a few minutes later. She tells me I can go home if I want, but I say I'm okay here. Despite the coffee, she falls asleep a few minutes later, perhaps some of her restlessness disappearing when I arrived.

I don't feel particularly tired, so I grab the Italo Calvino book I bought with Emma and try to read, using the book for company more than distraction. Mostly, I just sit there, staring out the window at the parking lot. A few times a nurse comes in to check on Dad, young, stern but with a nice smile, which she offers when she sees I'm awake. Mom snores beside me, curled up beneath her blanket. She looks even frailer than Dad.

It's hard not to think of death, and for once I don't try to stop it, just let my mind drift to the subject. I think of myself and everyone I love as living, breathing beings who will one day die. I think of the days I've lived, of the last two months, all that I managed to fill them with.

At dawn, Felix makes an appearance. Felix as Felix, in that stained white shirt, no bullet holes or blood or any evidence that he's gone. Almost at the same time, Dad stirs. Mom seems to sense this and jolts awake, scurrying to his side, to give him some water. She cradles his head as he drinks baby sips from a straw. Then his eyes flit toward me.

"Mijo," he says, moving the straw away from his mouth. He tries to sit up, but Mom tells him no. She readjusts the pillow so he can see me a little easier, but she doesn't let him work himself up.

"Hey," I say, rising a little.

"Come give me a hug," Dad says. "A kiss. I'm so happy to see you."

And just like that, whatever ill will I felt toward my father, whatever rancor or resentment or disappointment, it's gone. It practically floats right out of my chest and through the window. I get close and lean over Dad and we embrace to the fullest extent a hospital bed will allow. Relief finds its way to every corner of my body. Dad's still alive.

When I finally pull away, I can tell Dad is trying to hang on, to move an arm toward me. But Mom says no, again. "You have to take it easy."

"Why? The surgery was hours ago, and it was only a single bypass," he says with a wink. I forgot this about him, his sense of humor. Felix got it from somewhere.

Felix has summoned himself a chair, and he's sitting on the other side of the bed, his body turned slightly away from me, angled toward Dad. He's leaning forward, arms on the railing, chin on his arms, eyes glazed over, stuck on some distant point.

"I'm gonna get the nurse to sedate you again," Mom says, raising a threatening finger at him.

Dad smiles and rolls his eyes. "Fine, fine. Can I hear about my son's trip then? Is listening too strenuous?"

"Being a smartass is," Mom says, but she relaxes into her chair, looking happy. Felix says nothing, moves not an inch.

So I talk. I run through the whole summer, even if I'd already told Mom most of it over the phone. I start from the very first day and this time don't skip a thing. Going to Provecho in Felix's honor, how delicious the food was, yet how unsatisfying the meal itself. The motel room, the trips with Emma to the lake. Dad gets a funny look on his face when I go into detail of the long hours standing at the sink but refrains from comment. I talk for nearly an hour without any interruptions other than the occasional question. Felix lays his forehead on his arms for a bit as he listens. He doesn't crack a joke, doesn't interject in any way. Mom doesn't stop smiling.

They beam when I regale them with the dishes I created for staff meals, mutter bilingual curse words when I tell them the kind of things Chef would say to me during our training sessions. Always vague about the girls I've dated, I surprise myself when I tell them exactly what me and Emma did on our first date, how things progressed from there.

I'd forgotten what it was like to have someone who inherently cares about what you're saying, who responds as if it'd happened to them. Yes, Emma helped bring that feeling back around every now and then. Elias too. But I didn't have a family on the island. Not one that was alive, anyway.

When I'm done talking, the stern nurse comes in again, a little more talkative now that everyone's awake. She fluffs Dad's pillow, checks the tubes in his arms. Even if he's still an imposing physical figure, it's hard to see him reduced to such weakness by his own body. He keeps his eyes on me, smiling. The nurse leaves, and I start to feel the exhaustion of staying up all night. I think maybe I'll go home, shower, eat something that Elias would appreciate. Before I get up, though, Dad clears his throat. "Right before the heart attack, I thought to myself, shit, I've done it again." I'm taken aback, not just by what he's just said but by the fact that there seems to be tears in his eyes. Mom stops fussing; Felix freezes.

"You know I hated myself for how things turned out with Felix, right?" Dad continues. The air doesn't quite leave the room, just comes to a standstill. The blinds don't sway in the breeze caused by the AC, because there is no breeze. The air's listening. "I hated that I couldn't find a way to keep him close to us and happy. Hated myself for not knowing how to do anything other than try to impose myself. I couldn't be happy for him. When you left, I didn't immediately realize I'd done it again. Pushed another son away." Dad wipes at his eye; Felix does the same. Beyond the door, an old lady in a hospital gown shuffles by, a younger woman holding her IV walks slightly behind her. I expect dozens of people to follow, pretending they're going somewhere so they can listen in on what Dad's saying.

"Look, I know how to do a few things well." He pauses to take a breath or to think. "Run a business. Provide for my family. Once upon a time, believe it or not, I could make a pretty decent omelet." He smiles.

"I wanted to give you and your brother a good life. I wanted to make sure your mom wouldn't have to worry about the safety or happiness of our children. So, I did what I thought was right, and I chased success. I used the things I was good at to achieve those goals.

"But in chasing success, I sacrificed a few things. Quality time with all of you. Humility, maybe." Another pause, the world at a further standstill. Cars looking for empty spaces in the parking lot have stopped moving; the clouds are still. "I never meant to sacrifice your and your brother's happiness, but it turns out that's what I've done."

I almost want to interject, but it feels like I'm frozen too. Only Felix is showing signs of movement, a shimmer in his eyes, which he turns his eyes downward to hide, resting his forehead on his arms. Mom's basically weeping.

Dad starts to reach for more water, but Mom admonishes him in Spanish and brings the glass toward him. After a few sips he lets his head go back to the pillow. "Felix did it too, you know. In a way." Another sip, waves Mom away. "My fault. I set the example.

"He chased after his dreams at the expense of his family. I never hated him for that, just hated that I did it first, and so it was easy for him to follow along. That whole time he was gone, the thing I was angriest about was that I couldn't say anything. It would make me a hypocrite. He did exactly what I did and instead of understanding him, I ignored him. I got mad that he rejected what I'd spent so long working to provide him, not realizing that he went after exactly what I wanted for him: his own joy. Not a day goes by that I don't hate myself for that."

At the same time, Mom and Felix both reach for Dad's hands. He grasps Mom's on his right, but I can't tell if he reacts to Felix's touch, if he can sense it at all. "Enough about my mistakes, though." Dad closes his eyes for a moment, and when he opens them I swear he glances at Felix for a second.

Then he's looking at me again. "You don't have to push us away to chase what you want, Carlos. Because of me, you too were going to sacrifice your family for your happiness. I don't want that to ever happen again."

Moments go by before I realize Dad's done talking. He's practically snoring by the time Mom gets up to fuss with his sheets. The world regains its motion, though the words going through my head are: *Nothing will ever be the same.*

Then, as the hospital goes back to normalcy—sickly people shuffling down the hallway; doctors trying to keep others alive; harmless houseflies buzzing about, attracted by the fluorescent lighting; a line forming at the coffee shop, relatives with bags beneath their eyes—Felix's ghost stands up.

He wipes at his eyes. Gives me a grin. Raises his eyebrows and gives a little shoulder shrug, as if to say, *What are you gonna do?*

Kisses Dad's forehead.

Disappears.

CHAPTER 32

NASHVILLE HOT CHICKEN SANDWICHES

2 pounds pounded chicken
breasts

2 cups flour

2 large eggs

¼ cup buttermilk

4 tablespoons hot sauce

3 tablespoons brown sugar

6 tablespoons cayenne pepper

3 tablespoons garlic powder

FOR SLAW:

1 purple cabbage

2 tomatoes, diced

½ cup cilantro, chopped

1 julienned red pepper

2 carrots, grated

¼ cup mayo

4 tablespoons olive oil

3 tablespoons apple cider vinegar

METHOD:

"Carlos, put the fryer down."

"Mom, it's one meal."

"Your father just had a heart attack. We're not having whatever crazy concoction you think we're having."

"It's been long enough, no?" Dad chimes in. "Plus, it was all stress, you heard the doctor. I am no longer stressed, so I can have some fried chicken. In fact, it would probably help me relax."

I carry the fryer to the counter, plug it in defiantly, sharing a wink with Dad. There are a handful of grocery bags on the kitchen island.

Rosalba is fussing, trying to put things away and help out, but I tell her she can relax. I'll handle everything.

I grab the cabbage, chop it roughly, set it in a bowl with water and the disinfectant drops, a step I was always happy to be able to skip in the US. I crack a few eggs, passing the yolk back and forth between the halves so that the whites drip down to a bowl beneath.

How many times did I do exactly this at the house on the island, with Emma sitting nearby on the counter? I've cooked every day since Dad was released from the hospital, and every time I picture her there with me, sitting on the counter, making jokes, running a finger through a bowl to taste something. Or I think: *if you crack this egg perfectly, she'll respond to an email. If this omelet turns out perfectly golden, without a tinge of brown, she'll call.*

Dad watches intently as I whisk the egg yolks with some oil and lime. "What are you doing there?"

"Making mayo for the coleslaw."

"Making mayo? Don't we have some in the fridge?"

"Yeah, but it's tastier this way," I say. "Plus, this is my show-off meal."

"They're all your show-off meals," someone shouts. I turn around and see Danny, Nico and Poncho coming into the kitchen. They're tanned, shaggy-haired. Nico's got a new eyebrow ring and is carrying a case of beer with both hands. The three of them got back about a week after I did, and the overlap will last only a couple of days before they continue on to college. I'm staying.

They come around shaking hands, half hugging. The guys give

cheek-kisses to Mom, gentle shoulder pats to Dad. "Una chela?" Nico says, cracking a beer open and offering one to my parents.

"Nico, the man just had a heart attack."

"All the more reason," Nico says. "Life is short!"

"You offer my husband another beer and I will shorten your life."

I turn my attention back to the food. I grab a few more eggs, crack them into a bowl, turn on music that Emma might have chosen. Buttermilk was impossible to find, even at the fancy supermarket a few blocks away, so I use a mixture of whole milk and heavy cream. Danny steps over with a beer for me. "What are you making for us?"

"Nashville hot chicken sandwiches."

"Whatever that is," Danny says, looking at everything crowding the counter. "Anything we can do to help?"

"Call Emma. See if she wants to come over."

Danny laughs. "Still?"

"Hasn't been that long, man."

"Yeah, I get you. A little offended that our company won't suffice, but whatever."

"What can I say? She takes a joke a lot better." I smirk, walking over to rinse the egg from my hands. "Cuter too."

"Yeah, I'd replace you with Siene in a heartbeat too," Danny says, drinking from his beer, taking the opportunity to delve into the story of the Belgian girl he fell in love with overnight in Venice. How instead of joining the guys on a train to Munich, he just walked around the city with her, and ever since he hasn't been able to get her out of his mind.

I julienne carrots and bell peppers for the slaw while Danny talks about her. It goes on for a few minutes. Meanwhile, Nico and Poncho regale Dad with Eurostories. Then Danny seems to have exhausted himself of the topic. He leans back against the counter, watches me dredge some pounded chicken breasts in flour. "Anyway. Everything okay with you?"

I pause, think for a second. I still expect to see Felix showing up places. In the flour, in the condensation sweating off the beer bottle, in any corner of any room. "No, not everything," I say with a shrug. Then I add a smile, wash my hands again.

Danny seems content with the answer. We turn our attention to the main conversation. I switch the deep fryer on, and while that's heating up I cut the brioche buns in half and slide them into the oven. I make a quick dressing for the slaw, mix it with the mayo, a good amount of lime that I know will make the flavor of the chicken's seasoning pop as well as dissipate its heat. Chopped cilantro, olive oil, a little apple cider vinegar. I picture Elias scooping a tiny bit of slaw into his palm, getting that approving look in his eye. I picture the lake at night, Emma kicking pebbles as she walks, arms folded, glasses resting on top of her head. I picture life unfolding. Not in any particular direction or manner but just the sheer fact of it, the steady unraveling of time. Outside, the summer storm is unusually late, patches of blue sky still visible out in the valley. I wipe the counter clean, carrying plates to the sink.

The thermometer on the fryer dings, and so I turn to it, setting up the chicken to go in in batches. I prepare a bowl with an absurd amount of cayenne pepper, some sugar, garlic powder, paprika. I pull the quick-pickled cucumbers from the fridge. This, I'll always have. The joy of a dish come together.

We eat on the balcony, taking advantage of the weather. As best as we can over the sound of chewing, of drinking, of sharp intakes of breath when the spice is almost overwhelming, we talk. Of Europe and the island, of the guys going off to school in a few days, of my application to a culinary school in the city. We talk about Felix, how sweaty he got anytime he had spicy food but how he never shied away from it.

Later, when everyone has left, I walk by the kitchen, getting ready to do the dishes, a little conflicted about the fact that they've been washed and stored away. It is, of course, a relief. But I was looking forward to the nostalgia of it all. Which is insane. I was doing dishes for twelve hours a day only a couple of weeks ago. But I haven't seen my fingers wrinkle in a while, and I somehow miss the sight. My lower back is relaxed, and I do not get to enjoy the relief of being done with the small, temporary pain of standing at the sink. There's something to be said for discomfort that doesn't last.

I go to my room, try to read. I still get too aware of life in those moments, see my fingers holding the book up, see my hands attached to my wrists, feel way too close to any of it. I grab my computer, set it atop my hamper as I search for some show or movie to fall asleep to. I end up reading through old emails Felix sent me, looking at pictures from his travels. Just because I expect the pictures to move, to speak to me, there's no reason they ever will again. I let the sadness crush me for a moment, then quickly click on the first movie my fingers find and lie back in bed, trying to calm my mind.

While the movie plays on, I grab my phone, looking up random reci-pes, just to see what people are trying out. I look up, again, stuff about the culinary school I'll be attending. Then I move on to random pic-tures I took on the island. A bunch of the dishes I made. Emma in the meadow, eating a berry. The full moon from the top of that one hill, its impressiveness in the photograph a sad imitation of the real thing.

We haven't talked since I left. Not a peep. She never answered any of my messages or calls, and once I got back home and was dealing with everything else, I didn't know what could possibly be the point of continuing to reach out, other than self-inflicted torture. But because it's three in the morning, and these things tend to happen at three, I open up my email. I type the first thing I can think of into the body of a new message and then immediately delete it because it was a soufflé-related joke which is intensely stupid. I go the exact opposite direction and tell her I love her. Then I delete the hell out of that.

Years of this, it feels like. The movie ends, credits roll. I still have my phone in my hand, the email perfectly blank. It feels like this will never go away.

I really wish you'd been in my life longer, I finally write. I wish you still were. I'm not entirely happy with all it does and does not say. It's something, though. I look around my darkened room for a second to see if Felix is about to show up with some words of wisdom, and when it's clear that's not going to happen and that I should just go to sleep already, I type Emma's name into the address line, send it off into the ether and rest my head on my pillow.

Food's not on my mind. Neither is Felix. Neither is death. Just Emma. It won't always be like this, I know.

Sleep finally takes me without my noticing, and in the morning, for a moment or two, I am unaware of anything at all except how it feels to be awake again. Then I reach for my phone, flick my fingers this way and that, tap the screen.

1 new email, my phone reads. Emma St. Croix, it elaborates.

What a world, I think.

* * * * *

ACKNOWLEDGMENTS:

First of all, I'd like to thank the chefs and cooks who read early drafts of the book and consulted on kitchen matters for authenticity. Agata Swinska, Sergio Rodriguez, Diego Valderrama and Kevin Todd, I'm indebted to you for your insight and time. Thank you to the staff at Cooper's Hawk in Cincinnati for letting me observe a shift in the kitchen. Same goes for Alex Souza and Pixza in Mexico City. I'm also indebted to a few wonderful books: *Blood, Bones and Butter: The Inadvertent Education of a Reluctant Chef* by Gabrielle Hamilton; *Yes, Chef: A Memoir* by Marcus Samuelsson; *Sous Chef: 24 Hours on the Line* by Michael Gibney; *Kitchen Confidential* and *Medium Raw* by Anthony Bourdain. Also, the dishwasher forums I perused online and all those who posted in them, which helped me shape Carlos's experiences in the kitchen.

A huge thanks and shout-out to my wonderful editorial team at Alloy, spearheaded by Annie Stone, who I'll dearly miss working with. Sara Shandler and Josh Bank, and all the people there who do wonders for my books.

I've got the pleasure of having a second lovely group of people championing my books at Harlequin Teen. T.S., who makes my books better, even if he loves hard shell tacos. Tashya, Siena and everyone at the NYC offices, as well as Bryn, Michelle, Lisa, Amy and all those I had the pleasure to meet in Toronto the summer while writing this book.

Thank you so much for all you do, for the countless hours you work on my behalf.

To all champions of books: librarians, booksellers, reviewers, publicists, sales reps, book club members, a bunch of titles I'm forgetting. Twitter users, Goodreads reviewers, anyone who can't contain their love of books, whether they're mine or not. Thank you for making this world a more bookish place.

Thanks to my family, their love. You should know my brother Shay almost derailed my interest in cooking by getting me angry one of the only times in my life, but he taught me plenty and probably fueled my interest more than either of us knows. I owe a great deal of my understanding about the world of restaurants to him. Many of my cooking skills come from my mom, and I'm eternally grateful to all the times she let me be her sous, and all the times she's returned the favor. My sister, who spent a rainy summer in Mexico City with me watching *Top Chef*, the show which made me jealous of people who can cook and made me want to try to myself. My dad eats everything I cook and says it could be served at a restaurant, so that's pretty sweet. Also, for being my constant cheerleader, and for being a probably severely underpaid business manager. Cat, for being the best reader in my family and maybe my biggest fan. Moms don't count.

To Laura, of course, and her love. Of me, my writing, travel, food, balconies, sleeping, all of it.

I've been so thankful to find a wealth of friends in the YA author community. I wish I knew you all better. There are so many opportunities in a profession like ours to be envious or jealous of talent and success, but you're such lovely people that I can only ever be jealous when you are hanging out without me. Come visit me in Mexico City. I'll feed you. Ask Eric Smith and Zoraida Cordova. Whom I want to specially thank for coming to hang out with me in my hometown and making a few days of writing that much better.

A few other friends who've helped in a variety of ways I could list but I'll save the space to list them instead: Chris Russell, Maggie Vazquez, Josh Zoller, Dave Rueb, Amy Olson, Bret Sikkink, Leslie Barnheizer, Perri Devon-Sand, The Dongers Crew for the travels and the meals (Laura Fairbank, Greg Fairbank, Steph Polvere, and Mackenzie Day), Jason and Mary Cornwell-Wright, John Powell, Dan Godshall, Jorge Brake, Federico "Bugs not Rico" Hernandez, Dawn Ryan, Leah Kreitz, Gonzala Scaglia, Claire Tinley, John McGrath. G and Berky, I wasn't going to forget you this time. I'm sorry for the other two. I understand if you still hate me.

My agent, Pete Knapp. Thanks for believing in my writing. I'm excited for all that's to come.

Lastly, and probably most importantly, thank you to my readers. I get to do what I do because of you, but your tweets, emails, Instagram posts, reviews and general support make it that much sweeter. Seriously, thank you for reading.